Margare *r*
weeks.

But was she really ready for this sort of complication?

Maybe she'd been a bit lonely during the past few years, but she'd been so safe. So sheltered from the heartache and turmoil she'd known before. Tucker wasn't safe. And turmoil seemed inevitable whenever he was around.

So why was she seriously considering recklessly ignoring her fears and throwing herself at him? Had she truly lost her mind?

The most seductive thing about Tucker, she realized, was the way he made her feel when he looked at her. She felt pretty. Sexy. Desirable. Even daring and impetuous. Funny—he was the only one who'd ever made her feel those things. And she was finding that these unfamiliar feelings were insidiously addictive.

Oh, yes, he was dangerous. And for the first time in longer than she could remember, she was contemplating taking a risk....

Dear Reader,

Happy Valentine's Day! Love is in the air, and Special Edition has plenty of little cupids to help matchmake! There are family stories here, there are breathtaking romances there—you name it, you'll find love in each and every Silhouette Special Edition.

This month we're pleased to welcome new-to-Silhouette author Angela Benson. Her debut book for Special Edition, *A Family Wedding,* is a warm, wonderful tale of friends falling in love…and a darling little girl's dream come true.

We're also proud to present Jane Toombs's dramatic tale, *Nobody's Baby,* our THAT'S MY BABY! title. Jane also has written under the pseudonym Diana Stuart, and this is her first book for Special Edition under her real name. And speaking of firsts, please welcome to Special Edition, veteran Silhouette Desire author Peggy Moreland, by reading *Rugrats and Rawhide*—a tender tale of love for this Valentine's month.

Sherryl Woods returns with a marvelous new series— THE BRIDAL PATH. Don't miss the first book, *A Ranch for Sara,* a rollicking, heartwarming love story. The second and third titles will be available in March and April! And the Valentine's Day thermostat continues to rise with Gina Wilkins's sparkling tale of opposites attracting in *The Father Next Door.*

Finally, Natalie Bishop presents readers with the perfect February title—*Valentine's Child.* This tale of love lost and then rediscovered is full of the Valentine's Day spirit!

I hope you enjoy this book, and each and every title to come!

Sincerely,

Tara Gavin, Senior Editor

Please address questions and book requests to:
Silhouette Reader Service
U.S.: 3010 Walden Ave., P.O. Box 1325, Buffalo, NY 14269
Canadian: P.O. Box 609, Fort Erie, Ont. L2A 5X3

GINA WILKINS

THE FATHER NEXT DOOR

Published by Silhouette Books
America's Publisher of Contemporary Romance

For Norma Kasper—a very special fan.

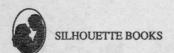 SILHOUETTE BOOKS

ISBN 0-373-24082-1

THE FATHER NEXT DOOR

Books by Gina Wilkins

Silhouette Special Edition

The Father Next Door #1082

Previously published as Gina Ferris

Silhouette Special Edition

Healing Sympathy #496
Lady Beware #549
In From the Rain #677
Prodigal Father #711
*Full of Grace #793
*Hardworking Man #806
*Fair and Wise #819
*Far To Go #862
*Loving and Giving #879
Babies on Board #913

Previously published as Gina Ferris Wilkins

Silhouette Special Edition

†A Man for Mom #955
†A Match for Celia #967
†A Home for Adam #980
†Cody's Fiancée #1006

*Family Found
†The Family Way

Silhouette Books

Mother's Day Collection 1995
Three Mothers & a Cradle
"Beginnings"

GINA FERRIS WILKINS

declares that she is Southern by birth and by choice, and she has chosen to set many of her books in the South, where she finds a rich treasury of characters and settings. She particularly loves the Ozark mountain region of northern Arkansas and southern Missouri and the proudly unique people who reside there. She and her husband, John, live in Arkansas, with their three children, Courtney, Kerry and David.

Dear Grandma Agnes,

Thanks for sending the cool new sneakers. Kitten likes the gift you sent her, too.

The new house is great. It has a lot more room than Dad's apartment. My friend Chuck lives close by. The only thing I don't like is the lady next door. She doesn't want me to take a shortcut across her yard to Chuck's house, in case I step on any of her stupid old flowers. And when my baseball went over the fence and landed in her fountain, she acted like I was going to throw it through her window or something. I don't think she's been around kids much.

Kitten saw her yesterday, when we were playing outside. She thinks she's pretty. She thinks Dad would like her. I think Kitten's nuts. Why would Dad want to meet a grouch?

I'll see you when we come for Aunt Cathy's wedding in November. Me and Kitten are really looking forward to spending the whole week with you and missing school.

Love,

Sam

P.S. Isn't my new computer really neat?

Chapter One

Margaret McAlister bent to retrieve her Saturday-morning newspaper from the bushes in front of her house. She muttered beneath her breath at the notoriously poor aim of her new paper carrier. During the past few weeks, she'd found her papers in the bushes, in the flower beds, in the fountain, on the roof—everywhere but on the front porch where they should have been.

Margaret had little patience with incompetence.

A fat black puppy suddenly dashed past her, stubby tail wagging, ears flapping behind him. She thought she recognized the pup as belonging to the little boy next door. Glancing at her neighbor's yard, she noticed that the gate to the chain-link-enclosed front lawn had been left open, providing an avenue for the dog's dash for adventure. She shook her head. Children shouldn't have pets if they weren't going to watch out for them.

Hearing the distant sound of car engines growing

closer, she tossed the newspaper onto her front stoop and hurried after the animal. "Here, boy. Come here, boy."

She tried to make her voice enticing, though she'd had little experience communicating with canines. Margaret didn't particularly like dogs, but she couldn't simply stand by and watch this little fellow be flattened by a heedless driver. "Come here, boy," she said again. "Or girl. Whatever you are."

She'd caught the dog's attention. It stopped, head cocked, tongue lolling as it eyed her.

She knelt and held out her hands. "Come on, pup. I'll take you home."

A moment later she was assaulted by six pounds of wiggling fur and lapping tongue. Jerking her face out of range, she snatched the puppy into her arms and stood. The little mutt squirmed so enthusiastically that she almost dropped it. She tucked it firmly beneath her arm and headed down the sidewalk toward the house next door.

Margaret had never formally met her new neighbors, though she had once had to ask the young boy to please not take a shortcut through her flower beds on his way to his friend's house down the block. And there'd been the time she'd had to retrieve his baseball from her fountain and return it to him over the fence. She hadn't lectured him, but she had asked him to be more careful in the future; the ball could have as easily gone through one of her windows.

Both times, the boy had ducked his head and muttered something unintelligible. Margaret would be the first to admit that she knew little more about talking to children than she did to dogs.

She pressed a finger to the doorbell of the redbrick Georgian home that was so much like her own and the others in this meticulously planned suburban Dallas neighborhood. The new residents had moved in about three weeks earlier.

Margaret had been very busy with work lately, so she hadn't paid much attention to her new neighbors, except on the two occasions when she'd spoken to the boy. She didn't even know what his parents looked like. There seemed to be a constant stream of people going in and out of the house, and Margaret hadn't bothered to try to identify the permanent occupants.

She waited curiously as the door swung slowly open. The little boy she'd encountered before, a stocky, dark-haired lad of eight or nine years, stared up at her with wide green eyes. And then he let out a bellow, turned on one sneaker and dashed away.

"Dad!" he yelled. "Dad, it's her! That mean lady from next door. And she's got Boomer!"

Stunned by the boy's reaction, Margaret closed her mouth with a snap. What the—?

"Hello?" she called out when the dog wriggled harder to get down. Should she set it on its feet and leave, closing the gate behind her? Should she wait here?

The dog wiggled and yipped. The boy was still yelling inside, and she heard a deep voice say, "Settle down, Sam."

"But, Dad, she's got Boomer!"

Margaret shook her head. This was getting her nowhere. Lifting her chin and taking a tighter grip on the pup, she stepped over the threshold, peering rather tentatively in the direction of the man's voice.

A large den opened off the foyer, much like her own floor plan. Stopping just inside the front door, Margaret could see a man sitting cross-legged on the carpeted floor. In her first glance, she noted his disheveled dark hair, outdoorsman's tan, incredibly broad shoulders and ruggedly handsome face—strictly as a dispassionate observation, of course. His concentration was focused entirely on his hands, which seemed to be tangled in the dark hair of the little girl who sat with her back turned to him.

An open book lay at the man's knee; it appeared to Margaret to be an illustrated instruction book on hair-styling. The man looked thoroughly bewildered. The boy had stationed himself behind his father and was bouncing up and down as he bellowed his indignation at being ignored. From Margaret's firm grasp, the dog yapped again, obviously anxious to play with his boy.

"Sam, take that dog outside," the man said, glaring at the book as though grimly determined to understand it. "And, Kitten, you're going to have to be still, or I'll never get this done."

"But you're pulling my hair, Daddy," the child wailed.

"You're the one who wanted me to— Oh."

Maybe it had been the dog's barking that made the man look up just then. His surprisingly green eyes locked with Margaret's, and he went very still, a look of startled curiosity on his face.

And then he smiled, and even Margaret's long-guarded heart jerked in response to the sheer male beauty of it.

Dimples, she thought. She'd always had a regrettably soft spot for them, a susceptibility she usually managed to ignore.

"Well, hello," he said, cocking his head in a manner that reminded her a bit of the puppy. "Do you, by any chance, know how to French braid?"

"I, uh…" Completely off guard, Margaret stammered a bit before she answered, "Yes, I do, but…"

A look of relief crossed his face. "Then would you mind showing me how? She wants to wear it to a birth-day party, and this blasted book doesn't make a lick of sense to me. I don't think it's written for single dads."

Margaret certainly hadn't come over for a hairstyling lesson. Nor had she realized her new neighbor was a single father.

"Your puppy got out of your yard and into the street," she explained, uncertain if he even knew why she was there. "I thought I should bring it back before it was run over."

"That was thoughtful of you," he said, carefully untangling his long fingers from the little girl's hair. "Was I supposed to put this up in a ponytail or anything first? The book doesn't say to, but..." He shrugged.

"No," Margaret answered, feeling a bit like Alice in Wonderland. "Mr., er...?"

"Hollis," he supplied, shoving himself to his feet. "Tucker Hollis. My friends call me Tuck."

He stuck out his right hand. She placed the puppy in it. He was forced to scramble to keep from dropping the wriggling dog.

"I'm Margaret McAlister," she said primly. "Your neighbor."

"Nice to meet you."

He turned to his son, who seemed to be trying to hide behind a chair. "Sam, take this dog outside. And make sure that gate's shut from now on, you hear? You want Boomer to get hit by a car?"

"No, sir," the boy muttered, taking his pet with a skittish look at Margaret. He all but bolted from the room as soon as he had his dog safely in his arms.

Margaret wondered if she'd been sterner than she'd intended when she'd talked to the boy about her flower beds and the ball in her fountain. He acted as though she were the malicious neighbor from *The Wizard of Oz,* scheming to steal his Toto.

Tucker Hollis planted his hands on his jeaned hips and studied her with a smile. "So you're the mean ol' lady next door. Gotta admit, you aren't exactly what I was expecting.''

She bristled. ''I am not a mean old lady,'' she declared, feeling compelled to protest. She was only thirty, after all.

He took a leisurely visual stroll from the top of her neatly brushed, chestnut brown hair to her sensibly shod feet, not missing an inch of her slender figure along the way. She realized that she had just been studied and cataloged—eyes, brown; nose, tip tilted; mouth, unpainted; legs, long; curves, practically nonexistent. She resisted an impulse to squirm self-consciously beneath his examination.

''No,'' he said, musingly. ''I can see that you aren't an old lady.''

She was appalled to feel her cheeks warm with a blush. She hadn't blushed in years.

The little girl still sitting on the floor squirmed impatiently. ''Daddy,'' she reminded him. ''My hair.''

''Oh. Yeah.'' He gave Margaret a look of appeal. ''Would you mind?''

She really would be a mean old lady if she refused to assist him, she supposed. Her Saturday-morning schedule had already been disrupted, so another few minutes couldn't make a major difference. She was wearing a knit slacks-and-top set, so she was able to kneel on the floor behind the child without concern for her clothing. She picked up the comb lying beside the useless instruction book.

''What's your name?'' she asked the little girl.

''Christine, but everyone calls me Kitten. I'm five. Almost six. What's your name?''

''Margaret McAlister.''

''What does everyone call you?'' Kitten inquired, looking curiously over her shoulder. ''Do you have a nickname?''

"No. Just 'Margaret.'"

"Oh." Kitten didn't seem to entirely approve of Margaret's answer.

Margaret turned the child's head gently but firmly forward, then slid the comb into her silky tresses. She looked up at Tucker Hollis before proceeding any further, finding him standing right beside her.

"Are you watching?" she asked, remembering that he had asked her to teach him how to make the braid.

He nodded. "I'm watching," he said, though his eyes were on her face, not on her hands.

Margaret hastily turned her attention to the task she'd taken on, nimbly gathering strands of hair and carefully explaining what she was doing. "You divide it into three sections, like this. Then you start to braid, picking up another strand of hair from each outside—"

"Say, would you like a cup of coffee or anything?" Tucker Hollis offered cheerfully, ignoring her careful instructions.

"No, thank you. I've already had my coffee this morning."

"So have another cup. Freshly made," he added enticingly.

She shook her head. "Thank you, but no. Now you take this strand here and—"

"You don't have any kids, do you, Mrs. McAlister?" Kitten inquired, turning her head to peer over her shoulder.

"No, I've never been married," Margaret responded, moving the child's head forward again. "You have to be still if you want your hair braided," she added.

"Yes, ma'am," Kitten replied with a nod that pulled from her fingers the strands Margaret had already gathered.

Margaret sighed and began again. "Now," she said,

trying to sound in control, "you divide the top section of hair into three equal strands and—"

"Dad." Still holding the active puppy, Sam burst back into the room. "The latch on the gate's broke. It won't stay closed. You'll have to fix it, or Boomer'll get out again."

"Darn," Hollis muttered, shoving a hand through his hair. The wayward strands at the front fell back over his forehead. He looked apologetically at Margaret. "Would you mind finishing this up without me? I'd better fix that gate so we can get the dog outside."

"But—"

"But, Daddy." Kitten's protest overrode Margaret's. "I'll be late to the birthday party."

"You won't be late, Kitten," he promised. "Ms. McAlister is going to do your hair, and I'll have the latch fixed in a snap. There'll be plenty of time to get you to your party."

"We'll be late," the child muttered as her father and brother hurried out. "We're *always* late."

After spending just five minutes in this chaotic household, Margaret wasn't at all surprised. If she'd ever seen a place in need of organization, this was it.

She quickly finished Kitten's hair, leaving the braid hanging down her back and tied at the bottom with a bright red plaid bow that matched the little pleated skirt the child wore with a crisp white blouse. At least the children looked clean, neat and well fed, Margaret noted, though the room around her was dismayingly cluttered with toys, books, magazines, newspapers, shoes and crayons. Several boxes rested in the corners, apparently waiting to be unpacked.

"Do you and your brother live full-time with your father?" Margaret asked impulsively. She immediately regretted the personal question, reminding herself that it was none of her business.

Kitten didn't hesitate to answer. "Yes," she said with a nod that made her bow bounce against her back. "Our mama was in a car wreck with Benny, and they went to heaven. Now Daddy takes care of us all the time. Well, not when he's at work, of course. He's a teacher. He teaches big kids—junior high. Our grandma picks us up after school and takes us to her house. We get to have a snack and watch television until Daddy gets through working and picks us up. Sometimes he has meetings and stuff at school and he has to stay late, so Grandma cooks dinner for us."

Margaret gulped, dismayed by the child's disclosure about her mother. "I—"

"I'm in kindergarten," Kitten went on. "My teacher's name is Ms. Clark. I like her 'cause she makes me laugh, but sometimes she yells at Tommy Perkins and she's really loud when she yells."

"Oh. Er…"

"Sam's in fourth grade. He's nine. His teacher's Mrs. Dixon. She makes him miss recess when he talks to his friends in class. Daddy said if it happens again, he's going to take Sam's Nintendo away for a whole month."

Margaret backed toward the door, wondering how quickly she could make her escape. She hadn't imagined that asking one simple question would unleash this artless flow of information.

"Daddy had an apartment when me and Sam lived with Mommy and Benny, but the apartment was too little for all of us, so we got this house. You want to see my room? I got a new bed and everything. It has a canopy."

"Not right now," Margaret answered a bit desperately. "I really should be—"

"Do you live all by yourself, Ms. Mc— Er…?" The child had obviously forgotten the last name.

"Just call me Margaret. And yes, I live alone."

"Don't you get scared? I get scared sometimes at night. Daddy lets me put my sleeping bag in his room when it thunders, 'cause I really hate thunder. It was thundering the night my Mommy went to heaven," Kitten added pensively.

Margaret had never felt more awkward or inept. Should she express her sympathy for the child's loss, or would that be inappropriate with a little girl so young? She decided to simply answer Kitten's questions instead.

"No, I don't get scared at night," she said. *Not anymore, anyway,* she could have added. Not since she'd carefully put together an orderly, controlled life for herself—a safe environment, a comfortably predictable routine, a steady, dependable income.

She didn't mention any of that, of course. Her life—most especially her past—wasn't open for discussion, even with this talkative little girl. She was relieved when Tucker Hollis strolled back into the room, rubbing his hands together in satisfaction.

"All done," he announced. "See, Kitten, I told you it wouldn't take long. Hey, your hair looks great."

Kitten preened and patted her braid. "I know. I can see it in the mirror over the couch," she answered immodestly.

"Did you thank Ms. McAlister for braiding it for you?"

"She said I can call her Margaret. Thank you, Margaret."

"You're welcome, er, Kitten." Margaret inwardly cringed at the silly nickname. "I hope you have a nice time at your party."

Kitten smiled brightly. "I will. Patty's mom always gives out cool party favors."

Her father groaned. "Materialistic brat. Go put on your shoes. We're supposed to be there in ten minutes."

Kitten sighed as she left the room. "We'll be late," she predicted. "We're *always* late."

"We won't be late." Tucker turned to Margaret. "Are you sure you wouldn't like a cup of coffee or something?"

She was inching toward the door again. "No, thank you."

He moved after her. "I've been meaning to get over and introduce myself, but everything's been so hectic since the move that there hasn't been time. I told Sam to stay on the sidewalks and out of your flower beds from now on, but if you have any more trouble with him, you let me know, okay? He's a good kid, but he forgets his manners at times. Like most kids, I guess."

"Yes, of course," Margaret murmured.

Tucker followed her to the front door. "Have you lived in this neighborhood long?"

"I bought my house five years ago."

"You were pretty young to buy a house, weren't you?"

"I was twenty-five." Margaret kept her voice just a bit cool, a subtle indication that she didn't particularly like answering personal questions.

"Then you and I are the same age. I just had my thirtieth birthday a couple of months ago."

"Congratulations," Margaret murmured, stepping outside.

Her mild sarcasm didn't seem to faze him—or to discourage him from his openly curious interrogation. "Where did you live before you moved here?"

"My family moved around a lot." She descended the porch steps, intending to end the conversation there.

Tucker Hollis followed her, leaving the front door gaping behind him. "Do you work out of your home? I've noticed that you don't leave often."

She didn't like the implication that he'd been watching her house. She frowned, telling herself she really should put him firmly in his place. Then again, she had no desire to antagonize her neighbors. She answered reluctantly, "Yes, I work out of my home. I'm a certified public accountant. I do contract work for several small local businesses that can't afford a full-time bookkeeper."

"No kidding. You don't look like a number cruncher."

She lifted an eyebrow without slowing as she walked briskly down the steps and onto the walkway. "Kitten told me that you're a schoolteacher. Physical education?"

"History," he corrected her. "Eighth and ninth grades."

"Really? You don't look like a history teacher."

His grin deepened. "Touché."

They had reached the gate. Tucker opened it for her. Margaret stepped through, expecting him to stay behind. Instead, he followed her again.

"You really don't have to walk me home," she said.

He shrugged. "Nice morning, isn't it? Going to be a beautiful day."

She hadn't really noticed before, but he was right. It was a lovely late-September morning, the sky clear and blue, trees awash in fall colors, an autumn crispness in the air that was especially refreshing after a very hot summer. "Yes, it is a nice morning."

"You aren't going to spend it inside with your spreadsheets and software, are you?"

"I work from ten until noon most Saturdays. I reserve Saturday afternoons for shopping and errands."

Tucker slanted her a wary look. "You aren't one of those organized types, are you? Every minute planned, every hour accounted for?"

She couldn't help but smile at his exaggerated dismay. "That pretty well sums me up."

He clucked and shook his head. "Could be a problem."

She frowned. "Why is that?"

His cheek crinkled appealingly with his grin—dimples deep enough to raise goose bumps on her arms in response. "I'm just the opposite type. And you know what they say about opposites attracting...."

The attraction was most definitely there—on her part, at least. But just because she'd noticed his masculine attributes didn't mean she'd completely lost her common sense. This man was trouble if she'd ever seen it.

"Yes, well," she said briskly. "I've never been one to go along with what 'they' say."

They'd reached her front porch. She scooped up her newspaper and tucked it beneath her arm. "It was nice to meet you, Mr. Hollis."

"Yeah. Thanks for bringing the mutt home." He didn't seem to be in any hurry to leave, though her hand was already on her doorknob. "You're sure I can't talk you into having a cup of coffee or something with me?"

"Thank you, but I still have work to do. And you have to take your daughter to the birthday party."

Tucker frowned and glanced at his watch. "Oh, yeah. Right. She's supposed to be there now, I think."

"Then you'd better hurry."

"I guess you're right. Rain check, okay?" He was already loping toward his own home, saving Margaret the effort of coming up with a suitably evasive response.

She shook her head as she entered her house and closed the front door behind her. Little Kitten had been right. They were going to be late for the party.

Tucker Hollis was most definitely trouble, she thought, picturing those dimples. Fortunately, she had become very good at avoiding that sort of risk.

* * *

Nearly every Saturday afternoon at four o'clock, Margaret took a forty-five-minute nap. It was a small indulgence after a day of doing housework and running errands, both part of her Saturday routine.

She always turned down the lights, put on classical music and stretched out on the antique fainting couch in her bedroom, covering herself with the luxuriously soft, hand-crocheted afghan she'd bought several years ago at a rural craft shop. She never slept deeply, just dozed, savoring the rare moments of idleness while the music she loved drifted through the room. It wasn't necessary to set an alarm; she never lay there longer than forty-five minutes.

At 4:25, she was brought abruptly out of her light sleep by a sudden blast of noise from outside.

It seemed to be coming from directly beneath her west bedroom window—music, laughter, cheerfully raised voices, children's shrill shrieks of laughter, a dog's manic yapping. It sounded as though a party had begun, one that would probably go on for a while.

She rubbed the remnants of her nap from her eyes and sighed, thinking wistfully of those twenty more minutes of self-indulgence she could have had.

She glanced out her second-story bedroom window, standing to one side so as not to call attention to herself. Several people had gathered in Tucker Hollis's roomy backyard. Wisps of smoke were beginning to rise from an outdoor grill, and portable picnic tables were being arranged on the lawn while children dashed among the adults in pursuit of the happy, tongue-lolling black puppy Margaret had rescued that morning.

Family, she thought with that old, familiar, bitter-wistful tug at her heart.

She let the curtain fall back into place and turned away. She had things to do. She might as well get to them.

Judging from the noise level, the party next door was

still going strong when Margaret's doorbell rang almost an hour later. She was expecting a friend to pick her up for an evening out, so she hastily finished brushing her hair, dropped the hairbrush and hurried downstairs. She smoothed a hand over her soft white blouse and gray pleated slacks before opening the door, a last-minute check for neatness.

She was caught completely by surprise to find her next-door neighbor on her doorstep. "Mr. Hollis," she said. "What—?"

"Tucker," he reminded her. "Or Tuck. I answer to anything but 'Mr.,' unless you're one of my students."

"Is there something I can do for you?" she asked.

"Actually, I came to invite you over for dinner. We're having a barbecue—real casual, just family. Sort of a housewarming party. Kitten's been telling everyone that you did her hair this morning, and I thought maybe you'd like to have a burger with us."

A low-slung black car pulled into the driveway behind them as he spoke. A tall blonde dressed in a brightly colored sweater and snug jeans hopped out.

"Thank you," Margaret told Tucker, "but I have plans for the evening. My friend and I are going to a movie."

"Hi, Margaret. Who's this?" Jackie inquired as she approached them.

"Jackie Shelton, this is my new neighbor, Tucker Hollis."

Jackie extended a brightly manicured hand. "Nice to meet you, Tucker. Come to borrow a cup of sugar?"

Tucker smiled—as Margaret had expected. Everyone smiled at Jackie. It seemed to be almost impossible not to do so. "Actually, I came to invite Margaret over for a barbecue party. I thought she might like to join us— but, of course, you and she already have plans for the evening."

Jackie shrugged, eyeing Tucker with a curiosity that

made Margaret wary. "We were just going to see a movie—hadn't even decided which one yet. A party sounds like a lot more fun."

"Er…" Margaret began.

"The invitation extends to both of you, of course," Tucker said promptly.

Jackie sniffed delicately. "Do I smell hickory smoke?"

He grinned, his cheeks tucking into the dimples that Margaret had noticed—quite objectively, of course—earlier. "You do. Burgers and ribs. My mom brought her world-famous potato salad, and my sister makes coleslaw like you've never tasted before. My brother's got two electric freezers cranking homemade ice cream even as we speak."

"Your brother?" Jackie asked with a birdlike tilt of her head. "That would be your married brother, Gus?"

Tucker chuckled. "No. That would be my single, currently unattached brother, Mick."

"Homemade ice cream," Jackie crooned. "God, it's been years since I had any."

She turned to her friend with a gleam in her blue eyes. "Ribs and ice cream, Margaret. You don't really expect me to turn that down, do you?"

I was rather hoping you would, Margaret almost said. She held on to her smile with an effort. "Well, I—"

"Great." Jackie turned back to Tucker with a grin. "We'll be right over."

He nodded, looking pleased. "We'll be in the backyard. No need to ring the bell or anything, just come through the gate when you're ready."

"Ten minutes," Jackie promised.

Tucker sent Margaret a vaguely apologetic smile, proving he was well aware that she'd just been manipulated into something she wouldn't have done otherwise. "It'll be fun," he assured her, then turned and loped across the lawn toward his own place.

"I," Margaret said, turning to her closest and dearest friend, "am going to strangle you. Slowly."

"Why didn't you tell me you had such interesting new neighbors?"

"I just met Tucker and his children this morning. I certainly wasn't expecting an invitation to a barbecue this afternoon. Why did you—?"

"Margaret, he is *gorgeous*," Jackie breathed, staring after Tucker in awe. "I guess he's married, since you mentioned kids, but did you hear? He has a single brother. We can share him."

Margaret rolled her eyes. "I don't share men, Jackie. And Tucker isn't married. He's a single father."

"Wow, even better. One brother for each of us. We'll decide who gets which after we meet the other one."

Had Margaret been the type to graphically express her emotions, she would have screamed. As it was, she drew a deep breath and shook her head, reminding herself that Jackie always carried on this way and didn't usually mean a word of it. They couldn't have been more different—nor could there be any better friend in the whole world, despite Jackie's occasional tendency to make Margaret consider screaming.

"Don't be ridiculous," she said. "I, for one, am not interested. You're welcome to both brothers, if you want them."

"Hmm. Brothers." Jackie seemed to consider the idea for a moment, then broke into an infectious grin. "I can handle that."

"Right. Now, since you've gotten us into this situation, I suppose we'd better go on over there. We'll make nice with the new neighbors, have a quick burger and then make a graceful, early exit. All right?"

Jackie shrugged. "Sure. But we can't go empty-handed. What have you got to add to the festivities?"

"Nothing."

"Oh, come on, you always have something. Let's go

look." Jackie scooted past her and headed for the kitchen.

Margaret followed hastily. "Really, Jackie, there's nothing. He doesn't expect us to bring anything, since the invitation was spur-of-the-moment. We—"

Jackie had already pounced on a couple of sealed containers. "Homemade chocolate-chip cookies! They'll go great with homemade ice cream. Looks like a couple of dozen here."

"Four dozen. And put them down—I made them for the church social tomorrow."

"So you can make more later. I'll help you."

Jackie, Margaret knew, couldn't boil water without scorching it. "But—"

Jackie had already tucked the containers beneath her arm. She eyed Margaret critically. "I don't suppose you want to change into jeans?"

"No, I do not."

Jackie sighed. "You look very nice, of course, just a bit prim for a backyard barbecue. But if that's what you want to wear—"

"It is."

"Then let's go."

"We planned this movie outing a week ago," Margaret muttered, tagging dutifully after her friend.

Jackie laughed. "Yes, I know. You really hate it when your plans are disrupted. But, as I keep telling you, it's good to be spontaneous sometimes. Keeps you from becoming an old fuddy-duddy."

"Thirty is not old," Margaret said defensively, peeved at having the word applied to her, even indirectly, for a second time that day. "And I don't mind being spontaneous on occasion. I simply like to be better prepared for it."

Jackie was still laughing when they closed Margaret's door behind them.

Chapter Two

Tucker had been watching for them, apparently. He rushed to welcome them when Margaret and Jackie came through the gate to his backyard.

Jackie handed him the plastic containers. "We brought homemade chocolate-chip cookies to go with the ice cream," she announced brightly, looking for all the world as though she'd slaved over a hot oven for hours to provide the treat.

"Hey, thanks. You didn't have to bring anything, but I know everyone will be glad to see these. This gang loves cookies."

Jackie postured modestly. "We hope they enjoy them."

Margaret gave her friend a look that promised a long private lecture later. Jackie grinned.

Tucker smiled at Margaret, that dimpled smile that made her insides do funny, unfamiliar things. "I'm glad you came," he said, sounding sincere.

Kitten bounced up to greet them, wearing a red T-shirt and jeans, her hair still relatively neat in the French braid Margaret had arranged that morning. The red plaid bow was a bit crooked, but still in place.

"Hi, Margaret. I didn't mess up my hair when I changed clothes. Everyone's been telling me how pretty I am," she added unabashedly. "Who's this?" she asked without giving Margaret a chance to respond.

"This is my friend Jackie Shelton. Jackie, this is Tucker's daughter, Christine."

"Everyone calls me Kitten," the child added. "It's a nickname."

Jackie smiled, comfortable with children in a way that Margaret could only envy. "My real name's Jacqueline, but everyone calls me Jackie. That's a nickname, too."

"My daddy has a nickname. Tuck. And my brother is Samuel, but we call him Sam. And Uncle Mick is really Michael, and Aunt Debbie's full name is Deborah. My cousin's Dennis John, but we call him D.J. Just about everybody in the family has a nickname," Kitten expounded without stopping for breath. "I don't know why Margaret doesn't have one, do you?"

"You know, I never really thought about it," Jackie said, struck by the observation. "Maybe we should give her one."

"I really prefer my own name," Margaret said quickly, before they could suggest anything. "Just plain Margaret."

Tucker grinned and took her left hand. "C'mon, Just Plain Margaret, I'll introduce you to the others."

Margaret had never truly believed any man's touch could make her tingle, no matter how attractive the man might be. She was astonished, and not at all pleased, to realize that her fingers were tingling like crazy in Tucker's big, warm grasp. Self-conscious, she tagged along as he pulled her into the crowd.

"Everyone, this is my new neighbor, Margaret McAlister, and her friend Jackie Shelton," he announced loudly, without releasing Margaret's hand. He took a deep breath and started introducing the others, pointing out each one he named.

His parents, Arnie and Lillie Hollis, were a nice-looking couple in their early sixties, both gray haired, neatly dressed, slim and fit. They looked to Margaret as though they'd just left their country club in crisp poplin slacks and matching white sweatshirts with tiny, crossed golf clubs embroidered on the left chest. They were the kind of parents she'd always fantasized about having, she thought with that old, painful ripple of regret.

Tucker's sister, Debbie Hendrickson, looked to be in her early thirties, with dark hair, green eyes and dimples that reminded Margaret forcibly of Tucker. Debbie welcomed Margaret and Jackie with a smile and a barely concealed curiosity.

Debbie's husband, Les, was a tall, sandy-haired orthodontist with flawless teeth and dark blue eyes that seemed to glow with an inner warmth. Margaret liked him immediately. Debbie and Les pointed out their three children, seven-year-old D.J., four-year-old Jake, and a baby girl, Emily, who lay in a plastic carrier, peacefully sleeping through the chaos around her.

Which left only Tuck's "single, currently unattached brother" still to be introduced.

Jackie zeroed in on the man with the unerring instincts of a homing pigeon. "You must be Mick," she said, her voice an octave lower than usual, her lips curved into an inviting smile. "I'm Jackie."

"And I," Mick promptly replied, "am in love." He took her extended hand and raised it to his lips, to Jackie's obvious delight.

Tucker groaned. "Mick is the shy one in the family,"

he said wryly. "Cut out the dramatics, Mick, and come say hi to my neighbor."

Mick, Margaret noted as he approached, had the same dark hair as his sister and brother, but his eyes were hazel. Unlike his siblings, he had more of his mother's features than his father's. He was a couple of inches shorter than Tucker's six feet, two or three years younger, and some thirty pounds lighter than his brother's muscular build, but he fit in well enough with this strikingly attractive family.

He took Margaret's right hand. "Tuck's been telling me what a beautiful neighborhood this is. Silly me, I thought he was referring to the landscaping. Now that I've seen you, I know what he *really* meant."

Margaret blushed, uncertain how to respond to the outrageous line of blarney. A chorus of groans came from Mick's family.

"Ignore him," Tucker advised. "He's insane. It's a great embarrassment to us, but what can we do? He's family."

There was that word again. *Family.*

Margaret disengaged her hands from the Hollis brothers and somehow managed to keep her strained smile in place. "It's very nice to meet you, Mick," she said politely.

"I hope you're both hungry," Lillie Hollis said to Margaret and Jackie. "The guys are cooking enough ribs and hamburgers to feed the entire neighborhood."

Tucker laughed. "You always say that, Mom. And then you're always amazed when there aren't even a few scraps left over afterward."

"I'm starving," Jackie said promptly, moving to Mick's side. "The smell of those ribs is making my mouth water. And did I hear something about homemade ice cream?"

"My specialty," Mick bragged. "Since it's probably

one of the last warm, sunny days of the season, it seemed like a good time to make some."

"Any time's a good time for ice cream," Jackie assured him.

Mick sighed gustily. "I am *definitely* in love."

"And I am going to be sick," Debbie muttered as she turned away. "C'mon, Tuck, help me take those ribs off the grill."

The Hollis family seemed to grow even more exuberant during the meal, everyone talking at once, the children vying for attention, the dog begging for scraps. Jackie blended right in as she flirted outrageously with Mick and Tucker and even their father. Margaret, on the other hand, found herself growing quieter as the evening wore on, feeling very much the introverted misfit among a crowd of extroverts.

It was hardly a new feeling for her.

Kitten stayed close to Margaret's side, chattering like a hyperactive magpie. It wasn't long before Margaret had heard every detail about the birthday party and most everything there was to know about Kitten's friends and classmates.

Though she'd never been at her best around children, she found it easy enough to converse with Kitten. All she had to do was smile and nod a lot, throwing in an occasional "Is that so?" or "And then what happened?"

Young Sam pointedly ignored her. Margaret wondered if he would ever forgive her for chiding him about the flower beds and the baseball incident, then decided it really didn't matter whether he did or not. It wasn't as if they were going to be personally involved, other than as neighbors.

As far as she was concerned, this get-together was a onetime, welcome-to-the-neighborhood sort of thing. She certainly didn't want the Hollis clan to feel obliged to invite her whenever they had a barbecue, just because she was the single woman who lived next door.

She did have a life—and it was a perfectly satisfactory one. No matter what some people said about it—Jackie, for instance, with her constant nagging for Margaret to get out more. Specifically, with men.

She glanced at her watch. It was after seven. Dinner had been eaten, ice cream and cookies consumed, casual conversation exhausted. Her ears were practically ringing from Kitten's ceaseless prattle. The children were all beginning to droop, and the baby fussed in her mother's arms. Surely it was time to leave. She gave Jackie a meaningful look.

Jackie approached with a sheepish expression that made Margaret immediately suspicious. "Er, Margaret," she began, pulling her slightly aside.

"What is it?"

"Mick's asked me to the late movie with him this evening. You don't mind, do you?"

There was nothing Margaret could do except shake her head. "Of course not."

"I know you and I had planned to go out. Of course, you're welcome to go with us...."

"No," Margaret answered, as Jackie must have known she would. She had no intention of being a third wheel on one of Jackie's dates. "I'm really not in the mood for a movie now. And besides," she added wryly, "I have to bake cookies for the church social tomorrow."

Jackie had the grace to look guilty. "I said I'd help you with that, didn't I?"

"Don't worry about it. It really doesn't take two people to stir together a few dozen cookies."

"You're sure you aren't mad? It's just that Mick and I got to talking, and he's interesting and funny—not to mention great looking—and when he asked, I hated to turn him down."

"Jackie. Go to the movie. I'm not mad."

Jackie smiled in quick relief. "Thanks, Margaret. You're a pal."

Margaret's answering smile felt strained. "Yes, I know. Now, I'd better be going. I have several things to do."

The Hollis family protested politely when Margaret announced that she was leaving. Tucking the empty cookie containers into the crook of her left arm, she shook hands with Lillie and Arnie, Debbie and Les and Mick, nodded a farewell to the children—a nod that Sam pretended not to see—thanked everyone for the invitation and accepted their thanks for the cookies.

She turned then to take her leave of Tucker, but he took her free arm companionably in his and started walking with her, all but towing her after him. "I'll walk you home," he said, giving her little chance to argue.

She tried anyway. "That really isn't necessary—"

"No trouble at all," he assured her heartily.

She surrendered with a silent sigh. She was already learning that Tucker Hollis didn't easily take no for an answer.

Tucker was rather quiet as they left his house. Too vividly aware of the silence, Margaret felt a need to fill it with airy pleasantries. "Your family is nice. You seem to be very close."

"Yes, we get along very well, for the most part. It's always been important to Mom to get the family together fairly often."

"That's nice," Margaret murmured lamely.

"What about your family? Are you close to them? Do they live nearby?"

A cold ripple began somewhere deep inside her, in

that place where she'd long ago buried resentments and disappointments and regrets.

With the ease of much practice, she ignored the sensation and kept her voice carefully uninflected. "My parents are both dead, and I was their only child. I have a few cousins scattered across the country, but we do little more than exchange Christmas cards."

"I'm sorry." He seemed genuinely dismayed.

She managed a smile and shook her head. "I've been on my own for some time now. To be honest, it suits me. There's no need for sympathy."

"I didn't mean to offend you. I just can't imagine not having family around," he admitted.

"No offense taken," she assured him. "I have my friends and my work and a few hobbies. I'm quite content."

"What hobbies?" he asked, cocking his head with interest.

"I read. Do some needlework. And I love theater—I go every chance I get."

"Theater. You mean, like plays and operas and stuff?"

She smiled. "Yes. Plays and operas and stuff."

He grinned wryly. "I get to the movies occasionally, usually with the kids, but I tend to spend more time in sporting arenas than theaters."

That didn't surprise her. "I'm not much of a sports fan," she confessed.

They really had absolutely nothing in common. She'd suspected as much; Tucker probably felt the same way.

She was sure his invitation for her to join his family barbecue had been more a friendly, neighborly gesture than a sign of personal interest. It was glaringly obvious that there could be nothing between them. Which, of course, was fine with her.

She liked her life exactly as it was. Tidy. Orderly. Predictable. Safe.

Tucker Hollis, with his impulsive gestures and chronic lateness and wicked smile and two bewildering offspring, was obviously the very opposite of the type of man she would look for—if, of course, she were looking for a man. Which, she assured herself, she wasn't.

"Well," she said brightly, turning to him at her door. "Here we are again at my doorstep."

He smiled. "Three times in one day. It's becoming a habit."

She unlocked her door. "Thank you again, for everything."

He laid a hand on her forearm, gently detaining her when she would have slipped inside without further ado. "Margaret?"

She looked up at him. "Yes?"

"Will you have dinner with me tomorrow night? Just the two of us. I'll get a baby-sitter for the kids."

She nearly dropped her keys. She honestly hadn't expected this. Had convinced herself it couldn't possibly happen.

"Is it that hard a decision to make?" he asked, sounding amused by her hesitation.

"You caught me by surprise," she admitted.

He lifted an eyebrow. "It surprises you that I'm attracted to you? Or that I've acted on the attraction so quickly by asking you out?"

She almost choked that time. What did he expect her to say in response to *that?*

She supposed she was reasonably attractive. Other men had seemed to think so, though her innate caution had kept her from taking many of them up on their overtures. She'd dated, of course—though she realized now how long it had been since she'd last gone out—but she'd limited her choices to men who seemed to be more like herself. Predictable. Practical. She couldn't imagine either of those words being applied to Tucker.

His smile faded. "Have I stepped out of line? Are you involved with someone else?"

She shook her head. "I'm not dating anyone. As I said, I'm content with my life now. I really don't want to complicate it."

His ready grin quirked the corners of his mouth again. "And you see me as a complication?"

She focused rather grimly on those roguish dimples of his. "Oh, yes," she muttered. "I'm afraid I do."

He didn't look at all displeased. He caught her chin and lifted her face so that their gazes met. "I feel the same way about you. But I'm willing to risk it. How about you?"

Another ripple of sensation went through her in response to his touch. She had no trouble identifying it this time. Fear.

"I—" She moistened her lips. "Thank you for asking, Tucker, but I'll have to decline. Let's just keep things nice and neighborly between us, all right?"

"I can be *very* neighborly," he assured her. And then he brushed his lips lightly, lingeringly across hers.

He stepped back before she had a chance to recover. "I'll be seeing you around, Margaret McAlister," he murmured. "You can count on it."

"I—"

But he was already gone, strolling down her walkway with that rolling swagger that made her want to chase him down and hit him. Or demand another kiss.

She groaned and slammed her front door closed behind her, locking herself into the sheltered serenity of her solitary home. The evening hadn't gone at all as she'd planned—and she really didn't handle last-minute changes well. That was the only excuse she could give for the fact that she was still trembling from the feel of

Tucker's lips against her own, no matter how brief and chaste the kiss had been.

She hadn't planned on Tucker Hollis at all—and now that she'd met him, she hadn't the faintest idea what she was going to do about him.

Margaret's lights went out at exactly 11:00 p.m. Tucker checked his watch just to make sure of the time, though it wasn't necessary. One thing he'd learned about his neighbor during the week that had passed since his family barbecue—punctuality seemed to be her religion.

He'd been discreet about watching her. Nothing so crass as trying to peer through her curtains or anything like that. He just happened to notice things. Like the fact that she went out for her paper each weekday morning exactly at seven o'clock—eight o'clock on weekends. And she went to bed every night at eleven. Precisely at eleven.

Whatever she did between getting her morning paper and going to bed was a mystery to him. Of course, he was gone weekdays, himself, and more than a few evenings, so he didn't know whether she had visitors or how often she left, but it seemed to him that Margaret's single household ran exactly like clockwork.

He shook his head. A strict schedule like that would make him crazy. Hell, a schedule like that would be impossible for him, with the kids and all. Was Margaret really as content as she'd claimed with her rigidly predictable routines?

Lonely. The word had occurred to him the first time he'd looked into her soft brown eyes. And that had been before he'd learned that she had no family, worked out of her home and seemed to spend a great deal of time by herself.

He wouldn't have thought she was his type. Not that he'd even had a type lately. Taking care of the kids since their mother's death a year ago had kept him so busy that he hadn't had time to date, much less get involved in a real relationship.

But something about Margaret McAlister tugged at him. Made him think of her at odd times. Made him wonder what went on behind that politely detached expression on her pretty face. Made him curious about what in her past had made her live such a solitary existence when he suspected that she wasn't nearly as much the loner as she might have others believe.

She couldn't have been more different from Callie, his late ex-wife. Callie had been impulsive and scatterbrained. Cheerfully boisterous, a lot of fun. About as dependable as rain in the desert.

They'd been high-school sweethearts. Her uninhibited zest for life had appealed to him then, as had her stunning figure and lusty passions. They'd married during his sophomore year of college. Callie had worked as a checker at a discount store to help him earn his degree, even after Sam was accidentally conceived earlier than they'd intended to start their family.

Tucker had promised Callie that he would get a teaching job as soon as he earned his bachelor's degree, study nights for his master's, then go into school administration. That job would one day pay him enough for her to quit work and let him repay her for all she'd done for him, he'd said repeatedly.

Their marriage had gotten shaky sometime after Sam's third birthday. Kitten had been the result of their imprudent attempt to strengthen the commitment between them by adding to their family.

Kitten had been only six months old when Callie became involved with Benny Campbell, the head of the sporting-goods department of the discount store where she'd worked for so many years.

Tucker had received his divorce papers the day after he'd finally earned his master's degree.

To give Callie credit, she'd asked for very little in return for her sacrifices during their marriage. She'd told him regretfully that she blamed herself for many of their problems, that she knew he'd done all he could to keep their family together, that everything she'd done for him had been motivated solely by the love that had faded as the years had passed. There'd been no custody battles, no arguments over child-support payments or division of property. The divorce had been amicable, uncomplicated and relatively painless.

And yet Tucker still smarted from the wounds he'd kept well hidden during the ordeal.

He hadn't wanted the divorce. He'd liked being married, liked being part of a family. He'd still loved Callie, despite her flaws—and he was well aware that he had more than enough of those himself. It hurt him to see her with Benny, and to miss all those nights of tucking his kids in to bed, all those family breakfasts they'd once shared.

During the three years following the divorce, Tucker had gotten on with his life and the pain had faded, but he had still grieved along with his children when their mother died in the car accident with her second husband.

There'd been other women after the divorce, before Tucker had become a full-time single dad. A few brief, enjoyable affairs that had ended by mutual consent, leaving no scars behind. Pleasant, but somehow unsatisfying. He hadn't even had that since the children had come to live with him.

He'd begun to wonder if he would ever find another woman who'd make him think of permanence and commitment, of growing old together. He'd always thought if he ever did meet someone who made him think along those lines, she'd be a bit like Callie. Free-spirited. Vivacious. Extroverted.

He never would have imagined that he'd take one look at an obviously repressed, probably compulsive, decidedly introverted number cruncher and feel as though he'd just been punched in the stomach. But that was exactly what had happened when he'd looked up from tangling his daughter's hair and found a slender, brown-eyed woman holding his son's puppy and watching him with a lonely, cautious expression that had tugged at all his masculine instincts.

Letting his bedroom curtain fall into place, he turned away from the window. It was getting late, and he had to be up early to feed the kids, get them off to school and then make it to his own school in time for his first-period class.

It was a challenge every morning to get it all done in time—and his students had learned not to be surprised when he dashed in at the last moment, winded and disheveled and flustered. But hey, he managed somehow. The kids were healthy and seemed happy enough, thank God, despite his admittedly disorganized nature. He didn't really need anyone to help him raise them.

But it would have been nice, he thought a bit wistfully, to have someone waiting when he climbed into bed.

He reached over and turned off the lamp, letting darkness fall over the silent bedroom. And then he rolled over in the king-size bed, stretched full length and forced himself to sleep.

Chapter Three

Taking advantage of the beautiful weather on the first Sunday afternoon of October—two weeks after the barbecue with her neighbors—Margaret put on jeans and a long-sleeved knit top, pulled her hair into a neat ponytail and went out to work in her yard. Her hands protected by heavy gloves, she tugged at weeds and pinched back straggly shoots of the multicolored chrysanthemums she'd planted in a bed around the fountain.

Margaret enjoyed yard work, and took pride in her lawn and the flower beds that ran the entire length of her house and lined the driveway. After a childhood spent moving from grungy apartments to run-down, packed-dirt trailer parks, or sleeping in a beat-up station wagon when her parents couldn't pay rent, she treasured her neat, lovely home.

Some twenty minutes had passed when she heard a child's voice from behind her. "Hi, Margaret! Whatcha doing?"

Margaret swiveled on her heels to find Kitten peering through the chain-link fence that separated their yards. "I'm working in my flower beds," she answered, though she thought it should have been obvious, even to a child. Perhaps this was just the little girl's way of striking up a conversation, she decided.

"You have pretty flowers. I like the yellow ones best."

Margaret glanced with pride at the thriving yellow mums. "Thank you. I like them, too."

"Daddy hasn't had time to work in our yard yet. Sam mowed it last week. I told Daddy I wanted some flowers like you have. And a fountain. I 'specially like the fountain. Can I come over?" Kitten spoke without even pausing for breath.

Unaccustomed to being interrupted in her chores, Margaret hesitated. "Well..."

"I won't get in your way," the child promised hopefully.

Margaret couldn't find the heart to reject her. "Yes, you're welcome to come over. But you have to ask your father."

"Okay. Be right back." Kitten turned and sprinted toward her front door.

Margaret had time only for a few more snips with her trimming shears before the child reappeared, winded and grinning, dressed in a blue-and-white shorts set, a flowered baseball-style cap and—Margaret couldn't help noticing—a pair of thick green mittens.

Kitten held up her hands. "These are the only gloves I could find. Will they work?"

"You want to help with my gardening?" Margaret asked, rather surprised.

Kitten nodded, her ponytail bobbing from the adjustment hole at the back of her cap. "I want to learn how so I can help Daddy put flowers in our yard. What do I do first?"

"Well..." Margaret glanced around consideringly. She certainly had no intention of handing the little girl a pair of shears. She pointed to a shoot of hook grass that was the bane of any gardener's life. "See this sprig of grass? It has to be pulled up, roots and all. Like this." She demonstrated.

Watching intently, Kitten nodded again, then pounced on another shoot. "This one, too?"

"Yes. As you can see, they sneak up all through the beds. You can pull as many of them as you see. Make sure you only pull shoots that look exactly like this, though."

"'Kay." Kitten tugged intently at the first sprout. She looked chagrined when it broke off in her mittened hand. "It broke. I didn't get the root," she said, stricken.

"That's all right," Margaret assured her hastily. "Here, let me show you again."

She covered the child's hand with her own, directed her to another weed and showed her how to pull from close to the ground with a steady pressure that eased the roots from the loosened topsoil and the thin layer of mulch.

Her lower lip caught between her teeth, Kitten moved to the next weed, took hold and pulled exactly the way Margaret had demonstrated. Her little face glowed when her efforts were met with success this time. "I got it!" she exclaimed. "Roots and all."

Margaret couldn't help but smile in return. "That's very good, Kitten. You learn quickly."

The child beamed in response to the praise and went back to work with an enthusiasm that Margaret found secretly amusing. She returned to her own work, though she kept one eye on Kitten and tried to respond appropriately to the child's almost ceaseless prattling.

At one point, she noticed Sam in the next yard, holding his puppy and watching her and Kitten work. The boy's frown bothered her; she wished he wouldn't look at her as though she were going to climb on a broom and zoom into the air at any moment.

She decided to try to redeem herself with him. After all, if they were going to be neighbors, they might as well be friendly.

"Hello, Sam," she called out. "Kitten and I were just going to have a glass of lemonade. Would you like to join us?"

Sam shook his head and turned away.

"You're s'posed to say 'No, thank you!'" Kitten reminded him loudly, her disapproval of her brother's behavior quite clear.

Scowling, Sam muttered something that might have been the correct response—or maybe one Margaret was better off not hearing, she thought wryly. The boy had disappeared before she could decide what to say next.

"Sam can be a real jerk sometimes," Kitten pronounced with a long-suffering sigh. "Did you say something about lemonade?"

Fifteen minutes later, Margaret and Kitten sat companionably in the wicker rockers on Margaret's front porch. On the small wicker table between them rested a tray that held a pitcher of lemonade and a plate of homemade oatmeal-raisin cookies. A pair of grubby green mittens lay beside the tray.

Her little feet dangling, Kitten rocked energetically while she sipped her drink, chewed her cookies and somehow at the same time managed to suggest that Margaret might want to put some goldfish in the pool of her fountain. "I saw a fountain with fish in it once," she added. "They were great big orange fish—some of them had white and yellow spots—and they were real pretty. Don't you think you'd like some in your fountain?''

"I don't know if fish would live in my fountain," Margaret replied, never having considered the possibility. "I suppose I could look into it.''

And then she forgot all about fish and fountains when Tucker Hollis rounded the corner of the fence and started up her walkway.

The late-afternoon sun slanted over him as though holding him in a spotlight, making his dark hair glitter with hidden highlights. He wore a gray T-shirt and well-worn jeans, both of which fit him like a second skin. Muscles rippled as he walked with that sexy, rolling gait she'd come to associate with him, and he was wearing a smile that could fell a woman's heart at twenty paces.

Margaret swallowed a sudden lump in her throat and reminded herself that he was merely a junior-high-school history teacher. The prosaic observation had no noticeable effect on her racing pulse.

She supposed she should be relieved to know that she had the same reactions to an attractive male as any other healthy woman her age. She wasn't. She'd never asked for sweaty palms or hammering heartbeats or girlish goose bumps, especially where this man was concerned. She'd never asked for trouble.

"Hi, Daddy," Kitten called out. "We're doing yard work.''

His mouth twitching, Tucker glanced at the lemonade and cookies. "Oh, is *that* what you're doing?''

Kitten giggled. "Well, not right now, of course. We're taking a break. See that pile of weeds over there? I pulled them up all by myself, didn't I, Margaret?''

"Yes, you've been a big help," Margaret agreed, trying to keep her voice casual as she avoided Tucker's eyes by looking at his child.

"You'd better go wash up now, Kitten," Tucker suggested. "We're supposed to go to Grandma's tonight for dinner, and you've only got an hour to get ready."

Margaret bit her lip. "I hope it's all right that she had a couple of cookies. I didn't think about it spoiling her appetite."

Tucker smiled and tugged at the brim of his daughter's cap. "Are you kidding? Nothing spoils this kid's appetite."

"They're healthy cookies, Daddy," Kitten assured him. "Oatmeal and raisin. Margaret made them herself. She makes the best cookies in the whole world."

"Really? Maybe she won't mind if I sample one for myself."

"Please, help yourself," Margaret responded immediately, motioning toward the plate of cookies. "Would you like some lemonade to go with it?"

"Sure, if it's no trouble. Head on over and clean up, Kitten. I'll be there in a few minutes." Tucker took the rocker Kitten obediently vacated, and he looked as though he intended to linger awhile.

Margaret went inside to get him a glass of ice for his drink. When she came back out, Kitten was gone, leaving Margaret alone on the porch with Tucker.

"Thanks," he said, accepting the glass of lemonade and helping himself to a couple of cookies from the plate. "It was nice of you to put up with Kitten for the afternoon. I've been grading essays, and she was getting pretty bored cooped up in the house."

Shaking her head, Margaret smiled. "She was no trouble. As a matter of fact, she's pretty good at weeding."

He chuckled. "It's amazing how much kids can accomplish when they think it's something fun, instead of something they've been told to do. You should see how long it takes her to put away her toys when I ask."

"I have to admit I haven't been around children much,

but Kitten seems like an exceptionally sweet-natured little girl.''

"Thanks. I think so, too, but it's nice to hear an objective opinion.''

Margaret glanced toward the house next door, remembering the scowl Sam had given her. ''I don't think Sam likes me very much.''

Tucker sighed. ''Don't take it personally. He's going through that difficult stage of boyhood. My mom warned me that it starts at about his age.''

''And when does it end?''

His grin was rueful. ''She said she'd let me know as soon as I've passed out of it.''

Margaret laughed. She could almost picture Lillie saying just that with a wry shake of her head.

''You have a nice laugh, Margaret McAlister. And an utterly beautiful smile.'' His voice had lowered, deepened, giving the words an intimacy that belied his light tone.

Suddenly self-conscious again, she looked down into her nearly empty lemonade glass. ''Um, thank you.''

She was aware that he was watching her, and she bit her lip, trying to think of something to say to quickly change the subject. Preferably something that didn't embarrass her.

He spoke before she could. ''It's difficult for you to accept compliments, isn't it?''

''I'm not used to flattery,'' she admitted. ''I never know quite what I'm expected to say in return.''

''You see, there's your problem. You think I'm expecting something from you. You're wrong, you know. I was simply pointing out that I like your smile.''

She moistened her lips and looked again toward the front lawn. ''Kitten thinks I should put goldfish in my fountain,'' she said, seizing the first conversational gambit that came to mind.

Tucker obviously wasn't fooled by the ploy, but he went along cooperatively enough, to her relief. "That sounds like something Kitten would come up with."

"She said she saw one once with fish in it. I'm not sure they'd live. What do you think?"

"I think they'd do fine with a little effort on your part. The basin is deep enough for regular-size goldfish, though not for the big koi. If you decide to try it, let me know. I'll help you get started."

"You're a fish expert, are you?"

He smiled. "Let's just say I've learned a few useful tricks in my time."

Oh, she didn't doubt that. That smile of his could be considered a "useful trick"—if seduction was what he had in mind.

He drained his glass, set it on the wicker table and stood. "I'd better get on home. Mom's threatened to ground me for the rest of my life if I'm late for dinner again."

He didn't look particularly concerned by the threat, which made Margaret smile again. She really did like Lillie, she thought.

"Thanks for the cookies," he added.

"You're welcome. Tell Kitten thanks for her help."

"Hey, why don't you come with us this evening? Mom would love to have you join us for dinner. She always makes enough for a half-dozen extra guests."

Margaret kept her smile cool, polite. "Thank you, but I have things I need to do tonight."

"Got the evening all scheduled, hmm?"

"Yes, I suppose I do." She all but dared him to tease her about it.

"Okay," he said, instead. "Some other time, then."

She stood, looking directly at him now. "I've already told you I'm not interested in dating," she reminded him, just in case he thought she'd changed her mind.

He grinned and touched the end of her nose with the tip of his finger. "Not interested *yet*," he corrected her.

"Tucker—"

But he was already on his way down the walk. "I'll be seeing you," he called over his shoulder.

Frustrated, she rubbed at her forehead. She really should have bought a house in the country, she told herself ruefully. One where the closest neighbors were a mile or so away.

Dinnertime conversation was enlivened that evening by Kitten's cheery tales of her adventures in gardening. Her grandparents listened indulgently, but Tucker noticed that Sam's scowl grew more pronounced as the meal progressed.

"I've admired Margaret's yard every time I've driven past," Lillie commented. "She must work very hard at keeping it so nice."

"She says it's not so hard if she does a little at a time," Kitten said.

"She sure works hard at keeping people out of it," Sam muttered.

Tucker gave his son a warning look.

"Margaret's nice," Kitten insisted. "She knows all about flowers and plants and stuff. And she makes good cookies. And she's got a nice smile."

Sam snorted. His grandparents looked at him in surprise.

"I don't like her much," he admitted. "I think she's mean."

"Need I remind you that she saved Boomer from being run over?" Tucker asked mildly. "She didn't have to chase him down and bring him home, you know. She did it because she didn't want him to get hurt."

Sam wasn't impressed. "She probably just wanted to meet *you*."

It didn't take a child psychologist to figure out that

Sam had noticed his father's interest in their attractive neighbor—and wasn't at all pleased about it. Tucker ran a hand over his jaw, wondering whether he should try to talk to the boy or just keep quiet and hope the initial belligerence would pass.

Since he hadn't dated since the kids had moved in with him a year ago, this was the first time the issue had come up. He wanted to handle it correctly. Though his children would always come first with him, he wanted Sam to know that he didn't intend to live the rest of his life like a monk.

"I *like* Margaret," Kitten stated, looking at her brother defiantly.

"Well, I don't."

"Yeah, well, you're a jerk."

"Dad!"

"Kitten," Tucker murmured. "Don't call your brother a jerk." He looked apologetically at his parents, who were struggling to control their amusement. Tucker could easily interpret the silent message his mother was sending him. *I warned you you'd have kids of your own someday. See what I went through with you and your brother and sister?*

Not for the first time, he acknowledged the wisdom of all those things she'd told him when he was a smart-mouthed kid himself.

Margaret found herself smiling at something Kitten had said as she ate her own dinner alone that evening. She really was a cute child, with a decidedly interesting outlook on life. Margaret had never imagined she would have enjoyed spending over an hour working side by side with a five-year-old, but oddly enough, she had.

She'd gone through a phase of wanting children in her early twenties. She'd hoped to find a man with whom she could imagine spending the rest of her life. Unfortunately, her few relationships had all ended in disillusion and disappointment.

She'd been told that she was too particular, that she expected too much from a man. She'd been told she should be willing to settle. She'd finally decided that she would rather live by herself, on her own terms, than settle for a marriage based on mutual discontent. She'd seen enough of that in her parents' marriage.

Since she'd stopped thinking in terms of marriage for herself, she'd convinced herself that she wouldn't have made a very good mother anyway. She didn't know anything about children. She hadn't had siblings or many playmates, had hardly had a chance to be a child herself. And her mother had certainly not served as a sterling example of motherhood.

Now there was only the occasional maternal tug, usually set off by those cute babies in diaper and baby-food commercials, or by the rare baby shower she felt obliged to attend, or by being forced to look at photographs of someone's children or grandchildren. And this afternoon, when Kitten had looked up at her so sweetly and asked her to show her how to pull weeds without breaking them off in her little mittened hand...

Margaret made a face and shook her head as though to dispel the fanciful thoughts that had lodged there. She was rather pleased to know that at least one child liked her, but that didn't mean she'd changed her mind about her goals.

She was content now. She didn't want to risk messing it up in pursuit of something that was probably wrong for her anyway.

Kitten was an adorable child. And her father was most definitely appealing. But all in all, Margaret thought she'd better keep her distance—even though both of them seemed inexplicably interested in making her a part of their lives, if only temporarily.

Chapter Four

Margaret was struck by a sense of déjà vu when she bent to retrieve her newspaper Monday morning and found herself distracted by a yapping puppy. The dog was out again. He came rushing up to Margaret when she stepped off her porch, his entire back half wiggling with his enthusiastic greeting. Cars passed on the street as neighbors left to brave the morning-rush-hour traffic.

It was a wonder, Margaret thought with a shake of her head, that Boomer hadn't already met with disaster.

She held out her hands to him. "Come here, boy," she said firmly.

He was in the mood to play. Tongue lolling, he evaded her grasp, though he stayed close, obviously teasing.

Margaret sighed. "Come on, Boomer, I really don't have time for this."

He got close enough to touch a wet nose to her hand, then dodged when she grabbed for him. Tail wagging wildly, he danced five feet away. She would have sworn he was laughing at her.

"It would serve you right if I left you to your fate," she muttered, scowling. She thought of calling Tucker to come get his dog, but she was afraid the pup would dash into the street if she turned her back on him.

She knelt and tried again, holding her hand out enticingly, making her voice as coaxing as she could. "Come here, Boomer. Come to Margaret. There's a good boy."

She felt like an idiot, but her persistence paid off. He dashed toward her, and she snatched him into her arms, getting a face full of tongue in reward for her efforts.

"Ugh," she muttered, jerking her face out of reach. "Stupid dog, don't you even know when someone doesn't like you?" But she cradled his wriggling body carefully as she carried him home.

The Hollises' gate was open again, the latch dangling. Obviously, Tucker wouldn't win any prizes in latch fixing. Restraining the dog beneath her arm, Margaret rang the doorbell.

Kitten opened the door. Her dark hair hadn't been combed yet, and there was a smudge of jelly on her cheek.

"Hi, Margaret," she said. "Does this match?"

It took Margaret a moment to figure out that the child was referring to the hunter green top she was wearing with black-and-turquoise-print leggings. "No, it doesn't," she replied honestly. The combination was really pretty awful.

Kitten sighed deeply. "I was afraid of that. Daddy hasn't had time to look at me yet. We're running late again."

"Then you'd better hurry and change. Maybe you could wear a pair of jeans with that top—jeans go with almost anything."

Kitten smiled. "Okay." She turned and dashed toward the stairs, leaving Margaret in the entryway with the puppy.

"Kitten, wait. Where's—?"

But the child was already gone. Margaret thought about just putting Boomer down and closing the door. If Boomer piddled in the hallway, too bad. It wasn't her responsibility to keep taking care of this dog.

She heard Tucker shouting from the back of the house, probably the kitchen. "Sam! Hey, Sam, are you ready yet? If you don't hurry, you're going to have to go to school without any breakfast, you hear? Sam, are you listening to me?"

Margaret couldn't help noticing Tucker's rather harried undertone. Were mornings always like this in the Hollis household? It seemed to her that Tucker needed to establish a better schedule. Not that it was any of her business, of course.

Hearing Tucker's voice, the puppy began to bark and squirm. "Sam, have you got that dog in the house again?" Tucker yelled. "Take him outside and get in here for breakfast."

Oops. It looked as though Sam would be blamed if Margaret dumped the dog and ran. That was all she needed to make him hate her forever.

"Tucker?" she called out, taking a step in the direction of his voice, leaving the door open behind her. "Hello?"

There was a crash from the kitchen, and then Tucker appeared in a doorway. His blue chambray shirt hung unbuttoned over his jeans, revealing a slice of tanned, lightly furred chest. "Margaret?" he asked in surprise. "What are you—?"

And then he spotted Boomer. He winced. "Don't tell me—"

"Kitten let me in. I—"

Sam barreled down the stairs. "Dad, I can't find my shoes. I know they were under my bed last night, but—"

He skidded to a halt, staring at Margaret.

Self-conscious at being the focus of their attention, she held the dog out to Sam. "Boomer got out again. I found him in my yard. I think your gate latch is broken again."

Sam took the dog, carefully avoiding any physical contact with Margaret. "Thanks," he muttered, then turned quickly to his father. "What should I do with him?"

Tucker groaned and ran a hand through his disheveled hair. Margaret made a conscious effort to keep her gaze focused away from his partially revealed chest.

"Damn," he said. "I really don't have time to fix the latch this morning. I'll have to tie the gate shut until I can work on it this evening."

He gave Margaret an apologetic look. "Thanks for rescuing him again. I'll try to make sure this is the last time."

"No problem. By the way, Kitten's gone up to finish dressing."

"Good. We're really running late this morning. Sam, your cereal's on the table, milk's in the fridge. You go eat while I do something with the mutt." He scooped the dog out of his son's hands, tucking it under his arm like a wriggling football.

"But, Dad, I can't find my shoes!"

"You can look for them after you eat. Hurry, now."

"Margaret." Kitten appeared at the top of the stairs, wearing jeans with the hunter green top. Her hair was still tangled, and jelly still streaked her cheek, but at least the fashion police wouldn't ticket her for clashing, Margaret thought wryly.

"Is this better?" the child asked, motioning toward her clothing.

"Much." Margaret looked at Tucker. "Is there anything I can do to help out?" she offered hesitantly. "I could do Kitten's hair, if you—"

"Would you?" He didn't bother to hide his relief. "Thanks, Margaret, that would be great. We've got to leave in about fifteen minutes, and as you can see, I'm not exactly ready."

She glanced at his chest, then quickly away. "Yes, I see." She turned to Sam. "Um, would you like me to…?"

"I don't need any help," the boy insisted, backing away.

"Sam, she was just offering—"

But Margaret didn't let Tucker finish the reprimand. "Take the dog out, Tucker. I'll help Kitten while Sam gets ready."

Tucker hesitated.

"Go," she ordered, pointing firmly toward the door.

Tucker grimaced but obeyed. Sam disappeared hastily into the kitchen. Margaret turned to the little girl. "Okay, Kitten, let's see about that hair."

Kitten led Margaret upstairs to her room. Margaret noted that the house was basically clean, but cardboard cartons were still stacked in several corners. She suspected that Tucker's system of moving involved unpacking things as he needed them.

Living in this household, she thought with a shake of her head, would quickly make her crazy. She'd seen too many packing cartons, endured too many hectic mornings during her childhood. Thank goodness she didn't have to live that way now.

Taking advantage of the situation, Kitten wanted her hair braided. Aware of the time constraints, Margaret worked quickly, finished off with a green bow and sent Kitten to wash her face and brush her teeth. "Better hurry," she advised. "I think your dad's getting frantic."

Kitten giggled. "What else is new?" But she headed for the bathroom without dallying.

Margaret found Sam sitting at the bottom of the stairs, tying the laces on a pair of scuffed sneakers. "I see you found your shoes."

Keeping his eyes on his laces, Sam nodded. "Uh-huh."

Margaret swallowed a sigh. "Well, I—"

Tucker barreled through a doorway, his shirt buttoned and mostly tucked in, his hands full. He tossed a brown paper bag at Sam, who caught it deftly. "Lunch," Tucker said, then raised his voice. "Kitten?"

"She's ready," Margaret assured him. "I'll get out of your way now."

He looked at her with a ruefully self-deprecating smile. "You must think you live next door to a circus. I promise you, it isn't always this crazy around here."

"I'm sure it isn't," she replied, hoping her lack of conviction wasn't evident in her voice.

He leaned over and kissed her cheek, as casually as if it were a familiar habit. "Thanks, Margaret," he said softly. "I owe you."

She knew she was blushing and hated herself for it. She knew Sam was watching, could almost feel the waves of resentment and disapproval coming from him. "Um, have a nice day."

And then she left. Quickly.

"Have a nice day?" she muttered, slapping her forehead as she closed herself into the quiet sanity of her own home. "Oh, great, Margaret. Very clever."

Not that she wanted to impress him with snappy repartee, or anything like that. It was just that...

She groaned. Her morning wasn't going at all as it should have.

That secluded house in the country was sounding better all the time.

His class was taking a test, so the room was quiet except for the shuffling of feet and papers, the scratching of pencils, the occasional cough or cleared throat or furtive whisper. Keeping a close eye on potential trouble-makers, Tucker wished he could put his chaotic morning out of his mind. But it was no use. He could still clearly picture Margaret standing in his hallway, looking as though she'd wandered onto the set of an old slapstick movie.

Even at just after seven in the morning, she'd been fully dressed—buttons and all, he thought with a wince—in a neatly pressed blouse and slacks and loafers that had looked freshly shined. Her hair had been tucked into its usual prim upsweep, her makeup had been done—she'd looked fresh and calm and collected. She couldn't have made more of a contrast to his family that morning if she'd deliberately tried.

He really should just admit defeat and stop even thinking about trying to persuade her to go out with him. She'd obviously already come to the conclusion that they were just too different. She couldn't have made her lack of interest in him more clear—but there had been that one moment when their eyes had met in his entryway and he'd thought he'd seen…something.

Or had he only convinced himself he'd seen something that hadn't been there at all? Maybe what he'd taken for attraction had been nothing more than bewilderment.

He really should let it drop. Resign himself to being neighborly on occasion, and nothing more.

But she'd smelled so good when he'd leaned close to her, her scent fresh and sweet, reminding him of the flowers that bloomed in her care. And her skin had felt so warm and silky against his lips when he'd impulsively kissed her cheek.

Maybe he should ask her one more time, he thought, loudly clearing his throat at a student who seemed to be trying to catch a glimpse of a classmate's test paper. The boy hastily turned his attention to his own paper.

Tucker spent the rest of the period contemplating his own multiple-choice problem. Ask her out again. Give up. Or maybe all of the above.

He was beginning to suspect that the results of this particular test could be terribly important.

Margaret realized that evening that she hadn't heard from Jackie for over two weeks now—since her friend had left the Hollis barbecue with Tucker's brother. Margaret suspected that the date must have gone well, judging by Jackie's silence. Jackie always tended to disappear when there was a new man in her life.

Margaret ate a light dinner of a grilled chicken breast, steamed vegetables and a wheat roll, cleaned up the kitchen and then wandered into her den to watch a nature special on the Discovery channel. Halfway through the program, she grew tired of watching nearly every carnivore in Africa stalk, kill and lunch on gazelles. She was beginning to think those poor creatures should be born with "golden arches" emblazoned on their side. Talk about fast food...

She snapped off the set and picked up a book, but that didn't hold her interest, either.

She'd bet it wasn't this quiet in the Hollis household on a typical Monday evening.

Reminding herself that she *liked* the quiet and solitude, she set her book aside and reached for the phone. Maybe she'd just make sure Jackie was all right.

She was rather surprised when Jackie answered; Margaret had more than half expected to reach her machine. "Hi," she said.

"Margaret, hi! I've been meaning to call you."

"Mmm. So, how's everything going?"

"Great!"

Margaret winced. Oh, yeah, she'd heard that tone before. Jackie fell passionately in love on an average of three times a year. It always ended in a blazing crash, followed by weeks of bitter self-recrimination. Until the next man came along.

Margaret and Jackie had been friends since they'd met in college, but they had nothing whatever in common. Neither of them quite understood the bond that had formed between them, the spiritual connection that held them together even when they didn't see each other for weeks at a time, even when their lives drifted in different directions. The truth was, Jackie was as close as Margaret had ever come to having a sister, and she loved her despite her occasional exasperation with her.

"Oh, Margaret, he's wonderful. Funny and smart and attentive. He's an assistant high-school football coach and he teaches health and physical education, so he's great with kids and in fantastic shape. And he cooks. Can you believe it?"

"Mick, right?"

Jackie laughed. "Well, of course Mick. Who else?"

"I take it you've seen him again since the barbecue."

"Every night. He'd be here now except that he had a meeting at school. He's coming over later. He promised to make pecan waffles for breakfast."

Margaret shook her head. Jackie certainly had thrown herself into this affair quickly enough. Usually, the hotter and faster the beginning, the more furious and explosive the ending, at least from what Margaret had observed of Jackie's previous experiences. Margaret wondered if the rest of the Hollis family knew that Mick and Jackie had gotten this deeply involved. Tucker hadn't said anything about it—not that she'd spent enough time with him to talk much about anything.

"What about you?" Jackie asked archly. "How's it going with your gorgeous new neighbor?"

"It isn't going any way in particular," Margaret answered coolly. "We hardly see each other."

"Oh." Jackie sounded disappointed. "You mean he hasn't asked you out or anything?"

"Jackie…"

"I felt sure he'd ask you out, especially after he walked you home from the barbecue. He definitely looked interested. Maybe if you—"

"Jackie, he asked me out. I turned him down."

Jackie growled. "You turned him down? Oh, Margaret, *what* am I going to do with you? Why in the world didn't you say yes? Here's this great guy with two great kids and a great family and everything and you turn him down. He's a definite serious prospect probably actively looking for someone to help him raise those kids. So what are you waiting for?"

"I'm not waiting for anything. Surely you can see that Tucker and I have nothing in common."

"No, I don't see that. And I don't know how you can say it, either. You haven't been around him enough to know whether you have anything in common or not!"

"Trust me. I know."

"Well, I think you're just scared," Jackie challenged.

Margaret refused to fall for the ploy. "Maybe" was all she said. "I'm content with my life now. I don't want to take a chance of getting involved with a man with two vulnerable children—a man who lives next door, by the way. Think how awkward it would be for everyone if it didn't work out. And besides, I'm not particularly interested in being selected to help raise someone's kids, as you put it."

"I didn't mean that would be the only reason he'd be interested in you. You're such a pessimist. If it doesn't work out, big deal. One date. You don't have to go out again, and you can still be neighborly. It doesn't have to be a disaster waiting to happen."

Maybe she *was* being a pessimist, but Margaret didn't think it would be that simple. For some reason, she was afraid that going out with Tucker, even for a simple dinner date, would be more risk than she was willing to take at this point in her life.

"Jackie," she said warningly, "promise me you'll let this be my decision. Don't get involved, all right?"

"I won't say anything," Jackie conceded reluctantly. "But I still— Oh. Someone's at the door. It's probably Mick."

"Then you'd better go let him in. And, Jackie, I hope everything works out for you this time."

"I have a good feeling about it this time, Margaret. Mick is special. Really special."

Margaret had heard that before, too. But she was being a pessimist again. "Keep in touch" was all she said.

"You know I will." Jackie already sounded distracted. "Talk to you later."

"Sure," Margaret said, but Jackie had already hung up.

Margaret cradled the receiver and sat for a while without moving, her thoughts grim. Her house was so quiet that she could hear a faint yapping coming from next door as Boomer stood guard over his yard, probably warning off a squirrel or a cat.

Margaret grimaced. Who'd have thought that the mere act of rescuing a puppy from traffic could lead to all this?

The one thing most likely to make Margaret crazy was sloppy bookkeeping. On the whole, she'd trained her clients to keep fairly decent records, but her newest account, an independently owned quick-lube shop, was proving more difficult than most.

It wasn't that the books were hard to keep—it was a small, fairly simple operation—but the owners, two young men in business for the first time, were haphazard record-keepers, to say the least. They brought their statements and receipts once a week, usually in a shopping bag. Their statements were handwritten, and Margaret couldn't even guess at their billing system. It was hard enough for her to read their writing.

As for their tax records...

She groaned and shook her head. She'd just found a receipt for a Hootie and the Blowfish CD. A scribbled note on the back said the CD was "for listening during business hours."

Margaret doubted the IRS considered Hootie and the Blowfish a legitimate deduction for a lube shop. She'd spent over an hour last week convincing one of the owners, Greg, that he couldn't deduct his new fishing boat.

"Just because you bought it from a regular customer," she'd explained as patiently as she could, "does not make it a legitimate business expense." She wasn't sure she'd ever convinced him.

It was after five on Thursday, and she'd spent most of the afternoon working on this account. She was about ready to put it away for the day. Her job wasn't a particularly exciting one, and the small businesses she worked for couldn't pay a great deal, but it gave her something to do with her time without having to go to an office every day.

She'd tried working for a large accounting firm when she'd graduated from college. She'd hated it—the office politics, the feeling that she wasn't in full control, the offhand work habits of many of her co-workers. She'd decided then that she wasn't a "team player."

As for money, her needs were easily met. After a childhood of insecurity and uncertainty due to her parents' problems, it was ironic that their deaths had provided security for her adulthood. Because of the insurance settlements she had received, her house was paid for, as was her car, and her simple life-style made her present income sufficient for her needs. She supposed she could earn more if she made an effort to broaden her client base, but she was content for now with the status quo.

Her unnervingly unpredictable childhood had left her almost obsessively wary of change now. She knew it, wasn't particularly proud of it, but her rut had become so calm and comfortable that she was afraid to make any drastic changes.

Cowardly—maybe.

Safe—definitely.

Now if only she could teach Greg and Jeff how to keep records...

Her doorbell distracted her from her work. She pushed away from the computer and went to answer it, half-expecting to find a delivery on her doorstep or one of her clients dropping off paperwork after business hours.

But it was Tucker Hollis's face she spotted through the leaded-glass pane in her front door. Her stomach immediately tightened, and she ran her hands down the legs of her dark slacks in a nervous gesture.

What did he want this time? Surely he wouldn't ask her out again. She really thought she'd made herself clear on that point. She was marginally relieved to find Kitten at Tucker's side when she opened the door. She didn't think Tucker would ask her out again with his five-year-old daughter as an audience.

"Hi, Margaret. I made you something at school today," Kitten announced proudly, holding out a sheet of paper.

"For me?" Margaret took the sheet carefully.

It was a drawing, colored with crayons. A rather crooked house was in the center, with what appeared to be mounds of wildly colorful flowers around it. What might have been a fountain had been drawn in the lower right corner. Looking closely, Margaret saw bright orange fish carefully drawn in the blue water. A yellow sun beamed wavy rays from the left corner, and the sky was an improbable blue, with two fat white clouds floating across the top.

"This is my house, isn't it, Kitten?" she asked, deeply touched by the gesture.

Smiling, Kitten nodded. "I drew it in art class. You can put it on your 'frigerator if you want. Do you like it?"

"I love it," Margaret said very sincerely. "Thank you. No one's ever drawn anything just for me before. I'm going to have it framed."

"Really?" Kitten looked delighted. "Did you hear, Daddy? She's going to frame it."

Tucker smiled. "I heard."

He looked at Margaret with obvious approval of her reaction to the gift. "I hope we aren't interrupting anything, but Kitten was eager to bring this over to you."

"I'm glad you did," Margaret said with a smile that included both of them. "You aren't interrupting anything. I was just getting ready to turn my computer off for the day. Would you like to come in for a soda?" she added, knowing it was the polite thing to do.

Tucker shook his head with what appeared to be regret. "We can't. Sam has a peewee football game tonight. We have to get on over to the stadium."

Kitten groaned. "Can't we stay a little while, Daddy? It's so boring at the stadium."

"Kitten, the game starts in less than twenty minutes. Sam will be disappointed if we're late."

The child sighed deeply. "I guess," she muttered. "But I wish I didn't have to go."

"She could stay here with me," Margaret suggested impulsively, still softened by the little drawing. And then she realized she shouldn't have spoken without thinking. "That is, if it's all right with you," she told Tucker.

Kitten caught her breath. "May I, Daddy? Please?"

Tucker hesitated. "You really want to spend your evening baby-sitting?" he asked Margaret.

She shrugged. "I don't have any other plans. Kitten is welcome to stay with me if she likes. And if you don't think Sam will mind her missing his game."

"Sam doesn't care if I'm there as long as Daddy goes," Kitten said quickly. "Really. I'd much rather stay here."

"She hasn't had dinner," Tucker told Margaret sheepishly. "I was going to get her a hot dog at the stadium."

"I haven't eaten, either. She can have dinner with me."

Kitten looked up at him imploringly. "Please, Daddy."

Tucker shrugged. "Okay. Sure."

Kitten squealed in delight and bounced on her little sneakers. Margaret smiled, bemused that the child would rather stay with her than go to a ball game.

She'd never thought of herself as someone children wanted to spend time with. She sincerely doubted that Sam would feel the same way as his sister.

"Be good," Tucker said warningly, touching the tip of his daughter's nose. And then he glanced at Margaret. "I'll pick her up after the game's over. It'll probably be around nine."

"We'll be fine, Tucker. Don't be late for Sam's game. I hope he wins."

Tucker grinned. "He'll be happy if he gets off the bench. The team is for nine- to twelve-year-olds, so he's one of the younger players.'' He reached out to touch her arm. "See you later, Margaret. And thanks."

She managed not to shiver in response to his touch, but it was a close call. "See you."

She closed the door behind him, then turned to the little girl who stood in her entryway, watching her expectantly. Only then did Margaret really realize what she'd done.

For the first time in her life, she'd offered to baby-sit. And she hadn't the foggiest idea how to begin.

"Um, I suppose we should start dinner," she said tentatively. "Would you like to help?"

"Sure. I help Daddy all the time. What are we going to have?"

Margaret thought quickly. What *did* children like to eat? "Do you like spaghetti?"

"I *love* spaghetti."

Smothering a smile, Margaret decided Kitten would have said that about whatever she'd suggested. She really was adorable.

"Let's go to the kitchen," she said, holding out her free hand.

Kitten slipped her hand into Margaret's and gave her a sweet smile that made Margaret's heart melt.

Being around this little girl could almost make her wish she'd had kids of her own, she thought with a touch of wistfulness.

Chapter Five

"Sam, why won't you go with me to pick up your sister? You can tell Margaret about your interception," Tucker coaxed.

Sam stubbornly shook his head. "I don't want to. I want to clean up and get ready for bed. I'm tired."

Tucker sighed as he parked the car in his garage. "Okay, go on in and get ready for bed. I'll walk over and get Kitten."

"Don't be long."

Tucker wondered if Sam wanted him to hurry because he didn't want to be alone, or because he didn't want Tucker spending any more time than necessary with Margaret. The boy was determined not to give Margaret a chance. But this wasn't the time to try to persuade him otherwise. "I won't be long."

It was a cool night, a faint scent of autumn in the air. Tucker stuffed his hands into the pockets of his leather jacket as he crossed into Margaret's yard. He wondered how she and Kitten had gotten along. Unlike Sam, Kitten had taken to Margaret right off—in a way that reminded Tucker uncomfortably of his own fascination with their new neighbor.

What was it about her that drew both him and his daughter? She certainly hadn't done anything in particular to gain their attention. Just the opposite, in fact. Both Tucker and Kitten had gone out of their way to get her to notice *them*. He thought ruefully that Kitten seemed to be making more progress than he was.

He stepped onto Margaret's porch and rang her bell. She answered almost immediately. Even after a day's work and an evening of baby-sitting, she looked neat and fresh and serene. Just once, he mused, he'd like to see her shaken out of her cool composure.

"Kitten fell asleep on the sofa watching television," she said as she let him in.

"She must have had a busy day at school. I'll carry her home and put her to bed."

She looked past him into the night. "Sam isn't with you?"

"No. He was pretty grubby after the game. He wanted to clean up."

"How did it go? Did he get to play?"

"He got to go in during the last quarter. Surprised everyone—himself included—by making an interception."

"Good for him. I'd offer you a drink, but I'm sure you don't want to leave him home alone for that long."

"Yeah, I've got to get home," Tucker agreed reluctantly. "Did Kitten behave herself?"

Margaret smiled. "She was a sweetheart. I can't imagine that she ever misbehaves."

Tucker rolled his eyes. "Let's just say she's a normal kid. She has her days."

"Well, I think she's delightful. She helped me make

dinner, and then we had a lovely meal together. Her manners are excellent. You're doing a wonderful job raising her, Tucker.''

He was both embarrassed and touched by her praise. He felt an unfamiliar warmth in his cheeks, an odd tightening in his chest. He'd worked very hard being a single parent to his kids during the past year, a year of worries and heartaches and sacrifices. It was nice to have someone tell him so sweetly that his efforts were paying off.

''Thanks'' was all he could say.

''You're welcome.'' She turned away. ''Kitten's in the den. I'll help you—''

Tucker reached out to catch her arm, stopping her in her tracks. ''Have dinner with me tomorrow, Margaret.''

A faint line appeared between her brows. ''We've been over this—''

''It's just dinner. I promise my table manners are at least as good as Kitten's.''

She didn't smile at the joke. ''I don't—''

''One dinner,'' he persisted. ''If you don't have a good time, just let me know and I won't ask you again.''

''I'm sure I would have a very nice time, but—''

He edged closer to her, so that his face was close to hers. ''I won't get out of line,'' he promised. ''No matter how much I might want to kiss you, I won't unless you ask me.''

Her cheeks flamed. Her eyes narrowed in what might have been a hint of temper.

At least he'd gotten a response from her rather than that chilly distance, he thought. Maybe making her mad at him wasn't exactly the standard approach to a seduction, but he had her full attention now.

''I have no intention of asking you to kiss me,'' she said, her tone edged with ice.

He only smiled. ''Fine. So, will you have dinner with me?''

She tilted her head, eyeing him speculatively. "If I say no, are you going to continue to ask every time we see each other?"

"Probably," he admitted. "It seems to be an irresistible impulse."

"More likely, it's become a challenge to your ego," she muttered. "Okay, fine, Tucker. We'll have dinner. We'll consider it a neighborly gesture, nothing more. And when it's over, I'll expect you to honor your promise not to ask again."

"Unless you want me to," he reminded her.

She sniffed delicately in answer.

He lowered his head until his mouth was only inches from hers. Okay, maybe it was ego, he thought, his searching gaze locked with her wary one. He suddenly wanted very badly to hear Margaret McAlister ask him for—well, for something. Anything.

Margaret stood very still. She seemed to be holding her breath. Remembering his promise, Tucker reluctantly stepped away. "Dinner tomorrow," he said, his voice just a bit husky. "Seven-thirty?"

"Fine." Her tone was casual, but she moved just a bit too quickly when she stepped out of his reach. "Kitten's in the den," she said, turning away from him.

He didn't detain her this time, but followed her into the den, where he found his daughter sprawled on a creamy sofa, sound asleep. She didn't even stir when he gathered her into his arms. "She really must have been tired this evening," he commented with a smile for Margaret.

Margaret's face softened. She moved close enough to stroke the child's sleep-flushed cheek. "Good night, Kitten," she murmured.

As though in response, Kitten murmured something incoherent and snuggled more comfortably into her father's arms.

Margaret led him to the door and all but shoved him outside, but he was smiling faintly when she closed the door behind him. At least he knew now that he would be seeing her the following evening—without his daughter or anyone else to distract them.

At six-thirty Friday evening, Margaret glared at the reflection in the mirror and berated herself for misplacing her backbone. Why had she allowed Tucker to talk her into this? She didn't know what to wear, how to act, what she'd say....

It was going to be a disaster.

Muttering beneath her breath, she jerked a plain black pantsuit out of her closet and told herself that somehow she would make it through the evening—and that would be that.

By seven, she'd redone her hair and swapped the severe-looking black set for a slightly more casual cream-colored outfit. She'd also worked herself into a healthy case of nerves. She could hardly remember the last time she'd been on a date. She hated dating; it was awkward and embarrassing and uncomfortable.

She should have stuck with her earlier refusals.

Seven-thirty found her pacing her den, smoothing her palms down the loose-fitting slacks she'd finally donned and wondering if Tucker would actually have the nerve to be late. He was the one who'd badgered her into this. The least he could do would be to show up on time.

The doorbell rang at seven forty-five. She took a long, deep breath before opening the door. She didn't bother with a fake smile.

Tucker stood on her doorstep, neatly dressed in a navy jacket, pale blue shirt and gray slacks, a small bouquet of mixed flowers clutched in his right hand. He held them out to her, his expression comically begging her not to throw them at him. "I'm late."

"Yes, I know." She took the flowers without touching his fingers.

"Thank you," she said because it was the polite thing to do. *She,* at least, practiced basic etiquette, she thought with a touch of superiority that calmed her nerves somewhat.

"I'm really sorry, Margaret. I dropped the kids off at Mom's for the night, and Dad asked me to help him fix a dripping faucet. It took a little longer than we expected."

"Apology accepted. I'll put these in water and get my purse and we can go." Figuring that the sooner they got this evening started, the sooner it would be over, she didn't waste any time.

They were just about to step outside when a shrill, repetitive sound came from Tucker's jacket. Margaret looked at him with a lifted eyebrow. "You're beeping."

He grimaced. "I know." He reached inside his jacket and pulled out a thin cellular phone. Flipping it open, he spoke curtly into it. "Hello?"

Margaret watched curiously as various emotions chased across his face during the disjointed conversation that followed.

"It did *what...?* Well, can't you call a... But I... She did? Is she okay...? Yeah, but..." Tucker groaned, looked apologetically at Margaret and spoke again into the phone. "Okay, tell them I'll be there in a minute."

He turned off the phone and stood holding it, still looking at Margaret. "You're not going to believe this."

"Try me."

He winced at her tone. "A pipe broke at my parents' house. Water's everywhere."

"Would this be the pipe you just fixed for them?"

"Well, uh, yeah."

"Have they considered calling a real plumber?"

He nodded. "They have. The problem is that Kitten fell on a wet spot and hit her head."

Margaret immediately abandoned her chilly tone. "She hit her head? Is she all right?"

"She's fine," Tucker said, holding up a reassuring hand. "Just a goose-egg bump on her forehead. Mom's got plenty of experience with that sort of thing. The problem is that Kitten and Sam got all upset and they—well, Sam in particular—want me to come make sure Kitten's okay. He seems to think they need me over there. Mom says she can't convince him otherwise."

"Then you'd better go."

"Look, I—"

"Tucker, I understand." She made a deliberate effort to soften her voice. "This sort of thing happens a lot when one has children, I expect. They need you. Go to them."

He looked torn. "You could go with me."

She shook her head. "No. This is a family problem. It's better if I stay here."

"Margaret, I'm really sorry. I was looking forward to having dinner with you."

"They're waiting for you," she reminded him.

"Promise me we'll do this another time."

She thought of the anxiety she'd suffered the past hour and a half in preparation for this nondate. Her utter certainty that she'd made a mistake agreeing to go out with him in the first place. This had to be a sign, she figured. An omen.

But Tucker looked fully prepared to stand right where he was until he had her promise. Knowing how stubborn he'd been before, she only nodded.

"Sure," she said, deliberately vague. "Some other time."

He didn't look satisfied, but they both knew he had to go. "I'll call you," he said.

"Fine." She moved past him to open the door.

He paused when he would have passed her, so close she could almost feel the frustrated heat radiating from him. He leaned close, his face only inches from hers. His gaze touched her mouth, rose slowly to her eyes. "I know I promised I wouldn't kiss you unless you asked...."

"That's—" She cleared her throat. "That's what you promised."

It wasn't easy to speak normally when her lips were throbbing with unwelcome anticipation.

"Ask me." His voice was a husky growl that made her knees go weak in response.

Her hands drew into fists at her sides, her palms cold. "No."

She couldn't for the life of her have said at that moment whether her refusal was motivated by prudence or fear. Fear seemed most likely.

The fleeting kisses he'd given her before had shaken her badly. She was afraid that if Tucker Hollis ever *really* kissed her, she'd never be able to think rationally about him again.

His sigh of resigned regret brushed her skin, almost like a physical touch. She trembled.

If she reacted this way just to the touch of his breath against her face, she didn't even want to think about what his kiss would do to her tonight.

"Some other time, then," he murmured.

She blinked. "Er..."

"Good night, Margaret." He moved then, quickly, as though forcing himself to do so. He pulled the door closed behind him.

This had to be the most bizarre evening of her life, Margaret mused dazedly as she stared at the door and listened to Tucker's car engine fade into the distance. She'd spent all that time getting ready and waiting for her date to arrive, and now here she was, all dressed up on a Friday evening with no place to go. And she was hungry. She'd been too anxious to eat lunch.

With a choked sound of exasperation, she turned away from the door, kicked off her shoes and headed for the kitchen. This was definitely a time for comfort food. Something delicious and sinful and completely bad for her.

And why did all of those adjectives make her think of Tucker Hollis, darn it?

"Damn." Tucker stood by his bedroom window, looking glumly at the lights next door.

It was late, and the kids were in bed, their sleepover at their grandparents' house abandoned after the chaotic evening. Kitten was fine, the bump on her forehead decorated with a cartoon bandage. She'd been openly disappointed that Tucker's date with Margaret had been called off.

Sam hadn't been.

Tucker frowned, thinking of how quickly Sam's exaggerated concern for his sister's welfare had faded once he'd been assured that Tucker wouldn't be going anywhere with Margaret that evening. He could still visualize the faint satisfaction in Sam's eyes when he'd said good-night and headed for bed.

Tucker supposed he was going to have to say something to the boy at some point. He still wasn't sure if Sam was opposed to Tucker dating anyone, or if it were just Margaret he objected to, but it didn't matter. Tucker would not allow his decisions to be dictated by the whims of a nine-year-old, no matter how much he loved the kid.

Tucker wanted to go out with Margaret, and Sam was just going to have to get used to it, especially since there was no rational reason at all for him to have developed such antipathy for her.

And then Tucker winced, looking again at those lights next door. He'd be lucky if he'd ever talk Margaret into another date. It had been difficult enough the first time. For some reason, she'd decided from the beginning that they were too different, that they should keep their distance. And now, after this evening...

He swallowed. He could still picture her standing in her entryway, looking so attractive in her pretty outfit, her hair soft around her face rather than pinned into its usual neat twist.

She'd obviously dressed up for the occasion, as he had. He'd wanted to look his best for her, wanted to impress her; he hoped she'd been motivated by similar reasoning. And then he'd left her standing there, after making her wait for him in the first place.

He wouldn't blame her if she never wanted to see him again. If he had a lick of common sense, he'd cut his losses, swallow his bruised pride and admit defeat. She had outspoken reservations about their dating, Sam was stubbornly opposed to the idea and even Tucker didn't know what it was, exactly, that drew him to her.

A sensible man would give up at this point.

Tucker had never been known as a particularly sensible man.

One more time, he told himself. He'd try one more time to pursue this inexplicable urge to learn more about Margaret McAlister. Maybe she and Sam were right. Maybe nothing would come of it. But he seemed bound and determined to find out for himself.

He only wished he hadn't made that stupid promise that he wouldn't kiss her unless she asked him to.

A delivery arrived at Margaret's house Monday afternoon. It didn't look like a business package. Curiously, she opened the square box, wondering who had sent her something marked Fragile.

Nested inside the box, protected by foam and tissue paper, was a red rose exquisitely crafted of fine porcelain. Catching her breath in surprise and delight, Margaret touched a fingertip to one delicate, dew-kissed petal. Lovely...

Studying every detail of the sculpture, she turned it over in her hands. A small brass key on the bottom caught her attention. A music box, she thought, and twisted the key. She listened carefully to the tinkling notes, then smiled when she recognized the tune. "All I Ask of You," from Andrew Lloyd Webber's *The Phantom of the Opera.*

Her throat tightened. This was one of her favorite songs. How had Tucker known that she—?

Tucker. She blinked, realizing that she'd automatically decided he'd sent the gift. She dug in the box and pulled out a card. The handwriting was a careless scrawl—she'd be willing to bet it was his, even before she read the words.

Margaret,
Please accept this as an apology for Friday night. I promise you next time will be different.

         Tuck.

Next time. She bit her lip. For the first time, she fully admitted to herself that this problem wasn't going to go away. Tucker, for some reason, had developed an interest in her—and he wasn't going to give up until he'd pursued it. That notably stubborn set to his handsome jaw wasn't just due to coincidence.

She tried to decide exactly what it was about Tucker that made her so nervous when she thought of being alone with him.

It wasn't that she didn't find him attractive. She did. Had from the first moment she'd laid eyes on him. What woman wouldn't?

It wasn't that she necessarily wanted to be alone all the time. She enjoyed going out, doing things, seeing people. She wasn't a hermit, after all.

As for the heat she'd seen in his eyes when he'd leaned so close to her Friday evening and somehow kissed her without ever touching her—well, she could handle that, too. She recognized desire when she saw it. Acknowledged that she'd felt it, too, though heaven only knew she'd had little enough experience with the emotion in her past.

It wasn't that she didn't have normal, healthy urges. She did. She just didn't meet many men who tempted her to set aside her innate caution and fastidiousness to take the risk of intimate involvement. Her past relationships had been rare, awkward, and had always ended with a disappointing fizzle.

And still, Tucker Hollis tempted her. So why did the thought of being with him scare her half-silly?

His kids? Okay, that was a legitimate concern. Children were so vulnerable, so impressionable. Margaret would hate to think anything she and Tucker did—or didn't do—would have a lasting effect on his children.

Sam already hated her, she thought with a sigh. Kitten, on the other hand, seemed to be developing a bond that made Margaret almost as nervous as the way Tucker looked at her. Getting involved with Tucker meant starting a four-way relationship, and that was enough to make any comfortably single woman nervous.

But it wasn't just the kids. And it wasn't just the awkwardness of being next-door neighbors, the uncomfortable ramifications that that could have in case of a dating disaster. It wasn't even her probably justified fear of having her heart broken.

She suspected she knew the real reason this thing with Tucker worried her so, and she wasn't at all sure she liked what the answer revealed about her. It was the lack of control she dreaded most intensely. That old, ugly feeling that the direction her life was taking wasn't entirely in her own hands.

It had taken years for her to feel fully in control of her own life. Years to overcome the deep scars that her chaotic childhood had left buried inside her. Years to get past the nightmares and the constant ache of nameless anxiety.

In some ways, Tucker reminded her of her parents. Impulsive, audacious, unconventional—maybe a little reckless. He was chronically late, and that drove her nuts. He displayed a marked aversion to the careful agendas that kept her sane.

True, he seemed more concerned about his children than her parents had, though even with them he was a bit careless where their schedules and routines were concerned. And she'd seen no signs that his energy and vitality were augmented by the chemicals—either legal or illegal—that her own parents had favored.

A young man she'd dated in college had once accused her of being a "control freak." He'd angrily told her that no one would ever live up to her ideals, that a man was destined to disappoint her because she set him up for failure with her unrealistic expectations. She hadn't bothered to argue with him, mostly because she'd secretly feared that he was right.

Maybe she was doing the same thing now with Tucker. They hadn't even been out yet, and already she was glumly anticipating everything that could go wrong if they did. He hadn't done a thing to really annoy her, but still she was trying to find fault in him. Nit-picking, as Jackie had labeled it on several occasions. Maybe she really was a control freak.

She was going to give him a chance, she told herself, suddenly deciding. There *was* going to be a next time, and she was going to enjoy herself. Have fun. If one date led to another, fine. If not, that was fine, too. She'd take it one day at a time.

She could be spontaneous, she told herself, remembering the similar protest she'd made to Jackie. Now that she'd had time to think about it, approve of it and plan it, a little spontaneity didn't seem so bad.

It was time to get back to work. She allowed herself only a twenty-minute break on weekday afternoons, and she'd wasted more time than that staring into space and fretting since the rose had arrived. She wound the little key on the bottom and let the tune play as she carried the rose with her to her office.

"Love me. That's all I ask of you."

The lyrics played through her mind in time with the notes. Swallowing a faint resurgence of nerves, she set the music-box rose on her desk and forced her attention back to the numbers on the pages spread out in front of her. Unlike people, numbers were so easily understood and manipulated.

Tucker called her that evening, after his kids were in bed. "How's it going?" he asked casually.

She set aside the book she'd been trying to read. "Fine. I got the rose today, Tucker. It's beautiful. Thank you."

"You're welcome. I thought it was kind of pretty."

He'd picked it out himself. She'd thought so, but hearing him confirm it pleased her.

"It's beautiful," she repeated. "How did you know my favorite song?"

"That's your favorite song?" He sounded startled. "What is it?"

"You don't remember?"

"No. To be honest, I just liked the way it looked. What song does it play?"

She smiled wryly. "'All I Ask of You.' From *The Phantom of the Opera*," she added when there was only blank silence on his end of the line.

"Oh. That theater stuff you like."

Her smile turned to a wince. "Yes. That theater stuff."

"Maybe you'll have to introduce me to it someday."

She changed the subject rather abruptly. "How's Kitten?"

"The lump on her head's gone. Didn't even leave a bruise in its place."

"I'm glad to hear that. And Sam?"

"Sam's fine."

"Good." And so much for *that* subject.

"I talked to Mick yesterday. He and your friend Jackie are really a hot item now, did you know?"

"Yes, I've talked to Jackie. She seems quite taken with him."

"Yeah, Mick, too. His relationships never tend to last very long, I'm afraid."

"Neither do Jackie's," Margaret admitted.

"Well, maybe this time it will work out for them."

"Yeah, maybe."

"Anyway," Tucker said after a moment, "Mick's taking Jackie out Saturday night for her birthday, and they want us to join them. A double date. What do you think?"

A double date. With Jackie and Mick. Margaret twisted the phone cord around her forefinger and imagined everything that could go wrong with *that* scenario. And then she told herself in annoyance that she was doing it again—predicting disaster with no reason to do so.

"Sure," she said, trying to sound enthusiastic. "That sounds like fun."

Tucker seemed rather surprised that she'd accepted so easily. "Yes?"

"Yes."

"Well, great. It's a date, then. I'll see you Saturday. I'll let you know a time as soon as Mick tells me their plans."

"Fine."

"So…" He didn't seem to know what else to say.

"So…?"

"Good night, Margaret."

"Good night, Tucker."

She hung up the phone and buried her face in her hands. She would *not* predict disaster, she told herself fiercely. She just wished she weren't so utterly sure she was headed for it.

Chapter Six

"Why do you have to go out with her again?" Sam asked rather belligerently as he watched his father button his shirt.

Tucker shoved the tails of the black denim shirt into the waistband of his black jeans. "I haven't been out with her once yet. You know what happened last time."

"That should have told you something," Sam muttered. "You shouldn't have asked her out in the first place."

Tucker picked up a comb and tried to smooth his unruly dark hair into some semblance of order. "When I want your advice about my social life, I'll ask you," he said mildly.

Sitting cross-legged on Tucker's bed, Sam scowled. "She's all wrong for you."

Tossing the comb in the general direction of his dresser, Tucker opened his closet door. "What makes you think that?"

"C'mon, Dad, you're a fun guy. You like to laugh and have a good time, ya know? I've *never* heard her laugh."

"You haven't spent much time with her," Tucker argued as he dragged his best black boots out of the closet. But, come to think of it, he'd only heard Margaret laugh once or twice himself.

He'd have to see what he could do about that tonight.

"She's too old."

"She's the same age I am."

"She doesn't act it."

Tucker grimaced. "I've been accused on occasion of not acting *my* age."

"What are you supposed to do? Be all serious and grumpy all the time? Like her?"

"She isn't serious and grumpy all the time. You heard Kitten say how much fun she had with her the night of your game. You haven't given her a chance."

"All she's ever done is yell at me."

"That's not true. She asked you not to walk through her flower beds and she asked you to be careful with your baseball. Both are perfectly reasonable requests. Do I have to remind you again that she's saved Boomer twice from becoming street pizza?"

"I don't think she even likes dogs," Sam grumbled, unfazed.

"Then it's all the nicer of her to watch out for yours, isn't it?" Tucker responded, determined to keep this light.

"I still don't see why you want to date her. Why couldn't you go out with someone different?"

Tucker shoved his left foot into his boot and smoothed the hem of his jeans down over it. "You have someone in mind?"

"Well, no," Sam admitted. "But you could probably find someone. You know, like those swimsuit babes on

TV. They're pretty and they're always laughing and having fun.''

"Bouncing and giggling and occasionally saving lives in slow motion," Tucker drawled with a half smile as he donned his other boot. "That's the kind of woman you think I should date?"

Sam had the grace to look sheepish. "Well, maybe not just like that. But—"

"Women are more than nice bodies and big hair, Sam, even though I happen to think Margaret is very pretty. But she's also intelligent and competent and successful at her business. I admire her, and I like her, and I want to go out with her tonight. I don't know if anything will come of it, whether we'll ever be more than friendly neighbors. But, whatever happens, I think you should try to get to know her before you make up your mind about her. That's only fair, son."

Sam ducked his head. "I already know she isn't anything like Mom."

The words were spoken very softly, but Tucker heard them. They went straight to his heart.

"No," he agreed, moving to sit beside his son. "Margaret isn't like your mom. I've never known anyone quite like Callie."

"She was the best." Sam's voice had grown husky.

"She was very special," Tucker agreed quietly. Sincerely. "I know you loved your mother, Sam. I loved her, too, even when that love changed and we weren't married anymore. Believe me, I'm not trying to replace your mom—not in your memories, or my own."

"Then why are you going out with *her?*"

Tucker wished his son would refer to Margaret by name, rather than that scornful pronoun. He let it pass for now. "You have friends, Sam. You like to spend time with them, don't you?"

"I don't have any girlfriends."

"Not yet," Tucker agreed with a faint smile. "Someday you will, I can promise you."

Ignoring Sam's look of disgust, he went on, "Margaret and I are friends. We're going out with Uncle Mick and his friend Jackie to have a good time. It's no big deal, just a little fun. Don't you think I deserve a little fun?"

Sam chewed his lip, neatly trapped. "Well, yeah, but—" he looked doubtfully at his father "—you really think you can have fun with *her?*"

"I don't know. But I won't ever know unless I give it a try, will I?"

Sam sighed. "Are you going to kiss her?" he asked, looking appalled by the idea.

Tucker shrugged. "I don't know. Maybe." *But only if she asks me to. And I'm not holding my breath for that.* "Men and women kiss sometimes. It's one way of showing that they like each other."

"You aren't thinking about marrying her or anything, are you?"

"Sam, right now I'm only thinking about going out with her tonight. Okay?"

Sam didn't look particularly happy about it, but he nodded. "Yeah, I guess it's okay."

Tucker ruffled the boy's hair, so like his own. "Thanks for giving me permission, 'Pop.'"

Sam wasn't quite finished. "What if something happens to me or Kitten?"

"Grandma and Grandpa can take care of it. If it's an emergency, I'll have the cell phone with me. But give me a break this time, kid. If you don't really need me, don't call me, okay?"

Sam muttered something that Tucker took as an affirmative. He gave his son a quick hug, then stood.

"C'mon, let's find Kitten and get over to Grandma's. I'd really hate to be late again tonight. Don't want to ruin my reputation for always being organized and punctual.''

A snort of laughter escaped the boy. "Yeah, right."

Tucker hoped he'd handled that exchange well. It was difficult knowing what to say to kids sometimes, how to calm their fears. When to stand tough, when to give in, when to resort to blatant bribery. He'd never expected to be a single parent, and he sometimes wondered if he was up to the task, but he was doing the best he knew how, under the circumstances.

He only hoped that was enough.

Margaret thought it boded well for the evening that the doorbell rang exactly on time. She'd refused to allow her nerves to overcome her this time. She'd chosen an outfit and kept it on, had only done her hair once and had managed not to pace before Tucker arrived.

She was making progress.

She really had overreacted the last time, she told herself a bit smugly. This date wasn't so special. Not much different than other dates she'd had in the past.

And then she opened the door and saw Tucker standing there, dressed in black denim and smiling at her. And she nearly swallowed her tongue.

"Hi," he said. "You look great."

She flushed self-consciously. "Thank you."

Jackie had called earlier and told her to dress casually, explaining that they would be going to a club with a country-western ambience. It wouldn't have been Margaret's first choice of destination, but she'd feigned enthusiasm for Jackie's sake.

After some consideration, Margaret had chosen to wear a long-sleeved denim dress with a wide leather belt. She didn't own any boots—almost unheard of from a Texan—so she made do with leather flats. She'd donned a pair of silver-and-turquoise earrings and had left her hair down, brushing it until it gleamed softly around her face. This was as close as she could come to country-western attire. Judging from the way Tucker was looking at her, he approved her choice.

"You, um, you look very nice yourself," she said, trying to keep her tone light.

"Thanks. Are you ready to go?"

Margaret suddenly realized that she had left him standing on the doorstep. What was wrong with her? She usually had better manners than that. "Would you like to come in?"

He glanced past her, then shook his head, his smile a bit crooked. "Maybe we'd better just go. Before something goes wrong again."

He was obviously thinking about their last attempt at a date. Margaret smiled at the reference. "Maybe you're right."

She picked up her purse and stepped out beside him. She didn't bother with a jacket, since it was a nice evening. A *very* nice evening, actually. Clear sky, scattered with glittering stars. A faint, fragrant breeze. A gorgeous man at her side.

No wonder she was beginning to feel just a bit unlike herself.

Tucker's black, four-wheel-drive Ford was parked in her driveway. He opened the passenger door for her and waited for her to climb in, and then he loped around the front and slid behind the wheel. "Mick said we're meeting at the Moonlight Rodeo. Have you been there before?"

"No. Have you?"

"No. I haven't been out much since the kids came to live with me," he explained as he backed out of the driveway.

Margaret wondered about that. She knew the children

had been with him a year. Had he really not dated during that time?

She had a sudden, uncomfortable concern that he'd asked her out only because she was convenient and available, but she quickly pushed that thought away. Tucker was a man who wouldn't have any problem finding women to go out with him, and she hadn't exactly thrown herself at him, she reminded herself.

She wouldn't worry tonight about why he'd asked her out or what would happen afterward. She would just relax and enjoy the evening.

Relax being the operative word, she thought, making a conscious effort to loosen her death grip on her purse.

She wished she could think of something witty to say. It had been quite a while since she'd been on a date herself, but she seemed to remember that casual conversation was expected.

"How are the children?" she asked, choosing what seemed to be the safest topic.

"Fine. They're spending the night with my folks. We'll just hope the pipes stay intact tonight," he added with a wry smile.

"I talked to Kitten a few minutes yesterday, over the fence. She was all excited about her field trip to the butterfly exhibit at the museum."

"Yeah. She had a ball. She got to see a butterfly emerge from its cocoon. And she said a big blue one landed on her shoulder and rode around with her for a while."

"I'm sure she enjoyed that."

"Tell me about yourself, Margaret," Tucker said, rather abruptly changing the subject. "Have you always lived in Dallas?"

"No. My family moved around a lot when I was growing up. I settled here after earning my accounting degree."

"You said you were an only child?"

"Yes." She toyed with the buckle on her purse. Her past was not a subject she wanted to discuss this evening. "Is it much farther to the club?"

"Not far. Have you known Jackie long?"

"We met in college. We've been friends ever since. Ten years now."

"Mick told me she's a speech therapist."

"Yes, a very good one. Children, especially, love her."

"What was your childhood like?"

Every time she thought the conversation had moved into a comfortable direction, he caught her off guard with another discomfiting question. She cleared her throat. "It was...okay," she said lamely. Inaccurately.

He slanted her a look that let her know he found the answer lacking. "That doesn't tell me much."

"I don't talk about my childhood a lot."

Tucker thought about that a moment. "I would have guessed you came from an academic background. Very structured, regimented, organized. Dinner at six, bedtime at nine, no snacks between meals."

"You'd have been wrong," she murmured bleakly. He had just neatly summed up the childhood she'd have given anything to claim as her own.

"Maybe you'll tell me about it sometime." He kept his tone casual.

"Maybe." But she doubted it.

"This is the place," Tucker said a moment later, nodding toward a neon-lighted building just ahead. "I think I see Mick's pickup."

"Pickup?" Margaret lifted an eyebrow. "Jackie came here in a truck?"

"She did if she rode with Mick. That's all he owns. Why?"

Margaret smiled. "I've heard her say several times

that she doesn't date pickup guys. Bad experience in her past.''

"Mick can be very persuasive." Tucker parked his four-wheel-drive between a Cadillac and a minivan.

"Runs in the family, I suppose," Margaret murmured.

He grinned, dimples flashing. "So they say."

Margaret's first impression of the club was that it was loud. The music was a few decibels higher than she would have liked, and the crowd of young patrons seemed determined to compete in volume. Mick and Jackie had been watching for them from their table in one corner; Mick stood and waved an arm to get their attention.

Tucker took Margaret's hand, ostensibly to keep her beside him as they threaded their way through the crowds. Whatever the reason, her skin tingled like crazy at every point of contact.

Just another date? *Sure, Margaret, keep telling yourself that. Keep trying to believe it.*

Jackie air-kissed Margaret's cheek. "Hi. You look great."

"Thanks. So do you."

Jackie always looked good, but tonight she was even more radiant than usual, Margaret couldn't help noticing. Jackie wore a sleek white jumpsuit studded with colored stones at the collar and belt. She'd braided her blond hair, tying it back with a jewel-toned scarf.

Margaret couldn't help but feel a bit dowdy next to her exotically lovely friend. It wasn't a new feeling for her.

"Happy birthday, Jackie," Tucker said in greeting.

"Thanks, Tuck," she said. "I'm glad you two could join us tonight. I've been looking forward to seeing you both."

"I heard about the last time you and Tuck tried to go out," Mick told Margaret with a grin. "Disaster, huh?"

She smiled. "Let's just say it was a very short date."

She took the seat Tucker held for her, wondering exactly how much he'd told his family and how they felt about him dating her.

And then she reminded herself that she wasn't going to worry about such things tonight. "Happy birthday," she said to Jackie.

Jackie groaned. "I'm trying not to think too much about it. Thirty-one. Yuck."

Mick grinned. "I keep telling her she looks pretty good for an older woman, but that doesn't seem to help much."

"Gee, I wonder why," Margaret said dryly, though she smiled. Mick was probably two or three years younger than Jackie, but that didn't seem to be bothering him, judging from the way he was gazing at her. He looked like a man who was thoroughly smitten. And, Margaret noted through her lashes, Jackie was looking a bit moonstruck herself.

Margaret sincerely hoped that this affair would turn out better for her impetuous friend than the past few had.

They ordered dinner from the rather limited menu of burgers and Tex-Mex. Conversation during the meal was definitely lively, with Mick, Jackie and Tucker cutting up and wisecracking while Margaret good-naturedly played straight man.

She wouldn't have known how to play any other role, she thought just a touch wistfully. She had never been as quick with a funny punch line as these three were.

Jackie pretended to be terribly embarrassed when a group of waiters gathered around the table after the meal to present a flaming birthday cake and sing a terrible rendition of a country-western birthday song. Margaret could tell that Jackie really enjoyed the attention, especially when Mick leaned over to help her blow out the candles and kissed her afterward.

"I brought you something," Margaret said, pulling a small wrapped gift out of her purse.

Jackie beamed. "You didn't have to bring a gift," she crooned even as she snatched the package from Margaret's hand and proceeded to tear into it.

"Yeah, I can tell she really hates getting gifts," Tucker drawled, smiling at Margaret.

Jackie squealed when she opened the box. "Earrings! Margaret, they're gorgeous."

"I'm glad you like them. I ordered them from that boutique in San Francisco that you like so much."

Jackie showed the dangling tiers of multicolored stones to Mick and Tucker, both of whom made appropriate noises for men confronted with utterly feminine baubles.

"They'll look great on you," Mick assured Jackie. "Of course, everything does."

Margaret was amazed to see Jackie blush like a schoolgirl.

After the cake had been divided and eaten, the two couples moved into the bar, where a band was playing for the dancers packing the small dance floor. Mick pounced on a newly vacated table for four.

"First round of drinks is on me," he announced, summoning a waitress. "What will everyone have?"

Jackie ordered a mixed drink, Mick and Tucker beer. "I'll just have a diet cola," Margaret requested.

"Margaret doesn't drink," Jackie informed the men.

"That doesn't surprise me," Tucker murmured.

Margaret lifted an eyebrow in question.

He smiled crookedly at her. "You wouldn't want to risk losing control."

She bit her lip, surprised that he'd shown such insight. Apparently, he was learning a bit more about her than she'd expected. Was he really studying her that closely, or was he just the perceptive type?

She could feel Jackie looking at her, and she made an effort to smile naturally. "That's part of it," she agreed.

"C'mon, Jackie, let's dance," Mick urged as soon as the drinks had been delivered, pushing back his chair and holding out his hand. Jackie joined him eagerly on the dance floor.

"Hard to believe they've only been dating for a month, isn't it?" Tucker asked, nodding toward Jackie and Mick, who were already intimately entwined on the dance floor.

Margaret lifted one shoulder. "I've seen Jackie get involved quickly before—but not quite like this," she admitted.

"Think it'll last?"

"I have no idea." She watched as Mick and Jackie engaged in a long, steamy kiss, either oblivious to or unconcerned about the people around them. She could almost feel the heat they generated.

Her cheeks warming, she quickly took a sip of her cola.

"Would you like to dance?" Tucker asked.

"I'm not a very good dancer," she confessed.

His dimples flashed. "That's okay. This isn't a very good band."

She smiled. "That's true."

He stood and held out his hand. "Dance with me."

She only hoped her knees would support her. Something about the way he was looking at her had made them go weak.

The mediocre band started a slow number just as Tucker and Margaret stepped onto the dance floor. Tucker drew her into his arms. For a junior-high history teacher, he was in excellent condition, she mused, feeling the muscles moving beneath black denim as he moved against her.

It had been a while since she'd danced with anyone.

A very long time since she'd been held this close to a man. She kept her gaze focused on his chin, moving rather stiffly as she worked at matching her steps to his.

"Relax," he murmured, his breath warm against her temple, a faint undercurrent of amusement in his deep voice. "You aren't being graded on this."

She smiled faintly. "Just as well."

"Trust me. You'd pass." He held her just a bit closer. "You feel very good in my arms, Margaret McAlister."

She blushed scarlet. "Don't flirt with me now, Tucker. I'm trying to concentrate."

He laughed. The sound was warm and rich and made her blush even hotter. A few dancers close to them turned their heads to look at them and smile, and Margaret knew they thought she'd said something clever and witty to make Tucker laugh that way. Little did they know...

"Have I mentioned yet that I really like you, Margaret?" he asked conversationally. "That practical accountant's mind of yours fascinates me."

She peered up at him suspiciously. Was he laughing *at* her now? "I'm not fascinating," she grumbled. "There's nothing at all unusual about me."

"Oh, I wouldn't say that." His gaze swept her face, seeming to take in every minute detail.

She looked down again. "You're making fun of me."

He rested his cheek against her hair. "No."

She wished briefly that she could believe him. Wished that she were the kind of woman who really could fascinate a man like this. Wished she were just a little more like Jackie, able to enjoy the pleasures of the present without always worrying about the future.

His shoulders were broad and strong beneath her left hand, his fingers wrapped snugly around her right hand. Slowly, she began to respond to the warmth, the music, the slow, sultry rhythm of the dance. Her rigid muscles began to relax—so much that she felt in danger of melting against him.

"Tucker?" she murmured after a moment.

"Hmm?"

"Have I mentioned yet that I like you, too?" The words amazed her even as she said them.

He lifted his head to give her a blinding smile that almost took her breath away. "No," he said. "You haven't mentioned that before."

Fiercely self-conscious now, she shrugged and glanced away. "It's always nice when neighbors can be friendly."

Tucker laughed again. "Yes," he agreed, sounding a bit choked. "That's exactly what I've been thinking."

She didn't know exactly what it was she kept saying or doing to amuse him, but she stopped worrying about it, deciding to just enjoy instead. He had such a nice laugh. Such a beautiful smile...

Tucker was pleased to discover that Margaret did know how to have a good time. He and Jackie and Mick wheedled her into trying a couple of new, fast-stepping line dances during the evening, and though she was hesitant at first, she gave it her best shot. Before long, she was flushed and breathless. And laughing.

Tucker couldn't stop looking at her. He'd always thought she was attractive, but tonight there was something beautiful about her.

And he wasn't the only man who noticed, he thought, slanting a glare of warning to a lanky cowboy who'd been studying her slender figure just a bit too closely.

Jackie was boldly, deliberately stunning. Tucker would have had to be blind not to notice Jackie's attributes. But still, it was Margaret to whom he kept turning, Margaret who intrigued and bemused him. Maybe because she was different from other women he'd known.

Or because she'd been so mysterious about her past the few times he'd asked about it. Maybe it was because she seemed so oddly oblivious to her own allure.

He could want her, he thought, watching the way her full skirt swirled around her shapely legs when she turned. He could want her very badly. But was this just a physical attraction—or was it more?

This wasn't the time to worry about the future, he decided, taking her hand as they made their way back to their table for a breather. He had finally succeeded in spending an evening with her, and things were going great so far. He would just enjoy while it lasted.

He was trying not to think about what might happen when he took her home that evening.

Margaret's laughter had faded by the time she and Tucker were in his vehicle, headed toward their neighborhood. Though she'd had a lovely time—much nicer than she'd expected—it had suddenly occurred to her that the date was coming to an end.

What did Tucker expect of her now?

After another few steamy slow dances, Jackie and Mick had suddenly grown visibly anxious to leave the restaurant. They'd managed to retain enough etiquette to take their leave of Margaret and Tucker politely. Jackie had hugged Margaret again and thanked her for the earrings. And then she and Mick had left, arm in arm, looking at each other in a way that had left no doubt about how their date would end.

Margaret knew Tucker's children were spending the night with their grandparents. There would be no reason for him to hurry away after seeing her home.

Surely he wasn't expecting a sleepover of his own.

"Did you have a good time tonight?" Tucker asked, breaking into her silence.

"Yes, very nice. Did you?"

"Yeah. Your friend's quite a character."

"So is your brother."

"They make a good match, I suppose."

"Perhaps."

The silence fell again.

Tucker glanced at her. "Margaret, is something wrong?"

She pasted on a smile. "No, of course not."

"Tired?"

"Maybe a little," she said, seizing the excuse.

He pulled into her driveway. "I'll see you to your door."

She nodded, wondering if he expected her to invite him in. She supposed she should offer a cup of coffee or something.

It wasn't that she didn't trust him in her home, she thought as she pushed the key into the lock. He'd given her no reason to be wary of him. She just wasn't quite sure what she was supposed to do now.

It really had been too long since she'd been out with a man, she thought ruefully.

"Would you like to come in...for a few minutes?" she asked, hoping she'd made the invitation specific enough.

His mouth twitched with what appeared to be wry amusement. "It's getting late," he said. "And you're tired. Maybe we'd better call it a night."

She told herself that what she felt was relief that he'd made it easy for her—not disappointment that he hadn't even tried for more.

"All right," she said with a forced smile. "Good night, Tucker. I had a very nice evening."

"So did I." He stood very close to her, smiling, apparently waiting for something.

She held the door partially open, wondering if he were going to kiss her good-night. Even if it was only the faintest touch of lips to cheek, most dates ended with a kiss on the doorstep, from what she remembered.

It wasn't that she was so anxious for Tucker to kiss her, she told herself primly. She was just following standard dating protocol. She wouldn't want to be gauche or anything.

Tucker raised a hand and touched a fingertip to her lips, his gaze locked with hers. His dimples deepened invitingly. "I think you've forgotten something," he murmured.

Puzzled, she frowned. *She* had forgotten something? What?

As though hearing her unspoken question, he reminded her. "I promised I wouldn't kiss you. Unless you asked me to."

Her face flamed. Oh, yes. She did remember that now. And she'd assured him haughtily that she wouldn't be asking.

Now, why had she done that?

Torn between pride and a wistful longing to have him kiss her good-night—just to end the date on a pleasant note, of course—she moistened her lips.

He watched her, his smile fading a bit. "Margaret?" His voice had lowered, roughened.

"What?"

He cupped her cheek in his hand, his face very close to hers. "Ask me."

What could it hurt? One kiss after a very nice evening. No big deal, right?

She opened her mouth to speak, but couldn't for the life of her come up with anything to say. It seemed easier all around to simply act instead.

She stretched upward, put a hand at the back of Tucker's head and pressed her mouth to his. She didn't intend it to be anything more than a quick brush of lips. But he felt and tasted so good that she couldn't resist lingering. Just for a little while. She tilted her head and kissed him harder. Enjoying.

He made a low sound of protest deep in his throat when she drew back.

He looked, she thought in pleased surprise, like a man who'd been rocked back on his heels. And it was she, Margaret Anne McAlister, who had brought that look to Tucker Hollis's handsome face.

Feeling the faintest ripple of feminine pride, she smiled. "Good night, Tucker."

He still hadn't moved when she walked inside and closed the door quietly between them.

And then she walked straight to her sofa, dropped heavily onto it and hid her face in her hands. God, she thought with a weary sigh, she really hated dating. She always did something incredibly stupid on a date.

Kissing Tucker Hollis that way had definitely not been one of her brighter moves.

Chapter Seven

Margaret was just pulling into her driveway the next day after church when she spotted Tucker's black Ford coming from the other direction. Both Tucker and Kitten waved to her. Sam looked the other way.

She was greatly annoyed with herself for letting just that glimpse of Tucker rattle her again. She'd spent part of the night and all of this morning trying to regain her perspective about their date.

It had just been dinner and dancing, she'd told herself. Nothing spectacular. Nothing magical. It certainly hadn't changed her life. He probably wouldn't even ask her again now that he'd satisfied his ego and his curiosity. She tried to convince herself that it wouldn't matter if he didn't.

It didn't take her long to change out of the dress she'd worn for church and into a more comfortable knit tunic-and-slacks set. The house seemed unusually quiet during her pasta-and-salad lunch; she turned on some music to entertain her during the meal.

In keeping with her craving for security and predictability, Margaret had developed a weekly schedule several years ago, and she followed it as faithfully as possible.

Monday through Friday, she woke at six-thirty, was showered and dressed by seven, had breakfast and read her newspaper and was in her office by eight. She took an hour for a lunch break, twenty minutes for an afternoon break at three o'clock, and finished work at five. She then prepared her dinner, which she ate at six. In the evenings when she didn't have something scheduled at church or one of her professional organizations, she read or watched television, sometimes caught up on any work left over from the day and was in bed by eleven.

Saturdays were for sleeping an hour later, catching up on work and household chores and running errands, her treasured forty-five-minute nap, often followed by an evening out with friends, usually at a theater or concert hall. Sundays, she attended church, had lunch—either with friends from church or, like today, at home alone—and spent the afternoon relaxing, working in her yard, catching up on correspondence and—her secret vice—watching old movies on cable.

She knew her routines would drive some people crazy with boredom. Jackie had said so often enough. Margaret couldn't help thinking that Tucker would probably feel much the same way. It wouldn't even be possible for him to schedule so precisely with two children to deal with. There were probably unexpected things always cropping up in the Hollis household—school events, children's parties, sports activities and so on. And Tucker seemed even less organized than most other parents of young children Margaret knew.

So, she thought, settling onto her sofa with an iced

tea and the television remote, it really was for the best if she and Tucker remained just friends. No more slow dances. No more kisses. No regrets.

Katharine Hepburn and Cary Grant were sparring on her television screen. Margaret sat back to enjoy, making a determined effort not to wonder what was going on in the house next door.

Later that afternoon, Margaret was seated at the desk in her office, writing a letter to a friend who'd moved to Seattle a few years earlier, when she was distracted by a noise from outside. She found herself drawn to the window, which faced her neighbor's backyard.

Tucker and his children and the little dog, Boomer, seemed to be engaged in a rowdy, breathless game of tag. Margaret could just faintly hear Kitten's squeals of laughter through her window. Sam, she noted, was grinning from ear to ear, playfully yelling something at his father that she couldn't make out. The dog barked and wriggled and bounced around their feet.

Tucker whirled and caught Sam in one arm, spinning the boy around and making him yelp happily. Kitten leapt into the fray, until all three of them—and Boomer—were tumbling on the ground, flushed and laughing. While Margaret watched, Tucker kissed Kitten's cheek, and then Sam's. The children both hugged him as they lay on the grass, catching their breath and sharing the moment.

There was a lump in Margaret's throat when she turned away from the window, suddenly feeling like a voyeur. An outsider. She returned to her desk and picked up her pen.

The words on the page in front of her were oddly blurred; she blinked them back into focus. And then she began to write again, the scratching of her pen the only sound within her tranquil home.

* * *

Margaret's telephone rang at just before five on Tues-day afternoon. Tucker's voice greeted her when she an-swered—the first time she'd heard from him since their date.

"I have an invitation for you," he said.

"Oh, I—"

"It's from Kitten."

She hesitated. "From Kitten?"

"Yeah. Sam's gone off to an Alan Jackson concert with his grandpa tonight, and Kitten's feeling left out. I rented a video for her and told her we'd order her fa-vorite pizza. She wants to know if you'd like to join us for a movie-and-pizza party."

An evening in Tucker's home with him and his daugh-ter? Both of whom she already found much too hard to resist. "Well, I had planned to—"

"Kitten would sure love it if you could come," Tucker cut in smoothly. "She's been wanting to see you again."

This really wasn't fair. And she suspected that Tucker was well aware of it.

Margaret sighed. "All right, I'd love to come. For Kitten," she added quickly.

"Of course. How does six o'clock sound?"

"Fine. Can I bring anything?"

"Just yourself. We'll take care of the rest."

Margaret hung up the phone and hit her forehead with her fist. This was *not* the way to keep a nice, neighborly distance between herself and Tucker.

Promptly at six, she rang his doorbell. Kitten yanked open the door, smiling broadly. "Hi, Margaret!" she cried, and then threw her little arms around Margaret's waist and gave her an enthusiastic hug.

Caught off guard, Margaret returned the hug a bit awkwardly at first, and then with more warmth as she realized how nice it was to be on the receiving end of a child's generous affection. "Hello, Kitten. It's good to see you."

"I got to play soccer at kindergarten today. Doug Vaughan kicked me in the leg, but I kicked him back."

Margaret smiled. "I thought the object of soccer was to kick the ball, not the other players."

"That would take all the fun out of the game," Tucker said, appearing behind his daughter. "Come on in, Margaret."

"Hello, Tucker," she said, praying that her cheeks didn't look as warm as they felt. She found that she couldn't quite meet his eyes as she passed him.

She still couldn't believe she'd kissed him. She hadn't even had an intoxicating drink to blame as an excuse for her behavior. She could only conclude that the spinning turns of the dances he'd taught her had temporarily addled her brains.

Thank goodness for Kitten. There could be no awkward silences with her in the room. The child immediately launched into a play-by-play account of her soccer game, followed by a lengthy complaint about the amount of work kindergartners were forced to do and a detailed review of the video her father had rented for them to watch that evening.

By the time she paused for breath, the pizza had been delivered and the three of them were seated at the kitchen table with paper plates and napkins and glasses of soda in front of them.

Tucker took advantage of his daughter filling her mouth with pizza to turn to Margaret and say, "And how was *your* day?"

Margaret smiled faintly. "Not nearly as exciting as Kitten's. I only worked on the books for a little clothing boutique in Irving. Nothing very interesting."

"Sam got to go see Alan Jackson," Kitten announced

grudgingly around a mouthful of pizza. "They said I was too little."

"Don't talk with your mouth full, Kitten," Tucker instructed.

Kitten swallowed with a gulp, then smiled at Margaret, her little face streaked with cheese and tomato sauce. "I didn't want to go to the dumb old concert, anyway," she said. "I'd rather be here with you and Daddy."

Margaret didn't quite know what to say in response, so she took another bite of her own pizza to give her an excuse.

"I'm going to be in a wedding," Kitten announced brightly. "I'm going to be a flower girl. I'm going to wear a blue dress with lots of ruffles that go all the way to the floor and I get to miss a whole week of school and fly to Houston on an airplane. Sam's going to be in it, too. He's going to wear a...what's it called, Daddy?"

"A tuxedo," Tucker supplied.

"When is this going to happen?" Margaret asked, giving the child her undivided attention—at least, as much as possible while she was so intensely aware of Tucker.

"How long, Daddy?"

"Ten more days. You leave the day after Halloween."

"I'm going to be a fairy princess for Halloween," Kitten said, immediately diverted. "Grandma's making my costume. It's bee-yoo-tiful."

Neither Tucker nor Margaret tried to turn the conversation along more-adult lines during the meal, both accepting in unspoken agreement that this evening was for Kitten. It was Kitten who brought up the subject of nicknames again.

"You call Daddy 'Tucker,'" she declared to Margaret, looking endearingly serious.

"That *is* my name, Kitten."

She shook her head at his comment. "Most people call you Tuck. Just about everyone has a nickname."

Realizing where the conversation was going, Margaret wondered why it seemed to bother Kitten so badly that Margaret answered to her given name. "Not everyone has a nickname, Kitten," she said. "Not everyone wants one."

"What are nicknames for 'Margaret'?" Kitten wanted to know, oblivious to the hint.

"Peggy," Tucker said.

Both Margaret and Kitten shook their heads.

"She doesn't look like a Peggy," Kitten declared. Margaret heartily agreed.

"Margie," Tucker supplied.

Kitten thought about it, then rejected that one, too.

"Marge?"

"No."

Tucker seemed to be enjoying Margaret's discomfiture as his daughter debated each of the names he suggested. "Maggie."

Kitten wrinkled her nose. "Uh-uh."

"Meg."

That one seemed to tempt Kitten a moment, then it, too, was spurned. "They just don't sound right for her," she said with a sigh.

Margaret shrugged. "Obviously, it's best if I stick with my given name."

Kitten didn't look at all satisfied. "There's got to be a nickname that's just perfect for you."

"I really don't think so."

Tucker came to Margaret's rescue. "Finished with your pizza, Kitten?"

The child nodded, still distracted.

"Then how about ice cream for dessert?"

Nicknames were abruptly forgotten. "With chocolate sauce?" she asked eagerly.

"You bet."

"And a cherry on top?"

"Okay."

"And some sprinkles."

Tucker exaggerated a scowl. "Don't push your luck, kid."

Kitten giggled.

He turned to Margaret. "Ice cream?"

She started to decline, thinking of the fat and calories she'd already consumed, but Kitten's expectant look was hard to withstand. "Maybe a little."

"Chocolate sauce and cherry on top?" Tucker asked, those wicked dimples appearing.

"And sprinkles," she returned mildly, carefully hiding her reaction to his grin.

Kitten seemed delighted that Margaret was getting into the spirit of the evening.

They moved into the den after dessert, settling onto the couch to watch the animated Disney video. By request, Kitten sat in the middle, Margaret on her right, Tucker at her left. Not long after the film began, Tucker draped a casual arm along the back of the couch.

Margaret was all too vividly aware that his fingers were only an inch or so from her shoulder. Occasionally, he flexed them. She wondered if it were only by accident that he brushed against her each time.

Whatever his intentions, she couldn't have been more physically aware of him if she'd been snuggled against his side, the way his daughter was.

The video was only an hour and a half long. By the time it ended, Kitten was almost asleep.

Smiling, Tucker rewound the film and gathered his daughter into his arms. "Let's go get you ready for bed," he said. "You've got school tomorrow."

"But I'm not sleepy," Kitten said around a huge yawn, rubbing her eyes with one little fist.

"I'd better go," Margaret said, edging toward the door.

Both Kitten and Tucker protested.

"Stay and say good-night when I'm in bed," Kitten pleaded.

"I'll make coffee," Tucker said. "We can talk."

That was what worried her. Tucking Kitten in, sharing late-evening coffee with Tucker—both prospects unnerved her in a way she couldn't have explained had she tried.

"Well, I..."

"Please, Margaret," Kitten said drowsily.

Margaret gave a silent sigh of resignation. "All right. I'll stay. But only until you're in bed," she added, glancing at Tucker.

"I'll call you when she's ready," he said, apparently unperturbed.

It was only about fifteen minutes later when Margaret was summoned upstairs to Kitten's bedroom. Dressed in frilly pink pajamas, the little girl lay against the pillows of her canopy bed, a floppy cloth doll tucked against her side. Her eyelids heavy, she lifted her face for a kiss from Margaret.

"Good night, Margaret," she murmured. "Tonight was fun."

Margaret pressed a kiss against the child's impossibly soft cheek. "Yes, it was. Thank you for inviting me. Sleep well, Kitten."

"Okay. Night, Daddy."

Tucker had been standing on the other side of Kitten's bed, watching them with a sudden frown that Margaret couldn't quite interpret.

He smoothed his expression into a smile as he bent over his daughter. "Good night, Kitten. See you in the morning."

"Watch out for those under-beds."

"Yeah. You keep an eye peeled for those closet-things."

Kitten giggled softly and snuggled more deeply into her pillows.

Tucker and Margaret left the room quietly; Tucker turned out the overhead light on his way out, leaving only a dim night-light burning in Kitten's room.

"What was that about under-beds and closet-things?" Margaret asked curiously when she and Tucker were downstairs.

He grinned rather sheepishly. "We say it every night," he explained. "One of those bedtime rituals kids seem to like. Sometimes we read a story when it isn't too late or Kitten isn't too tired."

"I see. But...under-beds and closet-things?"

He chuckled. "Didn't you ever think there were monsters living under your bed or in your closet? Kitten deals with her fears by turning them into a joke with me. She knows I'll be there in a heartbeat if she calls out."

"Oh." Margaret didn't answer his question about her own childhood fears. Hers hadn't involved imaginary creatures. The realities of her life had been frightening enough without make-believe monsters.

Pushing away the grim memories, she squared her shoulders. "I'd better go. It's getting late."

"It's just after eight," he argued, glancing at his watch. "Hardly late, except for a five-year-old."

"Yes, well, I have some things to do this evening."

"One cup of coffee?" he coaxed. "Sam won't be home for a couple of hours yet. I thought it would be nice to have some adult conversation now that Kitten and her hyperactive mouth are asleep."

She couldn't help smiling at his wry tone. "That isn't a very flattering way to talk about your own child."

"Have *you* ever met anyone who could talk more or faster?"

"Well...no. But she's adorable," Margaret said loyally.

"I know. So does she."

Margaret couldn't argue with that one, either. Little Kitten was a bit pampered, but still sweet natured. Though Margaret's exposure to children had been limited, she hadn't met many—maybe not any—that she liked as much as this one.

"So, how about it?" Tucker prodded. "Coffee?"

She was tempted. She really was. But the evening had been just a bit too comfortable and domestic already. She didn't want to start something she was terrified to finish. "Not tonight, Tucker. But thank you."

He didn't bother to hide his dissatisfaction, but he surrendered without further argument. "All right. I'll walk you home."

"You will not. I don't want you leaving Kitten here alone."

He nodded. "Okay. Be careful."

"I'm only going next door."

"Be careful anyway."

He walked her to the door, pausing a moment before opening it. He gave her one of those melt-your-knees, dimpled smiles. "I don't suppose you want to kiss me again before you go?"

She cleared her throat. "No. Not tonight."

He lowered his voice to a sexy croon. "Are you sure? I wouldn't object. Far from it, in fact."

She wondered briefly if Arnie Hollis had ever taken Tucker behind the woodshed when he was a boy. And then she wondered if it was too late for someone to do so now. Sometimes he could look just like a mischievous kid. A cocky, smart-aleck, altogether-too-charming kid.

"No, Tucker."

He exhaled deeply and touched a finger to her mouth. "Can't blame a guy for trying," he muttered.

Her lips tingled as wildly as though he had indeed kissed her. "I've got to go," she said, her voice a bit strangled.

He opened the door.

"Good night, Tucker," she remembered to say on the way out. "Er, thanks for the pizza."

She was halfway down the path before he could answer.

Tucker had never met anyone more skittish than Margaret McAlister. For every step they took forward in their developing friendship, she jumped two steps backward.

He could still remember the way she'd felt, the way she'd tasted when she'd kissed him. To be honest, she'd stunned him. Though he'd been wanting to kiss her all that evening, he'd been totally unprepared for the impact when it happened.

He still didn't know what had made the kiss so spectacular. It hadn't been as long or as deep or as passionate as others he'd known. He hadn't even had his arms around her. But it had left him hungry and restless and needy, so much so that he'd hardly slept that night.

He wanted her.

He only wished he could come close to understanding her.

She was afraid of something—visibly afraid. Of him? Ridiculous. He was hardly the type of guy a woman should fear. No hardened heartbreaker, no slick con man, no practiced seducer. Just an average Joe, a schoolteacher, a single dad with two kids and a mortgage. There was absolutely no reason for Margaret to fear him.

So what was the problem? Why did she sometimes look at him as though he were a threat to everything she held dear? And why the hell couldn't he just cut his losses and forget about her?

Women, he thought, shoving a hand through his tousled hair. Would he ever understand them? He really should just stop trying.

He wondered how long he should wait before he called Margaret and asked her out again.

Chapter Eight

It wasn't that Greg Jessup was a crook, Margaret decided sometime late Thursday afternoon. It was just that the happy-go-lucky young man had absolutely no understanding of accounting practices and tax laws—and no inclination to learn.

She'd spent the past hour with him in her home office, going over the so-called records that he and his partner in the quick-lube shop had provided her for that month's business. She looked at the jumble of torn receipts, oil-stained envelopes, fast-food hamburger wrappers and paper towels on her desk—all scribbled with notes and figures that Greg assured her were vitally important.

She was beginning to be very sorry that she had taken this account, no matter how much she secretly liked the guys.

She drew a deep breath, reminding herself that she had a dinner meeting of her professional-business-women's organization that evening and she wanted to wrap this up in time to change. She picked up a scrap of paper. "This says 'Mike—forty dollars.' What does that mean, Greg?"

The twenty-five-year-old entrepreneur scratched his sandy head and frowned. "Um, oh, yeah. That's for supplies."

"Supplies?" she repeated.

"Yeah. Mike's a buddy of Jeff's. He was hanging around the shop last Saturday when business was crazy and we ran out of hand cleaner and paper towels in the men's room. He volunteered to run to the store. I gave him a couple of twenties out of the register. I remembered to write it down," he added a bit smugly.

"The purchase was exactly forty dollars? That seems high for hand cleaner and paper towels."

Greg frowned uncertainly. "Well, I don't know. He didn't give me any change."

"How about a receipt?"

"Uh, isn't that a receipt in your hand?"

She struggled for a patient tone. "No. This is a scrap of adding-machine paper with a very vague memo written on it. A receipt is issued by the store and lists the items purchased and the total price. The IRS tends to prefer those to notes like this one."

"I don't think he gave me a receipt. He probably threw it away."

"Greg, we've been over this before. You and Jeff have *got* to start keeping better— Darn." She set her pencil down in response to the summons of her front doorbell. "Would you excuse me for a moment, please?"

He looked delighted to do so—like a schoolboy given a reprieve from the principal's lecture, Margaret thought wryly.

"Sure. Take your time," he said.

It took Margaret a moment to recognize the dark-haired woman standing at her doorstep holding a large shopping bag. She'd only met her once, over a month earlier.

"Debbie," she said, finally remembering the name. "Why, hello."

"Hi, Margaret. I hope I'm not interrupting anything."

Margaret wondered why in the world Tucker's sister had come to see her. She managed to restrain her curiosity as she spoke. "I'm meeting with a client, but it shouldn't take much longer. Would you like to come in and wait?"

"No, thanks. The kids are all waiting in the van," Debbie explained, gesturing toward the blue minivan parked behind her in Margaret's driveway. "I promised Tuck I'd drop some things off for his kids this afternoon, but I guess he's late getting home today. I worry about leaving the package on his doorstep. Would it be okay if I leave it here and let him get it from you later?"

"Of course."

"Thanks," Debbie said gratefully. "I've been shopping all afternoon and I'm ready to get home and put my feet up. Lord knows when Tuck will get back, so I don't want to wait for him. I'll stick a note on his door, telling him I left the package with you."

Debbie couldn't know, of course, that Margaret had been carefully avoiding Tucker and his children since the intimate little pizza party Tuesday evening. Obviously, she couldn't avoid them forever. They were, after all, neighbors.

Margaret took the bag. "No problem. I have a meeting this evening, but I'll get it to him somehow."

"No rush. It's just some underwear and socks and stuff for the kids. Tuck hasn't had time to shop lately, and since I was going to the mall today anyway, I volunteered to pick up some things they needed."

Margaret thought again of how much responsibility

Tucker faced being the single parent of two young children. It had to be daunting for him at times. It must be nice to have his close family to count on, she thought a bit wistfully.

Debbie didn't linger. "The kids will be getting restless," she explained, already moving toward the van. "Thanks again, Margaret. Maybe next time we'll have a chance to visit."

"That would be nice," Margaret said automatically, though she wasn't at all sure she wanted to grow fond of yet another member of Tucker's intriguing family. She closed the door, set the shopping bag on the sofa in the den and returned determinedly to her own life, which awaited her in her office.

"Now, Greg," she said as she took her place behind her desk again, "about those withholding forms you were supposed to have filled out for me on your full-time employees..."

Greg winced and slumped a bit lower in his chair. Margaret glanced surreptitiously at her watch, wondering if she was going to make it to her meeting after all.

Tucker convinced Kitten to stay at home with Sam while he went to get the package the note on his door had informed him could be retrieved at Margaret's house. It wasn't easy. Kitten wanted to see Margaret. Tucker finally promised he'd ask Margaret if she wanted to go out for a meal with them sometime during the weekend, to Sam's unconcealed displeasure.

As he walked across his yard to Margaret's, Tucker couldn't help worrying about Kitten's growing attachment to their neighbor. It wasn't that he didn't understand, exactly. After all, he'd become a bit obsessed with Margaret himself. But he didn't want Kitten hurt if something happened that put a permanent rift between himself and Margaret.

He knew it was a possibility. Their relationship...no, that wasn't the right word. Their friendship...no, not that, either.

Whatever it was that was growing between them was decidedly tentative. Balanced on the point of a toothpick. And he suspected that the feelings on both sides—however they might be described—were too strong to fade into a tepid, neighborly courtesy.

Something told him that this thing was more likely headed for an explosion than a bland fizzle.

If only she hadn't kissed him that way, maybe he could believe there wasn't that much between them. But she had. And he'd spent too many hours since, wishing she would do so again.

There was a strange car in her driveway. A sporty-looking red number. It wasn't her friend Jackie's—he remembered that hers was black.

He thought about waiting until her company was gone before calling on her, but since he was here, he couldn't resist stepping onto the porch and ringing her bell.

Margaret answered a moment later. Tucker wasn't at all pleased to see a man standing rather closely behind her.

The guy was tall and a bit lanky, a young, sandy-haired cowboy in jeans and boots and a denim shirt rolled up on his forearms. Some women probably would have found him good-looking. Tucker wondered with a scowl if Margaret agreed.

"You must be here for your package," Margaret said by way of greeting. "Wait just a moment and I'll get it for you."

She made him sound like the UPS guy or something, Tucker thought resentfully as she turned to the other man.

"I'll see you next week, Greg," she said.

Greg slung an arm around her shoulders and gave her

a hug. "I'll try not to make it so frustrating for you next time," he promised in an easy drawl. "Don't give up on me yet."

As Tucker jammed his hands into the pockets of his jacket, he noticed that Margaret's cheeks pinkened in response to the casual embrace. He told himself that he wasn't really fighting the urge to break the guy's face—but he knew he lied.

Margaret neatly disentangled herself from Greg's encircling arm. "Thanks, Greg. I'm sure you'll try."

"You've got my word," Greg said. He nodded to Tucker on his way past, seemingly unsurprised to find another man on Margaret's doorstep. "How ya doin'?"

Tucker growled something unintelligible in response.

"Come in, Tucker. I put your package in the den."

Tucker stepped inside the house and closed the door firmly behind him. "Who the hell was *he?*"

She'd already been moving toward the den. In response to Tucker's question—or more likely the tone in which he'd asked it—she stopped and turned slowly toward him. "I beg your pardon?"

It didn't help his mood that her tone had gone distant and cool. He jerked his head toward the door behind him. "That cocky kid who was all over you just now—who was he?"

Her chin lifted as her brown eyes narrowed. "I can't imagine what makes you think that is any of your business."

He was still too irritated to acknowledge her point. "You told me you aren't involved with anyone."

"That's true," she replied curtly. "I'm not involved with *anyone.*"

"Including me, you mean?"

"Including you. One double date and one pizza dinner do not give you the right to interrogate me, Tucker Hollis."

He moved two steps closer to her. She didn't back up. "Who was he, Margaret?"

"He's a client," she said, anger adding sudden heat to her voice. "I do the books for his business. He brings me his receipts—or what he tries to pass off as receipts—once a week after he closes his shop. I have nine other clients who occasionally stop by. Do you expect me to introduce you to every one of them?"

He should have had the grace to look sheepish. Somewhere inside, he acknowledged how unreasonable his behavior was. But he was still fuming at seeing that guy's arm around Margaret's shoulders. At seeing the stain of a blush on her cheeks in reaction to another man's touch.

"Look, I'm sorry," he said, knowing even as he spoke that he sounded too abrupt. "I know you don't owe me explanations—"

"I certainly do not."

He ignored her interruption. "It just caught me off guard, seeing him like that."

It had made him mad as hell, to be more precise. All he'd been able to think about was that Greg had felt comfortable giving Margaret a spontaneous hug when Tucker still felt he had to ask permission to touch her.

"I knew this was a mistake. I never should have gone out with a neighbor," Margaret complained.

"It wasn't a mistake, damn it. I just—"

She turned abruptly on one heel. "I'll get your package. And then you can go."

He caught her arm and whirled her around to face him. "There's something you need to understand before we finish this."

He didn't ask permission before he covered her surprise-parted lips with his own.

She stiffened against him as his arms went around her. He only drew her closer and let the kiss tell her everything he'd been trying to say since the first day he'd met her.

Maybe some of it got through to her. She relaxed—just a little. Her hands, which had clenched on his chest, opened. Her fingers spread.

He tilted his head and kissed her from a new angle, coaxing a response. He nearly groaned aloud when he got one. Her lips softened. Warmed. Moved beneath his in a tentative, rather hesitant response.

It was all he could do to resist the temptation to deepen the kiss. He wanted to taste her so badly he ached with it. But he figured he'd pressed his luck as far as he could—this time. Slowly, reluctantly he lifted his head.

"Now do you understand?" he asked hoarsely. "I don't feel 'neighborly' toward you, Margaret. It's a hell of a lot more than that."

He could see the fear in her eyes, though he still didn't quite understand what put it there. He could only hope she would someday trust him enough to explain—even after he'd made such a fool of himself with her today.

"I'm sorry," he said before she could find her voice. This time, the apology was offered sincerely. "I had no right to question you that way. It won't happen again."

"Tucker, I—"

As though suddenly aware that she was still plastered against him, she stiffened and drew back. He dropped his arms to his sides. "I really didn't want this," she whispered.

"I know," he said sympathetically. "I'm not sure I was ready for this myself. But here it is. What are we going to do about it?"

"I don't—I don't know."

"We could go on from here. See where it leads us."

"What about your children?" she asked, crossing her arms over her chest in a gesture that was both self-protective and defensive.

"What about them?"

"I don't want them to be hurt or confused by anything that might—that might happen between us. They're so young and impressionable. So vulnerable."

"Believe me, I'm fully aware of that," he said, irked again that she would question his dedication to his kids. "My children's welfare will always come first with me. But I have to have a life of my own. Other single parents have relationships without sacrificing their children's well-being. I don't see why I can't do the same, if I'm careful about it."

"It's not that. You're obviously a very good father. I know you'd never do anything to hurt those children. But I—well, I haven't had any experience with children. I don't know what to say, how to act—"

"How can you say that? Kitten's nuts about you."

She swallowed, as though his words made her even more nervous. "What about Sam?" she challenged.

"Sam hasn't had a chance yet to get to know you. We're all still getting to know each other. It's part of the process. It'll either work out—or it won't. But there's no reason to believe the kids will be hurt if you and I act like adults."

She exhaled through her nose. "And were you acting like an adult a little while ago?"

He winced as her point hit home.

"No," he admitted. "I was wrong. I've apologized, and I've promised it won't happen again. I'm not a complete jerk, Margaret. Despite the impression you might have gotten, I've never been the unreasonably jealous or abusive type. If I were, I'd have given Callie a lot harder time when she left me for Benny. We handled it all carefully, for the kids' sake. I've been dumped before, I can handle it again, if necessary. I'm just asking for a chance."

"Why, Tucker?" she asked, so softly he could hardly hear her, her eyes unguardedly bewildered.

"I thought I just made that clear."

She moistened her lips, which were still darkened from his kiss. "Oh."

"Yeah. Oh."

He managed a rather crooked smile. "Don't look so scared, Margaret. I'm only asking you to go out with me again. That's all. For now," he couldn't resist adding.

She touched her forehead, as though it were hurting her, then glanced at her watch. "I have a meeting tonight. I'm going to be late."

"Then I'll leave. I've got to get home to the kids anyway. I'll call you, okay?"

She nodded.

He turned to go.

"Wait—your package," she reminded him. She hurried into the den, retrieved the shopping bag and thrust it into his arms.

"Good night," Tucker said. "Drive carefully tonight."

"Yes. I will. Thank you." She opened the door as if she couldn't wait any longer for him to go through it.

He left without further delay, grimacing when the door closed a bit too hastily behind him.

Either he'd made some headway with her, or he'd just screwed up royally, he thought with a resigned sigh as he headed home. He supposed he wouldn't know for sure until the next time he talked to her.

He clung to the faint reassurance that she hadn't taken his head off when he'd kissed her. Had, in fact, kissed him back, even after he'd behaved like a total idiot. That had to be a good sign—didn't it?

He shook his head in self-disgust, then drew a deep breath and squared his shoulders before entering his house to join his children.

* * *

Margaret was late to her meeting. It was the first time since she'd joined the organization three years ago that she'd been late. She was aware of several curious, surprised faces turned her way when she arrived, breathless and uncharacteristically flustered.

She could blame that, too, on Tucker.

She'd thought of skipping the meeting altogether, but couldn't face the thought of staying home alone that evening, pacing the floor, worrying about the future and mentally replaying his kisses. She'd welcomed the distraction.

And then she spent the entire evening doing exactly what she'd tried to avoid. Worrying about the future. Feeling his lips on hers again. She would have hated to be tested on the topic of the guest speaker's talk; she didn't hear half of it.

Tucker was changing her life—interfering with her schedules, threatening her comfortably peaceful routines. She'd been afraid of that from the start, but now it seemed too late to stop it. Somehow, she knew this problem—this man—wasn't just going to fade meekly away because she willed it. And, even worse, she wasn't even still certain she wanted him to do so.

Did she really want Tucker to go away? Would she really choose never to see him again? Never again see that sexy smile creasing his lean cheeks? Or feel his arms around her, or his lips on hers? Or recognize the unexpected, unhidden desire in his eyes when he looked at her?

And Kitten—could she really wish the child out of her life now that she'd entered it and undeniably brightened it?

"Margaret?"

Something about the way her name was spoken made her aware that it wasn't the first time. She blinked and tried to pay attention to her surroundings. "I'm sorry, Gail, what did you say?"

The other woman was looking at her in concern. "Are you all right? You seem…well, out of it."

Margaret gave her a rueful smile. "I'm afraid I'm just tired this evening. I spent most of the afternoon with a difficult client."

Gail nodded sympathetically. "I can certainly understand that. You should try to get some rest tonight."

Margaret wondered what the odds were that her sleep would be undisturbed by restless dreams. She wouldn't want to place a bet on it. "Yes, I will," she said.

"Good night. Drive carefully."

So the meeting was over. Margaret couldn't even say what she'd eaten for dinner.

What was Tucker Hollis *doing* to her?

"Are you sure I look okay, Daddy? Is my hair bow straight?" Kitten fretted as she twisted in front of the mirror in her bedroom, fussing over her appearance. She wore a long-sleeved knit dress in bold red, yellow and purple stripes. The striped bow in her hair had come with the dress. Red tights and black Mary Janes completed the outfit.

Tucker thought she looked beautiful—and told her so. "Absolutely perfect," he assured her. "Grandma knew this outfit would look good on you when she picked it out for you."

"You think Margaret will like it?"

"I'm sure she will," Tucker replied patiently. "Now go downstairs and wait while I see if Sam's ready."

"Sam's in his room sulking. He doesn't want to go. He's such a jerk sometimes."

Tucker swallowed a sigh. "I'll talk to him. Go on down, now. And don't mess up your clothes."

"I won't." With one last, self-satisfied glance in the mirror, Kitten skipped away.

He was really going to have to watch out for his daughter's vanity before she turned into a spoiled little beauty-queen wannabe, Tucker thought wryly as he headed toward his son's room. Behavior that was cute at five wasn't so cute at fifteen.

Hell, he knew women his own age who couldn't think of anything but their appearance. He preferred a woman with more substance—a woman like Margaret, who seemed to somehow always look nice without fussing over it much.

He tapped on Sam's door. "Sam? You ready?"

An unintelligible mutter answered him. He opened the door.

Sam was lying on his stomach on the bed, still wearing the grubby jeans and sports jersey he'd had on all afternoon, a handheld video game glowing in front of him. The clothes Tucker had laid out for him to wear that evening were still untouched.

"Darn it, Sam, I told you to get dressed. We're going to be late if you don't hurry. Kitten and I are ready."

Sam glanced up sullenly from the game. "I still don't see why I have to go. Why can't I stay with Grandma and Grandpa?"

"Because I want you to go with us. This is a family outing, and that includes you."

"*She* isn't family."

Tucker held on to his temper with an effort. They had already gone over most of this argument, and though he'd tried to be patient and understanding then, he thought he'd made his point clear. This evening was not negotiable.

"Her name is Margaret. You may call her that or Ms. McAlister, but you will say it politely, is that understood?"

The boy nodded.

"Now get dressed. You *are* going with us and you're going to give Margaret a fair chance. You promised me earlier you would, and I'm holding you to your word."

Sam sighed gustily. "I still don't like it."

"That's your choice. You can have a good time tonight or you can make yourself miserable, but you will not ruin the evening for the rest of us. Clear?"

Tucker didn't flatly lay down the law for his kids very often, but when he did, they knew how they'd better respond. "Yes, sir," Sam mumbled.

"All right. Now get dressed and meet us downstairs in ten minutes. And don't make me come back up here to get you."

He closed Sam's door behind him as he left the room, then took a deep breath to restore his composure. There were times, he thought pensively, that he rather wished the old-fashioned rules of child raising still applied. If he or Mick had muttered at *their* dad that way, they'd have had a taste of the belt. And while he couldn't really imagine resorting to that form of discipline himself, he still had no intention of allowing his nine-year-old son to openly defy his directions.

He only hoped Sam wouldn't act badly during dinner. He'd always been a good boy, had never really embarrassed Tucker in public…but with preadolescents, there was always a first time.

Maybe taking his kids on a date with him hadn't been such a bright idea after all.

If there were undercurrents of tension during dinner, Kitten seemed oblivious to them. She was visibly thrilled to be having dinner at a nice, family-friendly Italian restaurant with Tucker and Margaret. As Tucker had anticipated, Kitten chattered incessantly, but—to his secret pride and relief—her table manners were pretty good for a five-year-old.

Sam ate his own meal neatly and quietly, contributing to the conversation only when directly spoken to, going out of his way to avoid eye contact with Margaret. Tucker could see that Margaret was making an effort to draw the boy out; whenever Kitten stopped for a bite or a breath, Margaret asked Sam something about school or sports.

Sam answered in monosyllables—not outwardly rude, which he knew Tucker wouldn't tolerate, but decidedly reserved.

The boy made no effort to hide his displeasure when the waiter naturally mistook them for a family and made a friendly comment to both Tucker and Margaret that they had unusually well-behaved children. Margaret merely smiled; Tucker thanked the waiter and asked for more iced tea.

There wasn't much opportunity for Tucker and Margaret to talk; Kitten's prattling made sure of that. But it didn't keep them from looking at each other occasionally, their eyes holding messages that probably bemused her as much as they did him.

He tried to tell her silently that he was glad she'd come, that he was pleased that she seemed to have forgiven him—at least provisionally—for his boorish behavior the day before. He attempted to let her know that he appreciated her warmth toward Kitten, her forbearance of Sam's resistance.

In return, she seemed to be telling him that she was trying to give him the chance he'd requested. That she still had doubts, and fears, but she hadn't completely rejected the possibility that there could still be something between them.

Or was he completely misreading her?

He concentrated on his dessert, telling himself firmly

that next time it would be just the two of them, no matter how beguilingly Kitten might beg to be included again.

They didn't try to do anything after dinner. By unspoken agreement, both Tucker and Margaret seemed to realize that they'd made as much progress as they could during one evening.

Tucker pulled into Margaret's driveway. "I'll walk you to the door."

"Me, too," said Kitten, reaching for the buckle of her seat belt.

"No, you wait here," Tucker said quickly. "I'll just be a minute."

Kitten sighed, but didn't argue. "Okay. G'night, Margaret."

Margaret turned in her seat to smile at the child. "Good night, Kitten. Good night, Sam."

"Night," Sam said, glancing away.

Tucker waited until Margaret unlocked her door before speaking. "I think the evening went well, don't you?"

Margaret looked discouraged. "Sam hates me."

"He doesn't hate you."

"He certainly doesn't like me."

"Give him time, Margaret. He isn't comfortable with change. It takes him a while to get used to someone new in his life."

She glanced over his shoulder toward his Ford. "I suppose I can understand that," she said slowly.

He couldn't help smiling wryly. "Somehow I thought you might."

She drew a deep breath. "Well...good night, Tucker."

He leaned over to brush his lips across hers. He figured the powerful kisses they'd shared Thursday had changed the ground rules—about some things, at least. "I'll call you."

"All right." She stepped back quickly, looking toward the driveway as though worried about what his children had seen, or their reaction to it.

Tucker waited until she'd closed the door, then loped back to his Ford and climbed behind the wheel. "You were both really good tonight," he said as he backed out of Margaret's driveway and pulled into his own. "I was proud of you."

He saw no need to mention Sam's reticence. As long as Sam hadn't been outwardly rude, Tucker thought they'd taken steps in the right direction.

"I had fun," Kitten said, climbing out of her seat after Tucker had parked in the garage. "Didn't you, Daddy?"

He opened the door that led into their kitchen. "Yes, Kitten, I had a very nice time."

"Margaret sure is nice. She always listens when I talk to her."

Tucker chuckled. "Mmm. That is nice of her."

His gentle barb sailed right over the child's head. "We looked like a real family tonight, didn't we? Even the waiter thought we were."

"We're not a family! Not with *her,*" Sam said loudly, slamming the kitchen door closed behind them.

"Sam——" Tucker began.

"We could be," Kitten shouted back. "Margaret likes us, even if you are jerky to her. Maybe she *wants* to be part of our family."

"Well, she isn't. And she never will be. We don't need her," Sam yelled, glaring down at his sister.

Tucker put a hand on his son's shoulder. "That's enough, Sam. We——"

Sam jerked away. "We don't need her," he insisted. "We're doing just fine without her, Dad."

Tucker might have gotten angry, had Sam looked defiant or openly confrontational. But he didn't. He just looked miserable.

Tucker ran a hand through his hair and exhaled slowly. "I think we're all tired," he said. "Kitten, go get ready for bed. And, Sam, all I'm asking is for you to give it some time, okay? Nothing's going to change right now. We simply have a new friend, all right?"

Sam bit his lip, looked at his feet and shrugged one shoulder, looking suddenly very small and very young. Tucker, on the other hand, felt suddenly old, the heavy weight of his responsibility for his children on his shoulders, along with a healthy dose of ambiguous guilt.

He put an arm around his son's shoulders and drew him close. "We're getting along fine, Sam. I promise you, nothing's going to come between us. Okay?"

Sam gulped and nodded, leaning into Tucker's embrace.

Tucker leaned down and kissed his son's forehead. "Go change and brush your teeth. Maybe you and I will watch a little TV after I put Kitten to bed."

Calmer now, Sam dashed at his eyes with the back of his hand. "Okay, Dad. That sounds good. Just the two of us."

Watching Sam leave the room, Tucker wondered glumly how other single parents managed to have a life of their own without feeling that they were permanently traumatizing their children. How come there weren't any instruction manuals for this job, anyway?

Chapter Nine

Tucker called Monday evening. It was late; Margaret had already dressed for bed and was brushing her teeth when the phone rang. She rinsed hastily and snatched up the receiver of her bedroom extension. "Hello?"

"Hi. It's Tuck."

Just the sound of his voice made her knees weaken. She sat on the edge of the bed. "Hello."

"I hope you weren't already in bed."

"No. Not yet." Though, according to her usual routine, she would just be climbing in had he not called.

"Good. I waited until the kids were in bed so we could talk for a few minutes without interruption."

She lifted an eyebrow as she glanced at her clock. "The children have just gotten to bed?"

"I got Kitten down about an hour ago. Sam remembered at the last minute that he needed a special costume for a school program tomorrow afternoon. We've spent most of the evening putting that together."

Sounded like another hectic evening in the Hollis household. Now, why didn't *that* surprise her?

"How was your day?" Tucker asked.

"Quiet," she replied, wondering why the word—which should have sounded peaceful and somewhat self-satisfied in comparison to his evening—came out sounding a bit bleak instead. She would have liked to modify it by telling him something interesting that had happened that day; unfortunately, she couldn't think of anything at the moment.

Tucker chuckled. "That's a word I hardly recognize these days," he admitted. "Maybe next week I'll be reminded of what it means."

"What do you mean?"

"The kids will be in Houston next week. For the wedding Kitten mentioned to you."

"Oh, yes. She's going to wear a long blue dress, with ruffles. And Sam's wearing a tux."

"Right. It's their aunt Cathy's wedding. Their mother's baby sister. Sam and Kitten are the only grandchildren on that side of the family, and everyone was anxious to have them in the wedding. Their grandmother took advantage of the opportunity to have them with her for the entire week. I'm putting them on a plane Friday morning, and they won't be back until the following Saturday."

"They'll miss school?"

"Yeah. I've already cleared it with their teachers and made arrangements for makeup work—not that Kitten will have much for kindergarten. Sam's doing real well in school, so a few days off shouldn't set him back."

Margaret figured that Tucker should know more about that than she, being a teacher himself. "Are the children close to their mother's family?"

"Yeah. There are only Cathy and her mother and a few extended relatives. They all dote on Sam and Kitten.

They're nice people. We all managed to keep a fairly close relationship even after Callie and I were divorced. Since she died, I've made an effort to keep them in touch with the kids. I thought it was important, for Kitten and Sam's sake especially.''

"It's good that you can all be friendly," Margaret murmured, assailed for a moment by unpleasant memories. "It's so painfully difficult for children when there is fighting and antagonism within their family."

Tucker was quiet a moment, as though digesting her words, or maybe the tone in which she'd spoken them. "Speaking from experience?" he asked a bit too casually.

"Yes," she answered shortly. "Is Sam looking forward to his visit with his grandmother?" she asked, abruptly changing the subject.

"Seems to be. There's a boy who lives next door to her who's about Sam's age. The two of them have been pals since they were toddlers, even though they only get to see each other a couple of times a year."

"That's nice." Margaret moistened her lips and made an effort to keep the conversation going. "I'm sure you'll miss them."

"Yeah. I'm used to having them underfoot all the time now. It's going to seem awfully quiet around here without them."

There was that word again. *Quiet.* It sounded just as lonely when Tucker said it.

Since the children seemed the safest topic—at least, not as personal as talking about themselves—Margaret doggedly continued. "I suppose they're looking forward to Halloween. I'm sure Kitten will look adorable in her fairy-princess costume. Is Sam too old to dress up?"

"Oh, no. He has grand plans to be a vampire. He's been after me to buy him some fangs and fake blood. I guess I'll take him shopping tomorrow."

Margaret wrinkled her nose. "Boys tend to prefer the more ghoulish costumes, don't they?"

"Of course." Tucker sounded amused. "I'm considering dressing up as a rotting corpse myself. How do you think I'd look?"

Probably gorgeous, Margaret found herself thinking wryly. She couldn't imagine Tucker looking any other way. "I'm sure that would be suitably grotesque," she said primly.

He laughed. "You're got a real talent for that."

"For what?"

"Royally dignified responses. Of the we-are-not-amused variety."

She wasn't sure if she was being complimented or insulted. "Um..."

"Maybe you and I can take advantage of next week to get to know each other better," he suggested, catching her while she was still nonplussed from his last comment. "Have dinner, maybe see a movie or something."

She swallowed. "I'll have to see. I have a rather busy week planned. Work, and a couple of meetings, and—"

"Margaret, I just suggested that we go out a couple of times, when you're available. We can try to work around your schedule. I do have a job myself, you know."

"I'm sorry, I didn't mean to imply that you don't have a busy schedule of your own."

"I'm sure it's nothing like yours," he said just a bit dryly. "I've always tried to remain flexible."

"I've found that planning and organization work best for me," she replied, a bit stung by the insinuated criticism.

"Fine. You can check your calendar to see if you can fit me in sometime next week. How's that?"

He sounded annoyed. Which made her wonder why

he persisted in asking her out when she only seemed to irritate him at times.

"I warned you that this wouldn't work out," she couldn't resist countering.

"And I asked you to give it a fair chance," he reminded her. "I don't think you've done that yet."

She bit her lip, uncertain whether to agree or disagree with his conclusion.

"Look, I'll call you later in the week, okay?"

"If you like."

"You know what, Margaret?" he asked conversationally, sounding suddenly amused again.

Wary of his mercurial mood changes, she asked cautiously, "What?"

"You really tick me off sometimes."

She couldn't help smiling. "So why do you keep calling?"

"Beats me. Must be that sexy mouth of yours. G'night."

"Good—"

But he'd already hung up.

She was rather dazed when she hung up the phone. She realized that she often felt that way after a conversation with Tucker Hollis. The man was definitely making her crazy.

But he thought she had a sexy mouth.

She lifted her fingertips to her lips, wondering what it was exactly that he found particularly appealing about them. And then she flushed and snapped off the light, embarrassed that she'd slipped into schoolgirlish dreaminess.

The man was dangerous. And she'd never in her adult life been drawn to danger. Safety, security, peace and tranquility were all she'd craved—

Until she'd met Tucker and discovered a hidden side to herself that she hadn't even known existed.

* * *

Starting before dusk on Thursday afternoon, Margaret had a steady stream of trick-or-treaters ring her doorbell. She didn't mind. She actually rather liked passing out treats on Halloween. Most of the children were cute and passingly polite, and she didn't allow the poorly behaved ones to spoil the fun for her.

She had resisted the impulse to buy healthy treats for the children; after all, it *was* Halloween. Instead, she'd bought several bags of popular chocolate candies and colorful bubble-gum balls.

She wasn't really the wicked witch of the neighborhood, she thought, picturing Sam's suspicious young eyes.

She didn't wear a costume—she didn't get into Halloween *that* much. Instead, she dressed in a black velour lounging set and embroidered black velvet slippers, making herself comfortable for an evening at home.

She'd started a new novel, so between visitors she settled onto her sofa to read and listen to music. Either because the occasion seemed to call for it, or because the little music box Tucker had given her had reminded her of it, she put a recording of the original-cast-production highlights of *The Phantom of the Opera* in her CD player. She let the dramatic music swirl around her as she read and answered the door.

The driving rhythm of the title song had just begun when the doorbell chimed again. Margaret set aside her book, picked up the big bowl of candy and gum and opened the door.

An adorable little fairy princess stood on the doorstep, smiling broadly. Several steps behind her, a vampire brooded, looking as though he'd rather be searching for blood anywhere but here.

"Trick or treat, Margaret!" Kitten sang out, holding

out a large plastic pumpkin already partially filled with treats.

"Why, who is this beautiful vision?" Margaret marveled, one hand to her cheek as she studied the child. "I don't think I've ever seen anyone more stunning."

Kitten preened. "That's what Grandpa said when we went to his house."

Margaret smiled and heaped a generous handful of goodies into Kitten's pumpkin. "Are you having fun this evening?"

Kitten nodded vigorously. "We went to a carnival at our school. I won a stuffed bear and a lot of this candy. Now Daddy's letting us trick or treat at houses where we know people. It's fun."

"I'm glad you're having a good time. I'm sure you're being careful," she added, hoping her words were correct.

"Sure. Daddy's sitting in the car at the curb, watching us. He's going to take us to some of our friends' houses."

Margaret hadn't even noticed the black vehicle at the curb. She glanced at it and moistened her lips. "Oh. Well…good."

"We're leaving tomorrow for our grandmother's house in Houston so we won't get to see you for a whole week," Kitten said, sounding torn between regret and anticipation.

"I'll miss you," Margaret told her. She realized that, while she'd said the phrase automatically, she meant it sincerely. She would miss seeing Kitten.

She glanced at the boy still standing back from the door. "Don't you want any candy, Sam?" Margaret offered enticingly, holding out the bowl.

He stepped forward slowly, opening the plastic bag he carried so that she could put in her contribution, which she carefully made sure equalled Kitten's. "Thank you," he said politely if without much warmth.

"You're welcome. Did you enjoy the carnival, too?"

"It was okay," he mumbled. "Come on, Kitten. Daddy said we had to hurry so it wouldn't get too late. We still have to finish packing tonight."

"Okay. Thanks, Margaret. I'll see you when we get back from Houston." Kitten had already bounced off the step, eager to be on her way for more Halloween bounties.

"Have a good time. Both of you," she called after them.

Kitten waved, but it was Sam that Margaret watched as the children hurried down the walk. She suspected that he'd only accompanied Kitten to her door because his sister had begged him to, or maybe because Tucker had insisted. She wished Sam weren't so aloof with her. She'd seen him laughing with his father and other members of his family; she knew he could be sweet and friendly.

If she could go back in time, change her first encounters with him, she would. Unfortunately, that wasn't possible.

Would he ever forgive her? Or was there more to his resistance than their less-than-auspicious beginning? Was it really her he disliked so intensely, or would he be suspicious of any woman he thought his father was interested in dating? She wished she knew how to reassure him that she had no intention of coming between Tucker and his children—as if any woman could.

She thought she saw Tucker wave to her as he pulled away. She lifted a hand in response, then turned her attention to the pint-size clown and slightly larger soldier who were just running up her walk, candy bags eagerly extended.

* * *

Margaret had just finished cooking her dinner Saturday evening when she was summoned to the door. She wiped her hands on a dish towel, suspecting that she knew who her unannounced caller might be. She found herself smoothing her hair and checking to make sure her blouse was neatly tucked into her slacks as she headed for the door.

Sure enough, Tucker stood on the doorstep, an endearingly sheepish grin on his face, his hair tumbled boyishly over his forehead. It would have taken a much stronger woman than Margaret to resist him when he looked like this.

She gave a silent sigh and held the door wider. "Come in."

He didn't give her time to change her mind. "Thanks," he said as he stepped past her. "It's lonely at my house."

"If you're trying for sympathy, forget it," she advised him, though she couldn't help thinking of how quiet his home must be without his children in it.

He shrugged, still smiling. "Well, it was worth a shot."

"Have you had dinner?"

He lifted an eyebrow. "Why, no."

"I was just about to eat. There's plenty for both of us, if you'd like to join me."

His smile deepened in pleasure. "Yeah. I'd like that. Thanks."

Telling herself she was only being neighborly, and calling herself a liar at the same time, Margaret turned for the kitchen. "Come on, then. You can help me set the table."

Tucker followed obediently.

She'd broiled a large steak and steamed vegetables to go with it. With the addition of a hastily put-together salad, there was plenty for two. Margaret had intention-

ally made enough for two meals, having planned to save
the leftovers for her own dinner the next evening.

"This looks great," Tucker enthused when they were
seated. "Do you like to cook?"

"I'm hardly a gourmet, but I do enjoy cooking at
times. Especially baking."

"Kitten certainly enjoys your cookies."

"I'll have to make her some more when she gets
home."

Tucker cut into his steak. "She'll like that."

"No problems getting them off on their trip yesterday?"

He smiled. "You mean, did we miss the plane or forget their luggage or leave the tickets at home or any
other typical Hollis-household disasters?"

"That's not what I asked."

"Well, anyway, I managed to get them off without
any real problems. At the last minute, Kitten got a little
nervous, but a nice flight attendant promised to watch
over her, which reassured her somewhat."

"It must have been hard for you to see them off,"
Margaret said, judging more by his tone than his actual
words.

"Yeah," he admitted. "It was a little tough, especially when Kitten looked up at me with tears in her
eyes and her lip quivering."

Margaret's throat tightened. "I probably would have
burst into tears myself."

Tucker grinned crookedly. "I didn't quite go that far,
but I have to admit it hurt. But Nancy assured me Kitten
would be fine once they were in the air, and apparently
she knew what she was talking about. When I talked to
Kitten on the phone last night, she said she'd had a great
time on the plane."

"Nancy?" Margaret asked casually, keeping her gaze
on her plate.

"The flight attendant."

"Oh." Funny, she thought. That little ripple that had coursed through her at his casual mention of another woman's name had felt suspiciously like jealousy. How ridiculous.

To distract herself from that line of thinking, she asked, "Did you take the day off yesterday?"

"No. I had to arrange for a sub for my first-period class, but I made it in time for second period. The kids' flight left early."

She realized that he hadn't talked about his career much. Maybe because she'd carefully avoiding asking personal questions about him, usually concentrating on his children when she and Tucker talked. Now she felt compelled to learn more about *him*. "Do you like teaching?"

"Most of the time. I've always intended to go into administration eventually, but teaching has its own rewards."

Margaret cocked her head and looked at him, thinking of his easy manner and appealing smile. "I bet you're a popular teacher with the students."

He looked a bit surprised, then shrugged. "With most of them, I suppose. I try to make classes interesting. To lend a shoulder when needed. Sometimes, I feel like I make a difference. Other times, it's more like swimming upstream in white water."

"Are all the horror stories I hear about today's schools really true? Are they really war zones?"

"It depends a lot on the school and the neighborhood, of course. Inner-city schools can be pretty bad. Mine's not so rough, though we have our share of hard cases. Eighth- and ninth-graders are old enough to feel that they have to prove something, young enough to be reckless about it. Some of them just need a firm hand, some careful guidance. Others are already headed for self-destruction, and there isn't a whole lot any teacher can do to stop them, though God knows we try. Mostly, it depends on their family situations.''

''Some of the stories I've read about the way children are being raised are enough to give one nightmares,'' Margaret murmured. ''I don't know how you can stay detached from the ones who are being abused or neglected or exploited.'' She almost shuddered at the unhappy memories her words conjured up.

''Who says I stay detached?'' Tucker asked grimly. ''I have one fourteen-year-old student who's pregnant. Rumor has it that it was her stepfather who got her that way. The counselors have tried to intervene, but their hands are pretty well tied by bureaucratic red tape and procedures. All they've been able to do is report their suspicions to the overburdened child-welfare services and pray that something will eventually be done for the kid. Both the kids.''

Margaret was appalled. ''How horrible.''

''There are nights when I can't sleep for pacing the floor and worrying about it, trying to come up with something—anything—I can do to make life better for just one or two of them. But all I can do is keep plugging away, trying to make them care about history when they don't even know if they're going to survive adolescence. I try to encourage them that they can make a better life for themselves if they want it badly enough to work for it, but their home lives and peer pressure make it difficult for them to believe me sometimes.''

Margaret thought of the few teachers who'd reached out to her, who'd recognized the difficulties of her family life and tried to help. She still clearly remembered the names and faces of the ones who'd cared, the ones who'd made her believe she could make her life better. That she had the potential to make more of herself than the depths her parents had allowed themselves to fall into.

She would be willing to bet there were a few former students who remembered Tucker as being one of the ones who cared.

"Where have you gone, Margaret?" Tucker asked quietly.

She blinked, finding him studying her intently from his side of the table. She flushed a little and lifted one shoulder. "I suppose I drifted into the past for a moment," she confessed, rather surprised at herself for telling him.

"You looked so sad. Was your childhood really so unhappy?"

"It wasn't...pleasant." The stark understatement probably told him even more than she intended.

His face warm with sympathy and understanding, he set down his fork. "Will you tell me about it?"

For the first time in more years than she could remember, she was tempted to talk about her past. She resisted. "No," she said quietly. "Not tonight."

He held her gaze. "Some other time, maybe?"

She bit her lip, aware that he was suggesting that their relationship would eventually advance to a point where she felt comfortable talking to him about such things. Maybe he was asking her to acknowledge the possibility that he was right. It felt oddly like taking a tentative step forward with him when she nodded and murmured, "Yes. Maybe some other time."

He looked curiously satisfied by her answer. "Okay. What's for dessert?"

She realized that sometime during their conversation he had emptied his plate. "Oh...well, I have chocolate cake."

His eyes lit up. "Chocolate cake?"

She smiled. "I take it you want some?"

"Please."

At that moment, he looked very much like Kitten when offered a plate of cookies. Unfortunately, Margaret's response to Tucker was much more disturbing than the warm, pleasant feelings his daughter evoked in her.

"What would you like to do now?" Tucker asked when dessert had been consumed, dishes rinsed and stacked in the dishwasher. "We could go out to a movie or something."

He didn't give her the option of sending him home just yet; he was enjoying this quiet time with her and he wasn't quite ready for it to end.

He found himself holding his breath, hoping she wouldn't retreat again now that she'd made a tentative step forward by inviting him to share her meal. He knew she was just as likely to panic now and send him packing—but he hoped that just this once she wouldn't.

She hesitated long enough to make him sweat—and then she smiled faintly and said, "If you like."

So she wasn't ready for the interlude to end, either. He managed not to punch the air in satisfaction.

Finding that he didn't really want to take her out in public and shatter the intimacy by mingling with other people, he pressed his luck a little and said casually, "Or we could stay in. Watch a little TV, maybe. There's a pretty good documentary on cable tonight."

She twisted her fingers in front of her, the only sign that she had doubts about spending that much more time here alone with him. He could only hope that her nervousness had nothing to do with qualms about her safety; surely she knew by now that he wasn't the type to demand more from a woman than she was willing to offer.

She drew a deep breath. "It doesn't have anything to do with gazelles being eaten, does it?"

He chuckled. "Why, no. Actually, it's about the Prohibition era. I recommended that my students watch it, not that I expect many of them will do so."

"Then I suppose the teacher should watch it."

He nodded. "That's what I sort of thought."

She tucked a strand of hair behind her ear, looking uncharacteristically shy. "You turn on the TV. I'll make coffee."

Oh, yeah, Tucker thought, snapping on the set and settling onto her sofa, leaving an invitingly empty place beside him. Things were going very well indeed this evening.

Now, if only he didn't do anything stupid to screw it up...

Halfway through the documentary, Tucker draped a casual arm along the back of the sofa, behind Margaret's back. He felt foolishly like a teenager with a skittish date, but he was beginning to think that if he didn't touch her soon, he was going to go crazy.

She didn't tense at his movement, but he knew she was aware of him. Her hands were in her lap, fingers linked. She had great hands, he mused. Graceful. Long fingers, slender wrists, a pale wash of color on her nails. Sitting this close, he could discern the light fragrance she wore. Nothing heavy or obvious—just a hint of the flowers she seemed so fond of.

Surreptitiously, he studied her profile. Her lashes were long. Her nose slightly uptilted—just enough to add a touch of cuteness to a face that was otherwise classically sculpted. Her skin was fair and flawless. She must take excellent care of it.

He admired the way she took care with her appearance without seeming vain about it. She always looked neat and fresh, but he'd never seen her primp or posture. His little Kitten could take a few pointers from Margaret, he thought ruefully.

"You aren't watching the program," Margaret murmured without glancing away from the television screen, proving that she was even more aware of him than he'd realized.

"No," he admitted, abandoning pretense.

Her fingers twisted more tightly in her lap. "Why?"

"I'm watching something much more interesting. You."

She glanced at him through her lashes. "You're making me self-conscious."

"Sorry," he said, though he wasn't particularly. He didn't look away.

She turned her head toward him, the program forgotten. "You're still looking at me."

"Mmm." He touched her lower lip with the tip of one finger. "You really do have a sexy mouth, Margaret."

Her cheeks darkened. "Tucker—"

He took a leap of courage. "I don't want to risk ruining a very nice evening, but I think I'm going to explode if I don't kiss you soon."

She was very still for a long moment, her gaze locked with his. And then she gave him a rather tremulous smile. "Well, we can't have that, can we? It would make such a mess in my den."

He was delighted. "Why, Margaret," he murmured, drawing her closer, "I do believe you just made a joke."

"You must be corrupting me," she whispered, laying her graceful hands lightly on his chest.

His laugh was part groan. "Honey, I'm certainly trying my best," he muttered.

And then he lowered his head and covered her mouth with his.

Chapter Ten

"Hi there, stranger."

Margaret smiled in response to the voice on her telephone Monday evening. "Hi, yourself. What have you been up to lately—or should I ask?"

Jackie chuckled. "Probably not. Let's just say that things are still...interesting."

Margaret settled back in her chair and lifted an eyebrow. "You mean you and Mick are still dating?" she asked, though she already knew they were. "What is it—six weeks now? That's some sort of record for you, isn't it?"

"C'mon, Margaret, I'm not that bad."

Margaret laughed. "No, maybe not quite that bad." But close. "So everything's still going well between you. I'm happy for you, Jackie."

"Oh, yeah, everything's great."

Margaret winced at the unspoken but implied *but*. "What's wrong?" she asked bluntly.

"Nothing's wrong," Jackie assured her hastily. "It's just that Mick can be…well, a little possessive."

Margaret swallowed a groan. "Possessive" was definitely a curse word in Jackie's vocabulary. If Mick was starting to act in any way jealous or controlling toward Jackie, he would soon find himself unceremoniously dumped. And he wouldn't be the first. "Have you tried talking to him about it?"

"Not really," Jackie admitted. "I hate to risk a quarrel when we've been getting along so well, for the most part."

"Jackie, if there's a problem between you, you should confront it now," Margaret advised. "The longer you allow it to fester, the worse it gets. Surely you know that by now."

"Yeah, well…I'll take care of it," Jackie promised vaguely, then promptly changed the subject. "So, how are you and Tuck getting along? You have been out with him again since my birthday, haven't you?"

"A time or two."

"And?"

"And…nothing much," Margaret answered nonchalantly. "We're friends, that's all."

She refused to think of the kisses on her sofa Saturday evening. Kisses that had come very close to shattering her control…until Tucker had suddenly muttered something about "not doing anything stupid" and had taken an abrupt leave of her. He'd left her all too aware of how shaky her willpower was when it came to him. And wondering exactly what he'd meant by "doing something stupid." She hadn't heard from him since.

"Friends, huh? That's not the way it looked to me when I watched you two together."

"Well, that's the way it is." For now anyway, she could have added, but prudently did not.

"Mick says Tuck's kids are out of town for the week."

"Yes, they're visiting their maternal grandmother in Houston."

"Sounds like a great time for you and Tuck to become more than 'just friends.' If you take my advice, that's exactly what you'll do."

"Jackie—"

"Hey, weren't you the one just giving *me* advice about my love life?"

Margaret had to admit that she was.

Satisfied, Jackie obligingly changed the subject, spending the next few minutes catching up since the last time they'd spoken. Margaret was the one who brought the call to an end.

"I'd better go," she said. "Someone's ringing my doorbell."

"Gee, I wonder who it could be," Jackie mused, obviously hoping it was Tucker.

Margaret suspected Jackie was right. She murmured a goodbye and hung up, making a quick check of her appearance as she moved slowly to answer the door.

Tucker stood with one arm propped on the doorjamb, his expression thoughtful. "Why is it," he asked conversationally, "that I can't stop thinking about you, Margaret McAlister?"

Her mouth went dry. "I don't know."

"Maybe the answer will come to us over dinner."

She placed her hands on her hips. "Is that your way of asking me out?" she asked suspiciously, wondering how often he'd used that particular line.

He dropped his arm, dimples flashing. "Please, Margaret, will you have dinner with me this evening?"

"You know, you could call every once in a while, rather than just showing up at my door."

"You're right. I apologize."

He was being much too cooperative. She didn't trust him an inch, and she let him know it with her frown. And then she sighed, surrendered and said, "All right. I'll have dinner with you. As it happens, I haven't eaten yet."

"Great."

"Come in. I'll get my jacket and purse."

He hesitated, then shook his head. "I'll wait here."

In response to her quizzical look, he gave her a slow, simmering smile and murmured, "Next time I come into your house, I'm hoping to stay awhile."

"You," she told him when she'd recovered her voice, "are impossible."

"Not impossible, honey. I just don't like to be too predictable."

She started to tell him she didn't care to be referred to as "honey." Something kept her silent as she turned and went after her purse, leaving him waiting patiently at the doorstep.

During the course of their dinner at a steak-and-seafood place not far from Margaret's house, she decided that "predictable" was a word few people would use to describe Tucker Hollis. It was almost as though she were out with a different man than the one who'd shared a quiet dinner and a television program with her Saturday evening. *That* Tucker had been courteous, friendly, perfectly well behaved, careful not to do anything to make her uncomfortable—at least until he'd kissed her. But even then he'd waited for permission.

The Tucker she was out with tonight, however, was anything but well behaved. He flirted outrageously from the time they left her house, showering her with compliments, touching her at every possible opportunity, giving her sizzling smiles that all but fried her mental synapses. By the time their leisurely dinner ended, it was all she could do to speak coherently.

Something told her that was exactly the result he'd set out to achieve.

The other Tucker had offered friendly companionship; this one made no secret of wanting more. And worse, he was making her want more, as well.

Even though Margaret knew what to expect by the time he walked her to her door, she still didn't quite know what to say when he cupped her face in his hands and asked quietly, "Are you going to invite me in?"

She knew he wasn't asking for coffee. Or conversation. Nervously, she moistened her lips with the tip of her tongue. His eyes followed the movement with a visible appreciation that made her limbs go heavy.

Something hot flickered in the pit of her stomach. Though it had been a very long time since she'd felt the sensation, she recognized it for what it was. Desire.

He didn't press her for an answer. Nor did he do anything overt to influence her. He just stood there. Looking the way he did. His hands warm on her face. Just a hint of dimple creasing his cheek.

No practiced lines of seduction could have swayed her more.

She wanted him. Had for weeks. But…was she really ready for this sort of complication?

Maybe she'd been a bit lonely during the past few years, but she'd been so safe. So sheltered from the heartache and turmoil she'd known before.

Tucker wasn't safe. And turmoil seemed inevitable when he was around.

So why was she seriously considering recklessly ignoring her fears and throwing herself at him?

Had she truly lost her mind?

"I—" She moistened her lips again.

He groaned. "Are you *trying* to make me crazy?" he

asked a bit huskily. "Because if you are, you're good at it."

The most seductive thing about Tucker, Margaret realized at that moment, was the way he made her feel when he looked at her like this. She felt pretty. Sexy. Desirable. Even daring and impetuous. Funny. He was the only one who'd ever made her feel those things.

She was finding that these unfamiliar feelings were insidiously addictive.

Oh, yes, he was dangerous. And for the first time in longer than she could remember, she was contemplating taking a risk.

He bent his head to brush her lips with his. "Never mind," he murmured, taking a step back. "I can see you aren't ready. Will you have dinner with me tomorrow?"

She made her decision right then. Maybe it was because he didn't press her, even seemed to understand her hesitation. Or maybe it was because she didn't like the thought of going into that empty house alone again tonight.

"Tucker?" she asked, not quite recognizing her own voice.

He smiled down at her. "Yes?"

She unlocked her door, then turned back to him. "Would you like to come in?"

He went very still. "For coffee?" he asked after a moment of studying her expression.

"Or whatever," she answered, surprisingly bold now that she'd made her decision.

His eyes flared. "That 'whatever' sounds mighty tempting. But I want you to be very sure, Margaret."

From somewhere, she found the strength to smile. Even to her, the smile felt rather wicked. "You should know by now that I never do anything unless I'm very sure," she murmured. And then hoped she'd told the truth.

He kissed her then, as though he couldn't wait another moment to do so. His arms went around her so tightly she could hardly breathe, his mouth moving on hers with a hunger he made no effort to mask.

Dimly aware that they were still standing on her doorstep, Margaret fumbled behind him and opened the door. They practically fell through it, still kissing. Tucker slammed it closed with his foot.

Even as she led him up the stairs to her bedroom, a tiny voice in her mind kept reminding her that she wasn't acting like herself, that she could be making a very big mistake. That she would surely be sorry. She ignored it.

Tucker didn't take time to study her bedroom decor. He pulled her into his arms beside the bed, touching her face with one hand. In wonder, she felt the fine tremors running through his fingers. She'd never imagined that she could make him tremble.

"Margaret," he said hoarsely, "I want you so badly."

Her smile was decidedly shaky. "I know," she whispered. "I feel the same way."

"I've wanted you since I first looked up and saw you holding Sam's dog."

The mention of his son sent a slight frisson of uneasiness through her; she ignored that, too.

He brushed his lips over hers, lightly, then again. She slid her arms around his neck and opened her mouth to him. A muffled groan rumbled in his chest as he deepened the kiss, surging into her mouth with a bold possessiveness that made her melt weakly against him.

A moment later, they were on the bed. Tucker made love to her mouth even as he deftly loosened the buttons of her blouse and reached for the fastening of her slacks.

Panic tried to set in when she found herself suddenly nude. Tucker struggled to undress himself while his hands and his mouth were busy exploring every inch of her. Already, her mind was whirling, her breath ragged and sharp, her nerve endings quivering with sensations of pleasure that bordered on pain. He kissed her throat and her back arched; he kneaded her breast and she gasped, her fingers clenching instinctively into his shoulders. He touched her thigh and her legs parted for him, totally without conscious effort on her part.

She was losing coherence, couldn't think clearly enough to act rationally, deliberately. She was no longer in control of his actions—or even her own. They seemed to be speeding without direction toward a destination she couldn't predict, couldn't dictate.

Out of control. Powerless.

She moaned and went rigid beneath him.

Instantly sensing the change in her, Tucker froze. "Margaret?" He lifted his head to search her face, his own flushed with the intensity of his emotions. "Honey, what is it? What's wrong?"

"I—"

She wanted him so badly. She could see—could feel—that he wanted her, too. How could she explain her fears to someone who'd never been where she'd been, whose past had been so different from her own? So safe and sheltered in comparison.

"Never mind," she whispered, reaching for him. "This is what I want. What I choose." As long as she kept reminding herself of that, the feelings of helpless vulnerability could be held at bay, she hoped.

Looking confused, he opened his mouth to question her further. She stopped him by the simple act of covering his mouth with hers, sliding her tongue between his lips to taste him as he'd already tasted her.

Apparently, she'd convinced him that the questions could wait. He pulled her close, letting her savor the full-length feel of him—his warmth, his strength, his textures. She trembled again, but this time need overpowered fear. She wrapped her arms around him and offered herself to him.

He fumbled with the condom he'd pulled from the pocket of his slacks. His hands were shaking visibly, and there was a stain of red on his tanned cheeks. "I'm not being very cool about this, am I?" he asked with a sheepishness that seduced her all over again. "It's been so damn long—"

She smiled. "Would you like some help?"

He gulped audibly. "I'm not sure I'd survive that."

She reached for him with a laugh that must have come from someone else. "Let's find out," she challenged him.

He survived—they both did. But, Margaret thought as she lay damp and exhausted on his chest a long time later, it had been a close call. The pleasure had been so powerful, so intense, so shattering, that she didn't think she'd ever be quite the same as she had been before Tucker Hollis made love to her. And while a part of her feared that possibility, there was another part that gloried in it.

Pushing reality away for just a little while longer, she gave a little sigh and buried her face in his throat, allowing herself to drift in a haze of satisfaction. His arms were warm around her, his heartbeat strong and rapid beneath her cheek. He murmured something she didn't even try to understand.

She closed her eyes and slipped into sleep, deliberately prolonging the blissful contentment she felt at that moment.

Margaret woke slowly, yet fully aware of what had happened, who lay in the bed beside her. She opened her eyes to find him propped on one arm, watching her sleep with a bemused expression that made her smile.

"What?" she asked, her voice husky.

"I seem to have misplaced someone," Tucker replied blandly. "Have you seen her? She's an accountant—a bit shy, a bit prim, rather cool at times. Your exact opposite, I would say, judging by what happened here earlier."

Margaret chuckled. "Dolt."

He pretended offense. "Is that any way to talk to a man who just made your heart sing?"

Her smile deepened. "Oh, is that what you just did?"

"Of course. Didn't you hear it?"

"No. I must have been...otherwise occupied."

He slid down to rest his ear against her left breast, almost taking her breath away. "Yeah...I still hear it," he murmured. "Still singing."

Margaret tried to speak lightly, but had to clear her throat first. "What—what's it singing?"

"It's either 'The Hallelujah Chorus'...or 'Bubba Shot the Jukebox,'" he proclaimed solemnly.

Skeptical, she lifted an eyebrow. "'Bubba Shot the Jukebox'?"

Grinning, he lifted his head to nod. "Mmm. A Mark Chestnutt hit from a couple of years ago. Haven't you ever heard it?"

"Can't say that I have."

"Too bad. It's a really sweet, sentimental number about a not-very-bright young man who takes a .45 and blows away a Wurlitzer. It was playing a song that made him cry, you know."

She tried to keep a straight face. "I see. And you think you're hearing that song now?"

He laid his head against her chest again. "Yup. That's the one."

"You're insane, you know."

"So I've been told on occasion. A vicious exaggeration, of course. It isn't insanity."

She couldn't resist stroking his thick, tousled hair. "Whatever it is, I hope it isn't contagious."

"Too late," he said, placing a light kiss just above her nipple. "You've already been exposed."

She swallowed, already aching for him again. "Then how do I protect myself?" she asked, only half-teasing now.

He gave her a tender smile. "You needn't worry. It isn't harmful. You might even find that you enjoy it."

"Insanity can be enjoyable?"

"Not insanity," he corrected her, nibbling at her lower lip as he slid one hand slowly up her bare side to cover her breast.

She squirmed beneath him. "What—what is it, then?"

He hesitated a moment, then smiled crookedly. "I'm not sure you're ready to hear the answer to that question just yet."

Something in his eyes made her breath catch in her throat. Before she could ask what he meant, he covered her mouth with his own and began to prove without doubt that it was possible for lightning to strike twice in one place all in the same night.

Margaret didn't invite Tucker to spend the night, nor did he ask to. He seemed to understand that she needed time to come to terms with the sudden, drastic change in their relationship. Still, he didn't bother to hide his reluctance to leave her.

He kissed her at the door to her bedroom. And again at the top of the stairs. And at the bottom. And at the front door.

"I'm not sure I could ever get enough of your kisses," he murmured, his smile curving against her lips. "Did I ever mention that your mouth makes me crazy, Margaret McAlister?"

"Oh, is that what does it?" she asked without drawing back.

He chuckled and seemed to force himself to set her away. And then he groaned and reached out to pull her robe together where it had slid open during their embrace. "Hold that," he said, placing her own hand tightly over the front of the garment.

She smiled and obligingly gripped the lapels.

"Now," he said with a deep breath, "maybe I can leave without falling flat on my face at your doorstep."

She put her free hand on the doorknob. "Good night, Tucker."

"G'night, honey. Sleep well."

She wondered if she would sleep at all. But all she said was, "You, too."

He stepped through the door, then turned, flippancy abandoned for a moment. "Margaret?"

"Yes?"

"Don't be sorry."

She moistened her lips. "No."

"Promise?"

"Promise."

His smile returned. "I'll hold you to that."

And then he turned on one heel and sauntered away, whistling something between his teeth. Though she didn't recognize the tune, she would have bet it had something to do with someone shooting a jukebox.

She found herself laughing softly as she closed the door. She was amazed at herself for doing so, considering the circumstances.

Tucker made her feel good, she realized, in more ways than one.

She suspected that he had just as much power to devastate her, if she didn't at least try to protect herself.

Chapter Eleven

Even without the kids to get ready and off to school, Tucker was almost late to work Tuesday morning. Maybe because all morning he'd had to fight an urge to stare into space with a sappy grin on his face.

He walked into his first-period class just as the bell rang for the students to be in their seats. The usual early-morning pandemonium greeted him; he ignored all of it except the boy and girl who were yelling at each other at the back of the room. "Marlon. Jessica. Zip it up and get in your seats," he said mildly, stripping out of his jacket. "Everyone else settle down so we can get started."

Still muttering at each other, Marlon and Jessica—whom Tucker knew to be a hot item for the past few weeks—took their seats, spending the rest of the period sulking and glaring at each other. Tucker refused to allow them to spoil his good mood.

"Problem, Marlon?" he asked as the students rushed out at the end of the period.

The boy sighed gustily. "Jessie's mad at me," he grumbled.

Tucker suppressed a smile. "That's what I figured."

Marlon scratched his red head. "You got a girlfriend, Mr. Hollis?"

"Um, yeah," Tucker replied, a bit startled. "I suppose I do."

"Are they all this much trouble?"

Tucker thought of the effort he'd gone to just to get Margaret to go out with him the first time. He knew his problems with her weren't over just because they'd made love. In fact, they were probably headed for an all-new set of problems now.

"Well," he said, resisting the temptation to indulge in a little sympathetic male bonding with the boy, "relationships take a lot of work, Marlon."

"Yeah, but is it worth it?"

A rush of warmth coursed through him as Tucker thought of the way Margaret had felt in his arms. Her delightfully surprising passion in response to his lovemaking.

He cleared his throat. "I suppose that depends on the couple involved. You're a little young to be getting tied down anyway, aren't you?"

"You got *that* straight," Marlon agreed vehemently.

The next group of students was beginning to file noisily into the room, jostling Marlon as they made their way to their seats. "You'd better go," Tucker advised him. "Don't want to be late to your next class."

"Okay. See you tomorrow, Mr. Hollis."

Tucker found himself smiling as he ushered his second-period students in and urged them into their seats.

He couldn't help wondering what Margaret would say

if she knew that he'd just referred to her as his "girl-friend."

Margaret found herself standing in front of a mirror at midmorning, staring at the woman who looked back at her. It was about the tenth time that day she'd been compelled to make sure she looked the same as she had yesterday morning—before some alien spirit had taken over her body and thrown her into Tucker Hollis's arms.

She still couldn't quite believe what they'd done. This time yesterday, she'd been debating whether to have dinner with him again, whether it was possible to date on a strictly friendly, nonthreatening basis.

Now he was her lover.

She gulped. Did one…well, two times, actually, qualify them as lovers? The word sounded rather serious. Committed. How did she know Tucker hadn't just been taking advantage of being free for the evening to engage in a pleasant one-night stand after a long period of abstinence?

She rejected the idea almost as soon as it occurred to her. Perhaps she was still getting to know Tucker in many ways, but she knew him better than that. Last night hadn't been casual sex for him, any more than it had been for her. She found that knowledge as unnerving as it was reassuring.

What did he expect from her now? What role did he foresee her playing in his life? Occasional bed partner? Significant other? She gulped—stepmother to his children?

Okay, she thought, fighting down the panic. Maybe it was way too soon to be thinking along those lines, for her *or* Tucker. Maybe the possibility hadn't even occurred to him yet.

Or maybe Jackie had been right. Maybe that was what he'd been looking for in a woman all along.

She knew it was difficult for him, being a single father. Knew there must be times when he wished for someone to help him. But…was he really considering her for the position?

Was it really so far-fetched to think otherwise?

He must have looked at her and seen someone who was stable, competent, successful in her own right, someone who would take responsibility and commitment seriously. She knew he was also attracted to her—she couldn't possibly deny it after last night—but had he seen that only as a nice bonus?

He'd seemed pleased that Kitten had taken to her so easily. He'd certainly encouraged their friendship. And, while it bothered Margaret very deeply, he didn't seem overly concerned by Sam's antagonism toward her. He kept assuring her it would pass, that Sam would come around.

Oh, God, *was* Tucker looking for a wife and substitute mother? And, even if she were willing to take on those responsibilities, did she really want to be pursued only because she seemed a good candidate for the job?

She turned away from the mirror in despair. She was making herself crazy this way. When would she ever learn to stop worrying about the future, simply enjoy the present? And she had enjoyed last night—immensely.

She'd promised Tucker she wouldn't be sorry. And she wasn't.

She only wished she could stop secretly anticipating disaster.

They spent Tuesday evening at her house. They ate take-out Chinese and talked about politics. They laughed together as Tucker relayed Kitten's moment-by-moment, hyperbole-laden description of her aunt's wedding. Tucker insisted that Kitten hadn't stopped talking for a good forty-five minutes; he winced at the mention of what his phone bill would probably run for that month. Margaret knew he considered the call worth every penny.

Though Margaret wouldn't have turned him down, Tucker didn't try to make love to her again that evening. She was torn between relief and disappointment when he left after only a few long, spectacular kisses. She knew he wanted to stay; he hadn't bothered to hide his desire. She finally decided that he was generously giving her time to be sure she wanted to go forward with this relationship. And maybe he was trying to show her that it wasn't just sex he wanted from her.

He really was a very special man, she mused dreamily as she prepared for bed. Ruefully aware that she was smiling like an infatuated schoolgirl, she tried to remind herself of all the problems facing them, but she simply didn't want to think of them then.

For the first time in a very long while, Margaret was almost blissfully happy. And she wanted to cling to the unusual feelings for just a little longer.

Margaret had choir practice at her church Wednesday night, and Tucker a building-committee meeting at his. They agreed to meet afterward at an ice-cream parlor approximately halfway between the two churches.

Tucker was waiting when Margaret entered. He waved to her from a booth in the back, and she hurried to join him.

She was dimly aware that her pulse was racing in response to the sight of him, that there was a flush of warmth on her cheeks, that she was smiling with a shy eagerness that was all new to her. She hadn't been this giddy over a guy even in high school.

It was as though a new Margaret had been born in Tucker's arms that night. One with hopes and dreams and enthusiasm that hadn't been beaten down by years of disappointments and broken promises. In one night, the habits of a lifetime of cautious self-protection had been threatened, despite her weak efforts to cling to them.

She knew it was happening too fast. Knew she wasn't approaching this thing logically and reasonably. Knew she wasn't preparing herself for the inevitable worst—but she couldn't seem to help it.

Seeing Tucker made her smile. And when he stood and kissed her tenderly in greeting, it was all she could do not to drag him out to the parking lot and attack him in the bushes. These feelings were new and exciting and a bit shocking, but she was enjoying them enough to ignore her fears, for the most part.

For the first time, she could understand why Jackie entered each new relationship with an optimism Margaret had always considered ill-advised, considering Jackie's track record. Maybe Jackie always felt the way Margaret did now—that this man just might be the right one, the one who would somehow make up for all the pain and disillusion of the past.

"How did your choir practice go?" Tucker asked when they'd settled into their booth with sinful ice-cream concoctions.

"Harmoniously," Margaret replied, straight-faced.

He groaned, then chuckled.

"And how was your building-committee meeting?" she inquired, a hint of challenge in her voice.

He didn't even hesitate. "Constructive."

They grinned at each other and dipped into their ice cream.

Margaret couldn't help wondering who this woman was who had possessed her. Whoever she was, she was certainly having a good time.

Friday evening, they went to the mall. Tucker needed to buy a birthday gift for his sister, and he talked Margaret into helping him pick it out, even though she protested that she didn't know Debbie well enough to know what she would like.

"She just likes things that are pretty," Tucker replied with a shrug. "You know, glass and stuff."

"Oh, *that* helps," Margaret grumbled.

He laughed and took her hand as they entered the mall. "Don't worry. We'll find something."

She looked down at their linked fingers, and then up at his contented expression. And again, she found herself fighting the fear.

After an evening together, holding hands and sharing long, intimate glances, the pressure of restraint was beginning to show in Tucker's expression. His eyes gleamed with a combination of need and caution, and there was an underlying tension in his voice as he tried to make casual conversation on the way to her house.

As much as she'd appreciated his patience during the past few days, his willingness to let her take things at her own pace, Margaret found that she'd had time enough to decide that she still wanted him. She didn't want to waste this night alone together because she was too afraid to take full advantage of it.

She turned to him at her doorstep. "Come inside with me," she said.

He lifted an eyebrow, trying to look nonchalant, though his eyes flared with anticipation. "That didn't sound like an invitation," he commented.

She smiled and took his hand. "Do you want me to beg?"

He seemed to consider it a moment. "Might be interesting," he murmured. Then he shook his head. "But not necessary. I'm the one who was prepared to beg tonight."

She smiled and opened the door. "That won't be necessary, either."

With an unconcealed eagerness, he followed her inside, closing the door behind him.

It was almost midnight when Tucker stirred against Margaret's pillows, brushed a kiss across her damp forehead and sighed contentedly. "You know," he murmured sleepily, "I could get used to this."

Her head pillowed on his bare shoulder, she stroked a lazy hand down his chest, her fingers gliding through the soft brown hairs. "It is nice, isn't it?"

"More than nice. What's happening between us is special, Margaret. You know that, don't you?"

The gravity of his tone made her shift uneasily against him. It was so much more comfortable when they kept it light, she thought wistfully. She could handle his teasing, his flirting, his nonsense...but serious conversation about their future overwhelmed her.

"It's, um, a little soon to be talking along those lines, isn't it?" she temporized.

"I would hardly say that," he replied dryly, motioning with one hand to indicate their intimate position. "I'd say it's definitely time to define where we're headed."

She cleared her throat. "We haven't really known each other very long."

"We've known each other seven weeks today—not that I'm counting," Tucker drawled. "And we've progressed a bit beyond the friendly-neighbor stage. I care about you, Margaret. Very much. I wouldn't be here now if I didn't."

She bit her lip.

Tucker sighed. "There you go again. Two steps back."

"I don't—"

"You know the old saying. 'One step forward, two

steps back.' That's what you've been doing with me from the first.''

"Not exactly.''

"Oh?'' He sounded mildly amused, with an undercurrent of exasperation. "Then what would you call it?''

"I'm just trying to be sensible,'' she said, hating the primness she heard in her voice.

"Sensible,'' he repeated. His hand slid down her bare side to cup her hip. "Oh, yes, we've been very 'sensible' tonight, haven't we?''

Almost hearing the echoes of her own cries of pleasure, Margaret flushed scarlet. "You know what I mean,'' she muttered.

"No, honey, I don't. Not exactly. I'd like to know that our relationship won't end when the kids get home tomorrow. I'm ready for the next step forward, Margaret. Spending more time together. Being seen together in public. I'd like you to have dinner with us at Mom's, and get to know my family. I want us to be a couple.''

"You mean go steady?'' she asked, hiding her fear behind a touch of sarcasm.

"If that's what you want to call it,'' he agreed evenly.

"I just think we should be discreet, Tucker. I don't want anyone hurt by whatever happens between us. Not your children—not us.''

"I'm not sure we haven't already passed the point of no return in that respect,'' he said quietly. "Serious involvements don't usually end without someone being hurt—trust me, I'm speaking from experience. But if it happens, we'll all survive. We have before.''

Serious involvement. Was that the way he would describe what was happening between them? And, yes, she assumed there'd been pain in his divorce from the children's mother—but he couldn't possibly understand why she still felt the need to protect herself from being hurt again. She still hadn't been able to share her childhood grief with him.

She lifted her head to look at him, knowing her expression was pleading. "I just need a little more time, Tucker. Please don't ask me to make any promises yet that I'm not at all sure I can keep."

His mouth twisted. "I'm afraid I'm not the patient type."

She managed a faint smile. "I know."

He sighed and stroked her hair. "I'll try not to push you. But I won't pretend I don't care about you, either."

She supposed that was all she could ask for tonight. Though she still worried about how Tucker would behave in front of his children and family, what he would unintentionally give away about what had happened between them, at least she'd let him know that she didn't want to be rushed into a commitment she wasn't sure was right for her.

That doubting little voice in her head asked skeptically if Tucker wasn't right—if it wasn't already too late for prudence. But Margaret had gotten very adept at ignoring that nagging whisper during the past few days.

"Will you at least go with me to the airport tomorrow to meet the kids?" Tucker asked after a moment of taut silence. "Kitten will be thrilled if you're there to greet her."

"What about Sam?"

He exhaled deeply. "You're always asking that."

"I can't help worrying about it. I don't want you to push Sam, either, Tucker."

"I'm not going to push him. But he might as well know that you're an important part of my life now. The sooner he accepts that, the sooner he'll stop resisting you."

Margaret wasn't so sure. "He's afraid, Tucker. He's

lost his mother and he doesn't want to risk losing his father."

"I thought you said you didn't know anything about children," he said with a faintly approving smile at her perception.

She shrugged and looked away from him. "I know about children's fears," she said with a touch of the old bitterness. "I just don't know how to make them go away."

"Someday," he said after another pause, "you're going to tell me about that. But in the meantime," he went on before she could prevaricate again, "you and Sam need to spend more time together. We won't push him, but I'm sure once he gets to know you the way Kitten and I have, he'll love you, too."

Love. Though lightly spoken, the word shimmered between them with a portentousness that almost made Margaret shudder.

"I had planned to do some work in the morning," she said weakly.

His sigh was explosive this time. "Damn it, Margaret, stop walking backward. I'm just asking you to go with me to pick up the kids, maybe stop for lunch somewhere on the way home. Surely you can take one Saturday morning off from your usual routines."

The implied criticism stung, but she pushed the irritation away. She really didn't want to spend what was left of this night quarreling with him. Who knew when they could be alone like this again?

"All right, Tucker," she said in resignation. "If it's that important to you, I'll go with you. I just hope Sam isn't too upset to see me there."

"He won't be," Tucker assured her brashly. "Trust me, I know my kid. He'll come around."

He kept saying that. Margaret hoped he knew what he was talking about. She and Tucker had enough problems to face without worrying about a nine-year-old boy's disapproval.

"And now that we've got that settled," Tucker said, turning to her purposefully, "have you realized that we've been wasting time talking when we could be communicating in another way?"

She opened her arms to him, relieved that the conversation was at an end—temporarily, at least. When they were making love, the future didn't matter. Only the present. And for now, that was all Margaret wanted to think about.

Margaret found Tucker's eagerness to be reunited with his children the next morning both amusing and endearing. They arrived at the airport forty minutes before the plane was due to land, and then she watched as Tucker paced restlessly around the waiting area. When the announcement finally came that the plane had landed, he was the first at the gate to meet the passengers.

With a lump in her throat, Margaret stood back and watched as Kitten and Sam ran forward into their father's arms, their young faces beaming with love. Tucker swung them both into his arms, planting noisy kisses, laughing as both of them chattered at once about their trip.

Kitten was the first to spot Margaret. She squealed and wriggled out of Tucker's embrace. "Margaret!" she cried, and embraced her with much the same enthusiasm she'd shown her father. "I didn't know you were going to be here. I'm glad you came."

The lump in her throat grew bigger as Margaret warmly returned the hug. "Did you have a nice visit with your grandmother? How was the wedding?"

"We had fun. I'll tell you all about it on the way home," Kitten promised earnestly.

"I'm sure you will," Margaret said with a smile.

Then, steeling herself for his reaction, she turned to Sam. "Hi, Sam. Did you have a nice time?"

Sam shrugged. "It was okay."

Margaret couldn't help noticing that the bright smile he'd worn for his father was conspicuously absent now. She wondered a bit wistfully if the boy would ever smile for her. And how could Tucker think they had a chance at making this work if his son was so unhappy about having her around?

Margaret's own childhood had been so miserable that she couldn't bear the thought of ruining Sam's. He'd already had to face his mother's loss; it couldn't be easy for him to have his father dating a woman he couldn't stand.

If only there was some way for her to reach him. But she simply didn't know enough about children to try.

With a suppressed sigh of regret, she turned back to Kitten, who was tugging at her hand for attention.

Kitten was drooping with exhaustion by the time Tucker got her settled down enough to tuck her into bed that evening. He thought her jaws had to be worn out; the kid had hardly stopped for breath since her plane landed, he thought with wry amusement.

He bent to kiss her freshly washed cheek. "Good night, honey. It's good to have you home again. I missed you."

"I missed you, too, Daddy," Kitten murmured. "And Margaret, too."

Tucker's smile felt a bit like a grimace. Sure, he wanted Kitten to like Margaret—he wanted both the kids to like her—but there were times when he could definitely feel a bit jealous of Kitten's affection for her. His daughter had always been the kind to give her love wholeheartedly and enthusiastically.

Tucker supposed she got that tendency from him, considering the way he'd fallen for Margaret himself.

He knew Kitten was hungry for a woman's care. Her grandmothers and aunts lavished her with attention, for sure, but it wasn't the same as having a mother in her home. Tucker suspected that Kitten had targeted Margaret as a likely prospect for that position. He couldn't fault her for that, either. Though he knew Margaret would be dismayed to hear it, he'd been thinking along those lines himself.

If only Sam weren't being so stubborn about it. Not to mention Margaret.

"Night, Daddy. Watch out for the under-beds," Kitten chanted around a huge yawn.

"Keep away from the closet-things," Tucker answered dutifully, smoothing the covers over her. "I love you, Kitten."

She murmured a response. She was asleep before Tucker left her room.

Smiling, he moved down the hallway and tapped on Sam's door. "Sam? You ready for bed?"

An affirmative murmur made him open the door. Sam was just crawling into bed. Tucker moved to smooth the covers over his son, who looked almost as tired as his little sister.

"Sure feels good to be in my own bed again," Sam said with a long sigh, snuggling into the Spider-Man sheets.

"Sure feels good to have you back in your own bed again," Tucker responded. "This place was way too quiet without you rug rats in it."

Sam chuckled. "Not a rug rat," he murmured.

"Are too," Tucker retorted, ruffling the boy's hair. This, too, was a familiar routine. "But I love you anyway."

"Love you, too." Sam rolled onto his side, pulling

the covers with him. The stuffed dog he would have fiercely denied sleeping with peeked out from beneath the sheets. ''Dad?''

''Yes?''

''You've been going out with her while we were gone, haven't you?''

Tucker, of course, didn't have to ask for clarification. ''Yes, I have. Margaret can be a lot of fun, Sam. Surely you noticed how much she and Kitten laughed during lunch.''

Tucker had also noticed the way Margaret's gaze had kept straying toward Sam. He knew she wanted to reach out to him, and he wanted to believe Sam felt the same way deep inside; it seemed that neither Sam nor Margaret knew how to make the first move. Tucker had promised Margaret he wouldn't push the boy, but he hadn't said he wouldn't drop a few hints.

''I won't make any trouble if you want to date her,'' Sam said unexpectedly. ''You deserve to have a life of your own, Dad.''

Tucker frowned. That sounded very much like a quote. Who had Sam been talking to about Margaret?

He started to say something, then noticed how tired Sam looked. He let it go. ''We'll talk about it again some other time,'' he said, kissing his son's cheek. ''Get some rest now.''

''Night, Dad.''

Tucker paused in his son's doorway for a moment before turning out the light and closing the door. ''Good night, Sam.''

Less than half an hour passed before the phone rang. Tucker snatched it up quickly, before it could rouse the kids. ''Hello?''

The caller was his former mother-in-law. ''I just wanted to make sure everything is okay with the children," she explained. "Did they have a good flight? Are they worn out?"

"Yes and yes," he answered lightly. "They're both sound asleep. Sounds like they had a great time with you, Agnes."

"Oh, I hope so. I had such a lovely time with them."

"Kitten told me all about the wedding. I'm sure Cathy made a beautiful bride."

"Oh, she did," Agnes agreed a bit mistily. "I wish you could have seen her."

Tucker had been invited to the wedding; he'd made excuses about being too busy. Though he liked his ex-wife's family, he felt awkward being around them much now, after all that had happened since his own wedding to Callie. And, as much as he'd missed the kids, he'd enjoyed having that time with Margaret.

"Christine told me you've been dating someone new," Agnes said, approaching the subject a bit cautiously. She was the only one who'd refused to adopt Kitten's preferred nickname, since "Christine" had been Callie's middle name.

Now Tucker understood who'd been talking to Sam. "Yes, I'm seeing someone," he admitted.

"Margaret McAlister. Kitten talked about her all week."

Tucker shifted his weight in his chair. "Kitten's very fond of Margaret. The feeling's mutual."

"Well, of course. Who wouldn't love that little girl?" Agnes asked as though scandalized by the very idea of anyone rejecting her adored granddaughter. "I understand that Sam is having a few problems accepting your new relationship."

"A few," Tucker admitted. "He and Margaret didn't get off to a good start, and now she's having difficulty getting him to accept her. I'm sure it's only temporary. Margaret's a very nice woman."

"I'm sure she is, or you wouldn't be interested in her," Agnes said firmly. "That's what I told Sam. I made him promise he would give your new lady friend a chance. You're too young to be alone, dear. You have so much to offer. I couldn't have asked for a better husband for my daughter, or a better father for my grandchildren. If only Callie hadn't let herself be taken in by that smooth-talking Benny…"

Tucker cleared his throat, afraid that Agnes was going to start crying. He knew she'd never approved of Callie's decision to divorce him and remarry. And he knew how desperately Agnes had grieved upon Callie's death. It hadn't been difficult for her to blame Benny for everything.

"Benny wasn't such a bad guy, Agnes. He was good to Callie and the kids."

He could hear Agnes take a deep, steadying breath before speaking briskly. "Well, that's all over now, and I thank you for letting me stay a part of the children's lives. I can't tell you how much this week meant to me."

"You're their grandmother, Agnes. They love you. You will always be an important part of their lives."

"Thank you, dear. I'll let you go now. I just wanted you to know that I think it's wonderful that there's someone new in your life. Be patient with Sam—he'll come around."

Hearing his own words repeated so confidently, Tucker hoped he and Agnes were both right. "I will. The kids will call you in a couple of weeks, okay?"

"I'll look forward to it."

Tucker felt rather tired as he hung up the phone. He should probably get to bed himself. He hadn't gotten much sleep the night before, not that he regretted a moment of it. He wondered if Margaret was sleeping now. If she missed having him in her bed as much as he missed being there.

He thought of Agnes's words of support as he turned out the lights on his way upstairs. It seemed that everyone thought he and Margaret made a good couple except Margaret and Sam.

Wryly, he wondered which of them was going to be harder to convince. Either way, he certainly had his work cut out for him.

Chapter Twelve

During the next week, Margaret discovered that having the Hollis family involved in her life made her carefully scheduled routines very difficult to follow. Tucker tended to call at all hours—late evenings, early mornings, during free periods at school. Kitten showed up unannounced on Margaret's doorstep twice to show her something she'd made at school, and then tended to linger until Tucker came to collect her. On both occasions, they talked Margaret into having dinner with them, her original plans discarded.

Sam wasn't outwardly hostile, and his manners during the meals were irreproachable, but Margaret couldn't tell that he was softening toward her, either. He rarely looked at her, and he spoke to her only to answer her questions—and then without elaboration. It was as though he'd decided there was nothing he could do to get rid of her without annoying his father, so he would tolerate her—but he wouldn't encourage her.

Margaret was falling behind in her work. Not seriously, but enough to concern her.

In all her years in business for herself, she'd never gotten behind before. She'd never allowed herself to. And she knew exactly whom to blame for her present disorganization.

She was on her way out for her newspaper Friday morning when she spotted Kitten's jacket lying on a chair in her living room, obviously forgotten after the child's impromptu visit the afternoon before. She frowned, wondering if Kitten needed the jacket for school. Should she call and ask, or just take it on over?

She glanced at her watch. Tucker and the children should be leaving soon. If Kitten needed the jacket, there wasn't much time to waste. On a sudden decision, Margaret folded the garment neatly over one arm and stepped outside.

Tucker answered his door, wearing only a pair of chinos. "Margaret!" he said with a smile. "Good morning."

"Good—" His enthusiastic kiss smothered the rest of the greeting.

The unexpected embrace shook her. It had been almost a week since they'd been alone together, almost a week since they'd done more than exchange quick kisses when the children weren't watching. Seeing him now, with his hair still tousled, his eyes still a bit sleep blurred, his chest bare, Margaret remembered in vivid detail what it had been like to wake up in his arms.

"Good morning," she managed to say when he finally released her. "I, um..." She cleared her throat. "Kitten left her jacket at my house yesterday. I thought she might need it today."

"Thanks. She's upstairs. She came down wearing red jeans and an orange sweater this morning. Even I knew that was a fashion mistake. I sent her back up to change into the red, white and blue sweater I bought to match those jeans.''

"And were you planning to wear a shirt today?" Margaret inquired, unable to resist running a finger lightly down the center of his chest.

His eyes darkened in response to her touch, but his smile wavered only a little. "Yeah. I thought I might. I was just about to iron one.''

She took a deep breath and stepped backward, out of temptation's reach. "You'd better hurry. You're going to be late.''

Tucker looked at his watch and grimaced. "Man, is it that late already?''

"Dad!" Sam's voice yelled from somewhere behind him. "I can't find my science book. And Kitten wants you to help her find her sweater.''

Tucker groaned.

"Have you ever considered getting everyone's clothes ready the night before?" Margaret asked tentatively. "It would save you time in the mornings.''

A quick frown creased his brow, but he smoothed it into a rueful smile. "I keep meaning to try that, but by the time I get everything done in the evenings and get the kids into bed, I always forget.''

"Daddy!" This time, it was Kitten wailing for his attention.

"I'll talk to you later," Margaret said, backing farther away.

"Yeah, sure. Later." He wasn't smiling now.

Margaret was aware that Tucker watched her from the doorway as she hurried down his walk. She heard the door close just as she crossed out of his yard and into her own.

Maybe she should have offered to help, she thought with a twinge of guilt, but she'd had a sudden, panicky urge to escape the pandemonium, let Tucker handle his own problems. He was the one who chose to live in what seemed to her to be utter confusion.

It was almost with a feeling of relief that she entered her own house, her newspaper under her arm. Her coffee was ready, her breakfast already on the table, waiting to be consumed at her leisure. She would then go into her office, where her files and accounts waited in the neatly organized piles she'd placed them into when she'd finished working yesterday.

Quiet, tidy and orderly. The way her life had been before Tucker and his children had crashed into it.

As she picked unenthusiastically at her breakfast, she found herself wondering what she would say if given a chance to put everything back the way it had been. She'd worked so hard to achieve security and serenity—was she really willing to risk giving it all up now? Was thirty too old to learn to be flexible and calm under stress?

She remembered once thinking that it would be difficult to maintain control when children were involved...or when Tucker was involved, for that matter. She repeated that observation now.

Okay, so Tucker made her feel with an intensity she'd never experienced, and Kitten had introduced her to the joy of childhood innocence. But living with either of them on a permanent basis wouldn't be easy. They both seemed to require a great deal of attention. And then there was Sam....

She sighed and rubbed her suddenly aching forehead, reminding herself that she was looking too far ahead again. It wasn't as though Tucker had proposed or anything. She just sensed that they were headed in that direction unless she decided now to change their course.

No wonder her work was suffering, she thought with a sigh. How could she concentrate on numbers and official forms and bottom lines when her whole life seemed on the verge of drastic change? If only she knew what to do. What she really wanted.

If only she weren't so torn between throwing all her long-time precautions aside and taking whatever the Hollises had to offer—or taking to her heels and running for safety and sanity.

The clan gathered at Tucker's sister's house on Sunday afternoon in honor of her thirty-fourth birthday. Tucker knew Margaret was a bit nervous about attending this first family function as his date, but he was insistent that she go. It was time, he'd decided, for everyone to realize that his intentions were serious—Margaret included.

She was welcomed warmly, and Tucker was pleased to see that she relaxed visibly within a few minutes. It was hard to resist his family when they poured on the charm, he thought a bit smugly—and they were certainly pouring it on for Margaret today. The whole family had been hinting for years that Tucker should find a nice woman and remarry.

"I really like her, Tucker," his mother murmured an hour or so after the party began. "She's obviously very clever and sensible."

"Surely you aren't implying that I've ever dated brainless bimbos," Tucker teased.

Lillie smiled and patted his arm. "Of course you haven't, dear. You've always had excellent taste in women, even if your marriage had an unfortunate end."

Tucker managed not to wince at his mother's unintentional tactlessness. "Er, thanks, Mom."

"Mick, now…" Lillie sighed, a slight frown of worry etched into her brow.

Tucker followed her gaze to where his younger brother stood tangled around Jackie, who looked more dramatically stunning than ever in a formfitting black

cat-suit and spangled red bolero jacket. Knee-high boots
with three-inch heels completed the outfit, making her
almost as tall as Mick.

"Jackie's okay, Mom," he assured her. "She just
likes to dress colorfully. She and Margaret have been
friends for years."

Lillie looked somewhat reassured by that reminder.
"Then she must be nice. It's just that Mick seems to
have fallen so hard. Debbie says it's almost as though
he's obsessed with this woman. She's older than he is,
you know."

"A couple of years," Tucker acknowledged, "but it
doesn't seem to bother either of them, so don't worry
about it. It probably won't last anyway. You know what
a short attention span Mick has."

"Yes, but this time could be different. He's already
been going out with her for a couple of months. That's
longer than he usually stays with any one girl."

"Jackie isn't a girl, Mom. She's a woman. And
Mick's twenty-eight. Both of them are old enough to
take care of themselves."

"I know," Lillie admitted with a self-conscious smile.
"I just can't help worrying about my children, no matter
how old they've gotten. You wait. You'll find out for
yourself what I mean someday when Sam brings a
woman home. Or when some longhaired, earringed boy
in leather shows up at your door to pick Kitten up for a
date."

"Over my dead body," Tucker replied without hesitation, intensely hating the very idea of any hormone-
ridden adolescent chasing after *his* beautiful little girl.

Lillie only laughed knowingly. "Yes, well, we'll see,
won't we?"

Tucker promptly changed the subject, bringing up the
five-day Caribbean cruise his parents were planning for

the coming week. Lillie was eagerly looking forward to the vacation, their first in several years.

She and Tucker had already made arrangements for him to pick the children up after school for the three weekdays that Lillie and Arnie would be out of town. He'd assured her they would be fine, that he could take a few afternoons off early to take care of his kids.

He was getting a bit tired of assuring everyone that he could handle all the responsibilities of single parenthood, despite his admittedly unorthodox style at times.

Debbie approached her brother after everyone had eaten birthday cake and ice cream. "Tuck, would you help me carry these things into the kitchen?" she asked, dumping a pile of dirty dishes into his arms before he could reply.

She smiled apologetically at Margaret, who'd been involved in a conversation with Jackie and Mick and Tucker while Sam and Kitten played in the backyard with their cousins beneath the watchful eyes of their grandparents. "I'll bring him right back," Debbie promised.

Looking a bit embarrassed, Margaret nodded and turned to respond to something Jackie had said.

"Okay, Deb," Tucker said as soon as they were alone in the kitchen. "What's up? Why'd you so subtly drag me in here?"

His older sister made a face at him. "How do you know anything's up? Maybe I just wanted a moment alone with my brother."

"Yeah? How come?" he asked suspiciously.

She grimaced and lifted a shoulder. "What do you know about this woman Mick's dating?"

He sighed gustily. "I've already been through this with Mom. I don't know Jackie very well, but I like her. She and Margaret are good friends, and Margaret wouldn't like someone who wasn't okay."

"No, probably not," Debbie murmured. "Margaret seems so levelheaded. She and Jackie certainly don't seem to have much in common, but if they've been friends for a long time, I suppose it's all right."

Tucker was bemused by the way everyone seemed to credit Margaret with such perceptiveness and discernment. Must be that competent air of hers, he decided. Margaret always seemed to know exactly what she was doing. The only time he'd seen her act awkward or uncertain was with him, when he'd boldly pursued her. He told himself not to worry about that; after all, he'd been successful so far with her, hadn't he?

"Why is everyone so concerned about Mick and Jackie?" he asked. "She certainly isn't as bad as that last woman he got tangled up with—you know, the exotic dancer?"

Debbie shuddered. "She *was* awful, wasn't she? Loud and abrasive and aggressive. The only thing he saw in her was— Well, it was obvious what he saw in her. Jackie's another flashy type, but she's a definite improvement."

"Then what's the problem?"

"It's Mick. He seems so…well, so obsessed," she said, choosing the same word she'd used with her mother. "Jackie is all he can talk or think about these days. He doesn't even act all that happy about it. I just hope he isn't heading for heartbreak."

"Happens to the best of us sometimes," Tucker murmured with a cynical shrug.

"Oh, Tuck, I didn't want to remind you of your divorce," Debbie said regretfully. "I know you were hurt when Callie left you, but you've gone on with your life. You're such a wonderful father, and now you have Margaret in your life—have I mentioned how much I like her?"

"I'm glad. She's very special to me."

"Well, anyone can see that," Debbie said with an arch smile. "It's written all over your face."

Tucker wasn't sure he liked that. "As bad as Mick?"

She shook her head emphatically. "No, not like Mick. You just look…well, happy."

He thought about it a moment. "Yeah," he said after a moment. "I guess I am."

His only problem at the moment, he could have added, was finding time to be alone with Margaret. His frustration was building with each day he had to say goodnight to her at her doorstep. He'd needed to spend time catching up with his kids after their week apart, but very soon he was going to find an excuse to allow him some private time with Margaret. And he wanted very much for at least part of that time to be spent in bed.

With just a touch of vexation, he told himself he'd have to let her know well in advance so that she could work him into that damn schedule of hers.

"Tuck?"

He blinked. "Yeah?"

"I was just saying how nice it is that Margaret and Kitten get along so well."

"Oh. Yeah, they get along great. And Sam's coming around," he added with an optimism he hoped was well-founded.

"Good. I wouldn't mind having another wedding in the family soon," his sister teased, patting his cheek.

He winced. "Just don't say anything like that around Margaret, okay? I'm not sure she's quite ready to hear it yet."

"I can see why she'd want to take her time," Debbie agreed, dropping the levity. "She's been living on her own for some time. Taking on a ready-made family would be a radical adjustment for her."

Tucker nodded glumly, remembering the dismay he'd

seen in Margaret's eyes when she'd caught him in the middle of yet another hectic morning two days before.

Okay, so maybe his household could use a little more organization. Still, they were getting by. He'd gotten the kids dropped off on time and hadn't been late for his own first class—well, not by more than a couple of minutes anyway. There'd been no need for Margaret to act quite so disapproving, he mentally grumbled.

He told himself his physical frustration must be making him surly, and he forced a smile. "May I get back to the party now, or was there anything else you wanted to grill me about?"

Debbie playfully punched his shoulder. "All right, if that's all the gossip you're willing to share with me, we might as well join the others again. Anyway, I'm ready to open my presents. And you'd better have gotten me something good, or you're getting plain white handkerchiefs for yours next month."

He grinned. Debbie knew how little enthusiasm he would have for getting plain white handkerchiefs as a birthday present. It was a threat she'd used often since his fifteenth birthday, when that had been the very gift his paternal grandmother had sent. "Trust me, you'll like your present," he promised. "Margaret helped me pick it out. And she has excellent taste, you know."

"Oooh." Eyes alight with greed, she gave him a little push. "So, what are we waiting for? Lead me to those packages!"

Something she saw in Jackie's eyes made Margaret want the chance to speak privately to her friend that afternoon, but after almost three hours had passed, she still hadn't caught Jackie alone. Mick was never more than a few inches from Jackie's side, and the rest of the family was often close by, as well.

The chance came late in the afternoon. The children

were in D.J.'s room, playing video games. Tucker, Les, Mick and Arnie had gone out to examine Les's new car, and Debbie and Lillie were upstairs in the nursery with baby Emily. Margaret and Jackie were alone in the den for a blessedly quiet interval.

"Jackie, is everything all right?" Margaret asked, taking immediate advantage of their privacy.

Jackie gave her a smile that was so patently false Margaret knew her instincts had been reliable. "Of course. Why do you ask?"

Margaret frowned. "Remember who you're talking to," she said warningly. "You can't fool me. I can tell something is bothering you."

Jackie sighed and ran a hand through her artfully tousled blond hair. "Really, Margaret. Nothing's wrong. Exactly."

"What do you mean by 'exactly'?" Margaret persisted.

Jackie drew a deep breath and then blurted, "It's Mick, okay? He won't even let me breathe. I can hardly go to the bathroom without him following me."

Margaret wasn't surprised. "I've noticed that he seems to like being close to you," she commented, her voice carefully uninflected.

"'Attached at the hip' is more like it." Jackie bit her lip. "I need more space, Margaret. I'd like to spend an evening with you at the movies, or a day shopping by myself, or just have a few hours at home alone. Every time I try to tell Mick that, he gets all tense and defensive and acts like I'm trying to dump him. I'm not, I'm crazy about the guy. It's just—"

"You need to breathe."

"Yeah," Jackie admitted despondently. "I need to breathe. And I'm terribly afraid I'm going to be forced to break up with him so I can."

By holding on so tightly, Mick was driving Jackie

away. Why couldn't he see that? Margaret wondered. Men could be so thickheaded at times. "I'm sorry, Jackie. I can tell you're unhappy."

"Not all the time," Jackie amended. "But it's building."

She shook her head when Margaret would have said something else. "That's enough about my problems for now," she said firmly. "I'll handle them somehow. Let's talk about you and Tuck."

Margaret looked away. "There's not so much to talk about."

Jackie cocked an eyebrow. In perfect imitation of Margaret, she said, "Remember who you're talking to. You can't fool me."

Margaret wrinkled her nose. "I was afraid you'd say that."

"Honey, any fool could see that you and Tuck are more than good neighbors these days. The way he looks at you...well, it's very sweet. I expect to see a ring on your finger any day now, and judging from the way they're acting, so does Tuck's family."

Margaret almost choked. "We certainly haven't discussed anything like that," she protested. "And what makes you think Tucker's family is, er...?"

"Anticipating a wedding? It's obvious by the way they keep beaming approval at you and Tuck. And Lillie nearly melted into a puddle of delight when Kitten snuggled into your lap while Debbie opened her presents."

Margaret had been a little surprised when Kitten had crawled so easily into her lap that afternoon. Kitten's action had been as natural as if she'd known Margaret all her life, utterly certain of her welcome.

Tired from running and playing with her cousins, she'd settled back into Margaret's arms with a contented sigh that had brought a huge lump to Margaret's throat. She'd been aware that Tucker was watching her with an expression she couldn't quite read, but she hadn't realized the others had paid much attention to the interplay between her and the child.

A ripple of panic coursed through her, but she refused to acknowledge it. "You're exaggerating," she accused Jackie instead.

Jackie's mouth twisted into a smile that held little humor. "Trust me, I've noticed the general approval you've gotten from this bunch. As for me...well, I'm that older woman who's chasing after baby brother. They haven't quite decided how to take me yet."

Dismayed, Margaret frowned. "Jackie, they've all been perfectly polite to you. I would have noticed if they hadn't."

"Oh, yes, they're a polite group. No one has said anything outright. It's just the feeling I'm getting from them."

"You're being paranoid. Just because you're having some problems with Mick, you're assuming that everyone disapproves of your relationship."

Jackie shrugged and made a production of studying her crimson-tinted nails. "You're probably right. I'm just being paranoid."

"Of course you are. And as for me and Tucker...well, we're a long way from a permanent commitment. I'm sure everyone realizes that. We've only known each other a few weeks."

"Two months and one day," Jackie murmured. "I was there, remember?"

Before Margaret could comment, Mick came back into the room. "Hi, gorgeous," he said, plopping onto the arm of Jackie's chair and throwing an arm around her shoulders. "Miss me?"

"Have you guys checked out the new car already?" Jackie asked, her smile suddenly bright again—and, to Margaret's familiar eyes, a bit false.

"Dad and Tuck are still looking it over. I wanted to get back to you," Mick murmured. Still holding Jackie tightly against him, he turned to Margaret. "Did she tell you about the ski weekend we're planning? We're going to Aspen, right after Christmas. I've already made reservations."

"No, she didn't mention it," Margaret replied, wondering if Jackie and Mick would still be together when that time came. She rather doubted it. It looked as though Jackie was headed for another painful breakup.

But Margaret didn't want to think about her friend's rocky relationship just then. She had too many worries of her own.

Margaret allowed herself to be persuaded to have dinner at Tucker's house that evening. They picked up take-out chicken and side dishes on the way home from the birthday party and ate from paper plates in Tucker's kitchen. The paper plates were his choice; he didn't like to wash dishes, he frankly admitted. Margaret got the impression that lots of paper plates were utilized in this household.

Giving in to Kitten's pleading, Margaret stayed long enough after dinner to help tuck the child into bed, though she kept telling everyone that she had things to do before she could turn in herself that night. Neither Kitten nor Tucker seemed overly concerned about Margaret's schedule.

"What are you going to wear to school tomorrow?" Margaret couldn't resist asking as she helped Kitten into her pajamas after the child's bath.

Kitten shrugged. "I dunno. I usually just pick something when I get up."

Margaret thought of some of the combinations Kitten had come up with on her own. "Why don't I help you choose something now?" she suggested. "We'll lay it on your chair so it will be ready for you to put it on in the morning.''

"Sure," Kitten said, bounding toward her closet. "What do you think I should wear?"

Together, they selected an oversize Mickey Mouse sweatshirt, leggings and socks that matched. "You'll look very cute," Margaret pronounced solemnly.

"This will sure save time," Kitten said.

Biting her lip at the naively accurate comment, Margaret only nodded.

"Daddy!" Kitten suddenly yelled as she crawled into bed. "I'm ready to tuck in."

Tucker appeared dutifully in the doorway a moment later. "You might want to call me a little louder next time, Kitten," he teased. "I'm not sure they heard you on the other side of town."

Kitten giggled. "Margaret helped me pick my clothes for tomorrow," she said, waving a little hand toward the garments on the chair. "I bet I beat you getting ready."

Margaret watched as a muscle twitched lightly in Tucker's jaw. "You might," he agreed. "Maybe I should have my own clothes ready, just in case."

"That's a good idea," Kitten told him gravely, looking as though it had all been her idea.

Tucker smoothed the covers to her chin and went through the good-night routine Margaret had watched before. Then it was her turn to kiss Kitten's cheek. "Good night, sweetie," she murmured. "Sleep well."

"G'night, Daddy. I love you," Kitten called out as Tucker and Margaret headed for the doorway.

"Love you, too, kiddo."

"I love you, too, Margaret," Kitten added sweetly.

Margaret's eyes suddenly stung with a prickle of tears. Her voice was rather husky when she replied, "I love you, too, Kitten."

Smiling contentedly, Kitten snuggled into her pillows with her floppy doll.

Margaret couldn't quite meet Tucker's eyes when he closed Kitten's door. "I'd better get on home," she said.

"I'll walk you. Sam's getting ready for bed. He'll be okay for a few minutes."

"That's really not—"

"I'll walk you," Tucker repeated, and while his tone was bland enough, something about the set of his jaw warned her not to argue.

She nodded and moved toward the stairs.

Instead of leaving her at her door, Tucker followed Margaret inside, closed the door and backed her against it. Planting a hand on the door at either side of her, he leaned down to capture her mouth with his. The kiss was so hot that Margaret wouldn't have been entirely surprised if the wooden door had burst into flames. By the time Tucker finally lifted his head to draw a ragged breath, she was quite sure she smelled smoke.

Her knees weak, she clung to the front of his shirt for support. "Wow," she said faintly.

He gave her a visibly shaky smile. "Yeah. Wow. I've been wanting to do that all day."

"I've wanted you to," she admitted.

He kissed her again, pressing her against the door so that she could feel his arousal. She couldn't resist moving against him just a bit.

He groaned and rested his forehead on hers. "Man, I wish I could stay."

"So do I."

He slid his hands down her sides, slowly, thoroughly, pausing at the swell of her breasts, her waist, her thighs. "You feel so good," he muttered. "I want you so much I ache."

It was all she could do to force her voice through her desire-tightened throat. "I know the feeling."

"Tell me you want me."

She pressed a kiss to his throat. "You know I do."

"Tell me."

"I want you, Tucker." About that, at least, she had no doubt.

His deep inhale brought him into closer contact with her breasts, which already felt heavy and tingly with need. "I'd better go while I still can," he said grimly.

Reluctantly, she nodded.

He held her tightly for a moment longer, then slowly drew away. "I promised Kitten and Sam I'd take them to a movie matinee after school tomorrow. It starts at four, I think. Want to meet us there?"

"Thank you, but I'd better not. I have to work."

"You can take off a little early, can't you? Don't make me sit through two hours of animated superheroes without adult companionship."

She smiled at his shameless cajolery, but resolutely shook her head. "I really should put in my full workday tomorrow. I've got quite a lot to do."

For a moment, she thought he was going to argue. She tensed, unavoidably thinking of Mick's smothering possessiveness of Jackie. Was it a trait that ran in the family? If so, both Hollis men had a lot to learn. Margaret could not simply ignore her responsibilities to her job because of Tucker—no more than she already had, at least. She refused to fall any further behind.

After a tense hesitation, Tucker nodded. "All right. If you can't, you can't. Let me know when you've got some free time, okay?"

"I have a dinner meeting with a client Tuesday night and a commitment at church on Wednesday. Why don't I cook dinner for the four of us on Thursday?" she suggested, thinking rapidly ahead.

"Thursday," he repeated without inflection. "Yeah, okay. We should be available then. So I'll see you Thursday."

"Okay." She searched his face, trying to read his emotions. Was he annoyed? Exasperated? Disappointed? She simply couldn't tell.

"I have to go," he said, reaching for the door. "Good night, Margaret."

She caught his arm. "Good night, Tucker," she murmured, and rose on tiptoes to kiss him.

He responded with a warmth that she found reassuring. But he left immediately afterward, closing the door firmly behind him.

Margaret walked wearily into her living room and sank gracelessly onto her couch. It had been a very long day.

Chapter Thirteen

Margaret and Tucker spoke only briefly during the next two days. Trying not to worry about their relationship, she threw herself into her work, and was beginning to catch up enough to feel comfortable again.

Her phone rang very early Wednesday morning, just as she'd finished dressing. She hadn't even gone out for her newspaper yet. "Hello?"

"Margaret."

"Tucker," she said in surprise. "Is something wrong?"

"Yeah. Look, I really hate to ask you this. I mean, I know you're busy with work and everything—"

"What is it?" she broke in, sensing his tension.

"It's Sam. He's sick. He's running a fever and has a painfully sore throat. I called the doctor, and he's prescribing an antibiotic, but I absolutely have to go to school today. There's a staff meeting I can't miss, since it has to do with next semester's funding—"

"Tucker," Margaret interrupted again. "Are you asking me to keep Sam today while you're at work?"

"Yeah," he admitted. "Mom and Dad have already left for their cruise and Deb has plans today, and I just don't know who else to call."

She was a bit hurt that he put it that way, as if she were his last choice. "He's welcome to stay here with me," she said firmly. "Or do you think it would be better if I come to your house so he can stay in his own bed?"

"No, I'll bring him over there. That way, you can go ahead and work. He won't need constant care or anything—he can sleep or watch TV. I just need you to make sure he takes his medicine and maybe take his temperature every so often."

"I'll make some soup for his lunch. Maybe he'll be able to swallow a little by then."

"I can't tell you how much I appreciate this. Any other time, I'd have been able to take the day off to stay with him myself, or Mom would've been around. Today was absolutely the worst day this could happen."

"Bring him on over as soon as you're ready. I'll be watching for you."

"Thanks, Margaret."

"You're welcome." Margaret hung up with a frown, a bit concerned about what she'd taken on. She knew nothing about caring for sick children; what if Sam's temperature suddenly shot up or he got nauseous or something? How would she know what to do? And how did Sam feel about spending the day with her, when he felt so badly and didn't like her much to begin with?

She hurried downstairs to start the soup stock cooking. Though her own mother hadn't been the type to make homemade soup when Margaret had been ill, Margaret knew that was the old standard practice. She figured it couldn't hurt.

* * *

Sam was scowling when his father pulled into Margaret's driveway. "I could've stayed home by myself," he croaked, huddling miserably into his jacket, his face flushed with fever.

"No, you couldn't," Tucker contradicted him. "You're not old enough for that, even if you were well. I'm really sorry I can't stay home with you today, but I promise I'll get back as soon as I can this afternoon. In the meantime, Margaret will make sure you have everything you need. You let her know how you're feeling, okay? I'll be calling to check on you."

"Can't I stay, too, Daddy?" Kitten asked pleadingly. "It's not fair that Sam gets to stay with Margaret today while I have to go to school."

"You aren't missing school, Kitten," Tucker said flatly. "You can see Margaret later."

"Wish she could stay here instead of me," Sam muttered.

Tucker reminded himself that the boy was sick. He tried to speak patiently. "I want you to be good for Margaret, you hear? She's being very nice to let you stay with her today."

Sam only shrugged.

Thoroughly harried, and aware that it was getting late, Tucker leapt out of the car and rounded the front to help his son to Margaret's door. Sam leaned gratefully against him, a bit unsteady on his legs. Margaret opened the door before they reached it.

She looked at Sam in visible concern. "Come in," she urged him. "Let's get you comfortable."

Sam looked up at Tucker, who nodded and patted his shoulder. "Go on in, son. Margaret will help you get settled somewhere."

The boy sighed and walked through the door.

"I've arranged to have the medicine delivered here,"

Tucker said, speaking quickly as he handed Margaret a small paper bag. "He'll need one spoonful as soon as it arrives and every four hours afterward. He had a dose of acetaminophen a half hour ago—the doctor said he could take that every four hours for fever. There's a bottle in the bag. He's having trouble swallowing, but he needs to get some liquids down so he doesn't dehydrate. I've written down the number of the school, and I'll tell the office to page me if you call. The doctor's number is also in there. And a thermometer. I didn't know if you had one."

"We'll be fine," Margaret assured him, her confident expression belying the hint of nerves in her voice. "I'll call if I need you."

"I'll be checking in with you whenever I get a chance."

"Fine. Now go, or you'll be late. I'll take care of Sam."

He leaned over to brush a quick kiss across her cheek. "I owe you one."

"You better believe it," she said lightly. "Go on, now. And try not to worry."

Fat chance of that, he thought as he sprinted back to his car, where Kitten waited impatiently. He couldn't really blame Margaret for being concerned that her life would be disrupted if she got any further involved with him. It seemed that everything that could go wrong had since he'd gotten to know her.

He wouldn't be surprised if she took to her heels after this. But if she did, he intended to be right behind her, he thought, slamming the car door and shoving the gearshift into Reverse.

Margaret closed the door and turned to Sam, who stood in the hallway, head down, shoulders hunched. He looked thoroughly miserable, poor kid.

"Would you like to lie down in a bed upstairs or on the couch in the den?" she asked. "The television set is in the den, if you feel like watching it."

"Okay," Sam muttered, his voice hoarse.

She nodded and ushered him into the den, where she'd already laid out a pillow and a warm blanket in anticipation of his choice. As soon as he was settled, she handed him the television remote. "I'll bring you some juice," she said. "Do you like apple juice?"

Sam touched his throat. "I don't think I can swallow it," he croaked.

"We'll try some cool water, then. I'll set it close by, and you can sip at it a little at a time. I have some cherry-flavored herbal throat lozenges. Maybe they'll make your throat feel a little better."

Sam shrugged and turned on the television.

Margaret didn't know whether to attribute his apathy to his illness or his dislike of her, but she told herself that she would not take it personally either way. He was just a child, she reminded herself as she fetched his water and the throat lozenges. A sick one, at that. She would do her best to take care of him, whether he cooperated or not.

Setting the glass on the coffee table within Sam's reach, she handed him a paper-wrapped lozenge. "Is there anything else I can get you?" she asked.

His gaze on the cartoon he'd selected, he shook his head. "I'm okay."

She suspected that he wouldn't appreciate her hovering over him all day. "All right. I'll leave you alone for a while. I'll be in my office if you need me. It's the first door on the left down the hall."

He nodded.

"I'll check on you often, but please don't hesitate to ask if you want anything, Sam."

He darted her a glance, then looked back at the screen. "Okay" was all he said.

She paused in the doorway, looking back at him. She found herself oddly reluctant to leave him alone in the room, though she would only be a few yards away. He looked so small huddled beneath the blanket on her sofa, his face flushed with fever, his eyelids heavy.

She'd never expected that the sight of a sick little boy would make her feel this way. So worried and protective and tender. Not that Sam would appreciate it if she showed any of those emotions, she thought, turning away with a stifled sigh.

The antibiotic was delivered half an hour later. Margaret carried it and a spoon into the den, where Sam had fallen asleep, the television blaring unnoticed. He was sleeping so soundly that she regretted having to disturb him, but she knew he needed the medicine.

"Sam?" she said quietly, kneeling beside him. "Sam, your medicine is here."

He stirred, but didn't waken.

She touched his face, frowning at the warmth of his skin. It would be almost three more hours before he could take anything for the fever. She hoped it didn't go up alarmingly in the meantime; she wouldn't have the faintest idea what to do about it if it did. "Wake up, Sam. You need to take this."

His eyelids fluttered, and then he squinted at her. "What?" he muttered, obviously disoriented.

"Your medicine is here," she repeated gently. "I'm going to help you take a spoonful, okay?"

He rubbed at his eyes with one hand, then nodded and wriggled upright.

Margaret carefully poured the sticky pink liquid into the spoon; Sam obediently opened his mouth to take it when she offered. He winced when he swallowed, both from the pain and the taste, she guessed sympathetically.

"Can you drink a little water?" she asked. "Your dad said you need lots of liquids today."

He looked doubtful, but didn't resist when she held the glass to his lips.

He managed only a couple of sips before he pushed the glass away. "It hurts."

"I know. I'm sorry. I hope the medicine works quickly to make it better."

He slid back onto the pillows. His eyes were bright, and his lower lip just a bit unsteady. He looked as though he might have cried had he not been working so hard at being brave.

Margaret smoothed the blanket over his shoulders, then couldn't resist stroking a damp strand of hair away from his forehead. She had the urge to gather him into her arms, but she wasn't at all sure he would appreciate that from her.

"I wish there was something I could do to make it stop hurting," she murmured, hating her inability to ease his discomfort.

How did parents deal with this? she wondered. They must feel so helpless and impotent when their children suffered, when there was so little they could do in response.

She knew how her own parents had dealt with their child, of course—they'd basically ignored her, being so wrapped up with their own real and imagined pains. She suspected that good parents, on the other hand, suffered almost as deeply as the children themselves.

She'd bet that Tucker did.

She couldn't help wondering which type of parent she would be—should the situation ever arise, of course.

"I'm going back to my office now," she told Sam, knowing there was nothing else she could do for him for now. "Let me know if there's anything I can get you."

He nodded. "Thanks," he said, the word little more than a hoarse whisper.

She was a bit startled. Was she wrong, or had that been a sincere expression of gratitude?

Not wanting to build false hope in herself, she merely nodded and repeated that she'd be close by if he needed her.

Tucker called at ten. "How is he?" he asked as soon as he identified himself.

"I just checked on him," Margaret reported. "He's sleeping on the couch in my den."

"The medicine arrived?"

"Yes, and I gave him some immediately. He still feels a bit warm to me. I'll give him another dose of acetaminophen at eleven. He's due for more antibiotic at noon."

"I hope he isn't giving you any trouble."

"No, not at all. He's been very quiet and cooperative. I just feel so badly for him. He obviously feels lousy."

"Anytime Sam is quiet and cooperative, you can bet he's sick," Tucker quipped, but Margaret could tell he had to make an effort to joke. She knew he must feel guilty that he'd had to leave the boy today.

"Is your meeting over already?" she asked.

"No. We're taking a break. I guess I'd better get back to it. You'll call if you need anything?"

"Of course. I'm going to try to get Sam to have a little soup after he takes his medicines. If that doesn't interest him, maybe a little ice cream would feel good to his throat."

"I can't tell you how much I appreciate this."

"I really don't mind. As I said, he's been no trouble at all."

"Taking care of a sick child is never easy," Tucker maintained. "You can't imagine what a relief it is to me to know that you're watching out for Sam. Thank you, Margaret."

As she hung up, she couldn't help wondering at the trust Tucker had expressed in her. It seemed a bit misplaced to her. How could he sound so confident about leaving his son with her, a woman who'd admitted that her experience with children was limited at best?

It was rather amazing how many new situations she'd experienced since Tucker Hollis and his children had moved next door.

Margaret managed to get Sam to eat a little soup for lunch, followed by a scoop of ice cream. She was relieved to note that he looked a little better, and hoped that the rest and medicine would work quickly to make him well again.

After lunch, Margaret went back into her office while Sam settled on the couch again with a *Goosebumps* book he'd brought with him, having lost interest in daytime television. Though he still hadn't said much to her, Margaret thought he looked a bit more comfortable in her presence now. She didn't try to force him into conversation, but she was pleased when he occasionally responded to something she said.

They weren't exactly friends yet, she decided, but neither did he act as though he needed a cross and a garlic necklace to protect himself from her. Surely that meant they were making some progress.

It was around two o'clock when a sound from the office doorway made her look up from the computer to find Sam standing there watching her, his book in his hand, an uncertain look on his face.

He cleared his throat and shifted his weight. "It's kind of quiet in there," he said, then motioned toward the leather love seat in one corner of her office. "Is it okay if I read in here?"

He was lonely, Margaret realized, both surprised and touched that he'd reached out to her this way. "Of course you may read in here," she said instantly. "I'll go get your pillow and blanket so you'll be comfortable."

As soon as he was settled, she placed a hand against his forehead. He still felt warm, but no more than before. "You'll need another dose of medicine in an hour," she murmured, making a mental note. "Is there anything you'd like now? How about a soda? A snack, maybe?"

"I'm not hungry," he replied. "But a soda sounds good," he added tentatively.

She smiled. "I'll be right back."

She returned carrying a glass of soda for him and another for herself. She pulled a small table close to him and set his drink on it. "Need anything else?"

"No, thank you." He opened his book, looking a bit embarrassed by her attention.

Some twenty minutes passed with the only sound in the office being the tapping of Margaret's fingers against her keyboard and the rustling of pages in Sam's book. When he started to squirm, she glanced around at him. "You okay?"

He nodded toward the expensive stereo system on the credenza behind her desk. "Do you ever listen to music when you work?"

"Yes, very often. What music do you like?"

"Country, mostly," he admitted.

Though it wouldn't have been Margaret's choice, she nodded obligingly and reached for the Power button. She paused when he spoke.

"Um, you know that music you were playing on Halloween?"

She frowned, trying to remember. "Halloween?"

He nodded. "I heard it while you and Kitten were talking. It sounded kind of interesting."

A glimpse of red porcelain at the corner of her desk jogged Margaret's memory. She glanced at the rose

Tucker had sent her. "I remember. It was music from *The Phantom of the Opera*."

Sam looked intrigued. "What's that?"

She rummaged through her CDs and found the one she wanted. "This particular version was produced by Andrew Lloyd Webber, who also wrote the music, along with lyricist Charles Hart," she explained. "It's about a young opera singer named Christine—"

"Like Kitten," Sam murmured.

"Yes, like Kitten," Margaret confirmed, trying to decide how to condense the story quickly. "Anyway, there's a man living beneath the opera house who has a deformity that makes him frightening to other people. He wears a mask to hide his face and he 'haunts' the opera house. He becomes obsessed with Christine, and he writes an opera for her to star in. Christine loves the musical soul of the phantom, but his violence frightens her. Then a man named Raoul comes along and also falls in love with Christine. The phantom kills some people and takes Christine down to his labyrinth, and then Raoul rushes to her rescue. The phantom orders her to stay with him or he will kill Raoul."

She winced at her ineptitude in summarizing the plotline. Though she loved the music, and knew the lyrics quite well, she'd seen the live production only once and she was having a hard time remembering all the details—and then translating them for a nine-year-old's understanding.

Sam seemed interested, nevertheless. "Cool," he croaked, setting his spooky book aside. "Then what happens?"

On a sudden impulse, Margaret turned to the CD player.

"The main songs from the musical are on this CD," she said. "Let's listen to it, and I'll try to tell you what's happening in each song. If you'd like that, of course," she added uncertainly.

Sam nodded. "Okay. Unless maybe you want me to go back in the den and let you work?" He sounded as diffident as she had.

Margaret shook her head. "There's nothing that can't wait until later," she assured him, not entirely accurately. "I can take a break to listen to this with you. It's about an hour long, so if you get tired or bored, just tell me and we'll turn it off."

Sam shrugged. "I'd like to hear it for a while."

She pushed the Play button.

Margaret closed her eyes and tried to remember each scene as it played out in song, describing the action as best she could to Sam, filling in when he didn't quite understand the words. He was particularly fascinated when the phantom came into the story, the bizarre behavior and emotions so eloquently expressed by Michael Crawford's brilliant singing.

Sam began to ask questions before Margaret could speak. "What's happening now?" he'd say. "Who's singing this part? Where's he taking her? Why is he saying that?"

By the time the story reached its breathless crescendo in the thirteen-and-a-half-minute final number, it was no longer necessary for Margaret to narrate. Sam had caught the gist of the tale and was listening avidly, curled on the love seat beneath the warm blanket.

Amazed by the boy's reaction to the music—he seemed so young to be caught up in the operatic drama—Margaret studied him surreptitiously.

He looked so much like Tucker, she realized, studying the familiar spark of interest in Sam's wide-set green eyes. Even the recalcitrant lock of dark hair on his forehead was so much like his father's that Margaret itched to brush it tenderly back, as she had a time or two with Tucker during the night she'd spent alone with him.

Margaret rarely listened to the end of the CD without an emotional response. When the tortured phantom sang, "It's over now," her throat almost always tightened.

She was fascinated to see that young Sam seemed to sense the intensity of the scene.

Only then did she realize that they had listened to the entire CD. Sam's attention had strayed only once or twice, and then briefly. She was frankly surprised.

"Did you like it?" she asked, though she guessed from his thoughtful expression that he had.

He nodded. "I'd like to see it sometime. I bet it's exciting."

"Yes, very. Do you like theater, Sam?"

Again, he surprised her by nodding. "Yeah. We take field trips from school to plays and things. And sometimes when we visit my grandma in Houston, she takes us to Galveston to the outdoor theater there. We got to see a show called *Brigadoon*. Do you know that one?"

"Why, yes."

"It's cool. These guys do a sword dance, and one of 'em runs away and falls off a cliff and gets killed and then the whole town disappears for another hundred years."

She smiled at his summary of the play. "Yes, I enjoyed that one, too. What other plays have you seen?"

"They do stuff at the children's theater all the time. I thought maybe I'd do some acting sometime," he added offhandedly.

Intrigued, she propped her elbows on her desk and openly studied him. "I love theater," she confided. "I go every chance I get. Maybe—" She hesitated only a moment before continuing. "Maybe you'd like to go to a play with me sometime?"

He studied her with a touch of his former wariness.

"Maybe," he said, trying to look casual, though she thought she saw interest in his eyes. "Dad doesn't like plays much. He'd rather go to movies."

"Maybe he just needs to try a few more plays."

"Yeah. Maybe." Sam put his head back onto the pillow.

Margaret thought of the comment Tucker had once made to describe his relationship with her. One step forward, two steps back. This felt like a definite step forward with Sam. Maybe they wouldn't have to take those back-steps.

She stood and walked over to him. His cheek felt a bit warmer to her now, so she coaxed him into letting her take his temperature again.

"One-oh-one," she murmured, reading the numbers. "You'd better take some more Tylenol."

"My throat's getting all sore again," he mumbled, rubbing at his neck. "Are there any more of those cherry things?"

"I'll get you one. Lie back and rest now."

"That's all I've been doing," he said with a sigh.

"It will help you get well sooner," she assured him. "I'll be right back."

Sam nodded, his eyes already getting heavy again.

Sam was still sleeping when Tucker arrived to pick him up at four. "I got here as soon as I could," he said when Margaret opened the door for him and Kitten. "How is he?"

"A little better, I think," she replied, automatically responding to Kitten's hug of greeting. "It's time for his antibiotic again, but he's sleeping. How was your day, Kitten?" she asked, not wanting the child to feel left out.

Kitten started to reply in detail.

Tucker indulged her a moment, then broke in to say,

"Where's Sam? I'll take him home and give him his medicine there."

"He's asleep on the couch in my office," Margaret said, motioning in that direction. "We spent part of the afternoon listening to music."

Tucker lifted an eyebrow. "You like country music?"

She smiled. "Who said we listened to country? We might have been listening to show tunes. Or opera."

Tucker snorted. "Sam? Opera? Not unless you tied him up first."

Margaret tilted her head, bemused by the realization that there was something she and Sam had shared that Tucker didn't yet understand. She suspected that Tucker had no idea that his son was interested in theater—not from lack of interest on Tucker's part, of course, but because the subject had probably just never really come up between them.

How utterly amazing that Margaret had discovered it first.

"Margaret," Kitten said, tugging impatiently at her hand. "I was telling you about what happened to me at recess."

"Oh, sorry, Kitten," Margaret apologized. "Please go on."

Maybe children weren't so very difficult to comprehend, after all, she thought dazedly. She was getting better than she'd ever anticipated at communicating with the Hollis siblings, though she was still cautious about how durable Sam's softening would prove to be once he was back on his feet and fully self-reliant again.

Tucker reappeared a moment later, his groggy son draped over his chest. Tucker carried the boy carefully, but casually, obviously from ease of habit. Sam had his head on Tucker's shoulder, his arms around his neck, the position so trusting and familiar that Margaret found her throat tightening again.

The sight of Tucker and his son made her chest feel warm and achy. If this wasn't love, she thought with a touch of panic, it was something much too close for comfort.

Chapter Fourteen

Margaret was *not* having a good day on Friday. For the first time in years, she overslept, which threw her whole morning off. She dropped her foundation as she was applying her makeup, and the sticky liquid went everywhere in her bathroom, making a terrible mess. She'd forgotten to set the timer on her coffeemaker— she had to wait for a pot to brew before she could have her breakfast.

Taking care of Sam both Wednesday and Thursday had made her fall behind on her work again. But she didn't regret the time she and Sam had spent together. He'd stayed close to her again on Thursday, sometimes reading quietly, other times actually initiating conversation. They weren't exactly bosom buddies yet, but Sam seemed to be thawing. They were making definite progress.

Tucker had arranged for a substitute teacher in his classes today, allowing him to stay home with Sam, who

wasn't quite well enough to return to school. Tucker had
gotten Sam's assignments from his teacher and had said
he would spend the day working with his son, getting
him ready to go back to school on Monday without having fallen too far behind after his weeklong visit with
his grandmother, followed by his unfortunately timed illness.

Margaret planned to spend Friday catching up on her
own work. And then Greg Jessup showed up at midmorning with a stack of tax forms he and his partner
had forgotten to file by the October 31 deadline.

"You know, of course, that you'll be assessed a pen-
alty," Margaret said with a long-suffering sigh. "You
were supposed to send a payment with this form."

"A payment?" Greg asked warily. "How much?"

She told him.

He groaned.

"Please tell me you have it set aside for this purpose," she begged. "We've discussed this, Greg. Taxes
have to be paid before all else."

"Well, I, er, I'll go talk to Jeff," he promised, and
made a hasty escape.

Margaret buried her face in her hands and told herself
it just wasn't worth it. She was going to have to ask
Greg and Jeff to find themselves a new bookkeeper. Unfortunately, they couldn't afford a full-time accountant
to write all their checks and file their forms. She did
everything else for them; why couldn't they handle those
simple little details? Frustrated, she opened the folder
he'd brought her to see what she could do.

She'd just gotten a good start on her day's work when
her computer died. Just blinked and went blank.

It was a sudden, unexpected demise; the computer
wasn't that old and hadn't even been ill. Frantic about
the hours of work she might have lost, Margaret tried

everything she knew to bring it back to life, but to no avail.

Thank goodness she was the type to compulsively back up everything each evening before she—

She suddenly groaned and hit her head with her fist. She hadn't backed up yesterday's work. Sam had been here, and then Tucker came, and Kitten lingered for a while, jabbering—and Margaret had forgotten to back up her work when she'd turned off the computer. It was the first time she could remember that she'd neglected to do so.

How many hours *had* she lost? She couldn't bear to think about it.

The telephone rang just as she was reaching for it to make an emergency call to a computer-repair shop. Automatically noting the time—just after noon—Margaret picked it up. "Hello."

"Hi, it's Tuck."

She pushed a strand of hair out of her face, momentarily distracted from her lousy morning. "Hello. How's Sam?"

"Much better. His throat's not nearly as sore as it was."

"Is he still running a fever?"

"A little this morning. His temperature's normal now."

"What a relief."

"How's your day going?"

"I've had better," she muttered, glaring at the lifeless shell of her computer.

"Problem?"

"Nothing serious," she answered, crossing her fingers.

He accepted the lie without question. "Good. Want to have a pizza or something with us this evening?"

"Thank you for asking, but I have plans. It might be late when I get home."

"Plans?" Tucker repeated, a frown in his voice.

She recognized that tone. It was the same one he'd used to question her about Greg the day he'd come over to find him here. She didn't like it now any more than she had then.

"Yes, plans," she said firmly, refusing to explain that it was only a club meeting. She didn't owe Tucker explanations about every moment of her time, she thought. He should understand that now.

She could almost feel him debating with himself about whether to question her further. She was relieved when he apparently made the prudent choice to let it go. "Okay, then I'll see you later," he said.

"All right. Now I really should get back to work. I have a few calls to make."

"Okay, sure. Oh, and by the way—"

"Yes?"

"Do you have plans for Thanksgiving? Deb called this morning to ask about Sam, and she reminded me that it's less than a week away. We'll gather at Mom's for a big dinner, and of course we'd all like it if you could be there with us."

Margaret froze. Thanksgiving dinner. She usually politely turned down all the obligatory invitations, preferring to indulge herself with a solitary feast rather than to endure the awkwardness of spending the holiday with someone else's family.

This situation was a bit different, of course. She and Tucker were involved—sort of. But she hadn't really thought about spending the coming holidays with his family. That would imply a commitment she hadn't yet made, wouldn't it? Encourage expectations that might not come through.

"I, um, I'll think about it," she promised.

"It would mean a lot to the kids if you join us," Tucker said enticingly. "But it would mean even more to me."

"I'll think about it, Tucker," she repeated, wondering how Sam really felt about it. Whether anything had really changed on his part, just because he'd spent two days in her company. "Now, I'm sorry, but I really have to go."

"Okay. I won't keep you any longer."

Was she being paranoid again, or did she hear resentment in his voice? She found herself trying to decide as the call concluded and she reached for her telephone book.

She didn't have time for this right now, she told herself, forcefully punching the numbers for the computer-repair service. She had a hectic day ahead of her.

The doorbell rang an hour later. Still at her desk—she hadn't had time for lunch—Margaret tossed down the pen she'd been using and hurried to answer it, pleasantly surprised that the computer-repair technician had arrived so quickly.

But it was Jackie who stood at Margaret's door, tears streaming down her face.

Margaret swallowed a groan, instantly recognizing her friend's woebegone expression. It was the same one she always wore when a romance ended.

"Margaret," Jackie sobbed. "He—he—he *dumped* me."

Margaret pulled her friend inside and closed the door. "Tell me about it," she said, trying to forget her computer woes for the moment. After all, her friend needed her.

Jackie was still weeping and hiccuping the details of her blowout with Mick when the computer technician arrived an hour later. Leaving Jackie sniffling into the sofa, Margaret escorted the man into her office, described the problem and begged him to perform a miracle. A fast one.

One of her clients called and asked a question that Margaret couldn't answer without access to her computer files. She had just completed that apologetic conversation when her doorbell rang again. It was Mick.

"Is Jackie here?" he demanded, looking a bit wild-eyed.

"She's in the den," Margaret began, "but—"

"Tell him to go away!" Jackie shouted from the other room.

"Not without talking to you, damn it!" Mick yelled back. He started to storm in, then paused and looked at Margaret. "Is it okay if I come in?"

"I don't know, Mick. Jackie's—"

"Jackie, I want to talk to you," Mick yelled.

"You've already talked to me!" Jackie shouted back. "I remember every cruel word you said!"

Margaret winced, wondering what the computer technician thought of the noisy exchange echoing through her house. "Please," she said to Mick, "go talk to her. I'm sure you can work this out. And try to keep the volume down, will you?"

"I'll try," he said grimly, already moving in that direction.

Margaret rubbed her aching temples and went to check the status of her computer.

Barely thirty minutes had passed when the doorbell chimed again. Passing the den, where two voices were still raised in heated discussion, Margaret answered the door.

"Hi, Margaret," Kitten sang out cheerily. "I just got home. Did I leave my library book here yesterday? I can't find it, and Daddy says if I don't, he's going to take it out of my 'llowance. I don't even get a 'llowance," she added thoughtfully.

Margaret looked distractedly around. "I don't remember seeing a library book," she murmured. "Are you sure you brought it in with you, Kitten?"

The child lifted both hands in a shrug. "I can't remember. Maybe. I think I was looking at it in the car when we got here. Or maybe I wasn't."

The computer technician appeared in the hallway. "Ms. McAlister? I need to talk to you," he said, his tone ominously somber.

Margaret drew a long breath. "You may come in and look for your book," she said to Kitten. "But I really don't think it's here. I have to go into my office for a minute. I'll be right back."

"Okay," Kitten said. "I'll start in the kitchen. Do you have any cookies?"

"Yes, but they're too high for you to reach. I'll get you some as soon as I can."

"Okay," Kitten said, already skipping toward the kitchen.

Even knowing that Kitten hadn't gone anywhere near the kitchen the afternoon before, Margaret didn't try to redirect her. She figured Kitten was better off rummaging in the kitchen for a few minutes than anywhere else in the house—especially the den.

The computer was in bad shape. The technician explained that it would have to be taken to his shop for a new part—which, of course, would have to be ordered.

"How long will that take?" Margaret asked, resigned for the worst.

"Today being Friday, it'll probably be Tuesday or Wednesday before you'll have it back," he said, packing up his tools. "Hope that isn't too much of an inconvenience."

He had no idea how inconvenient, Margaret thought with a swallowed moan. A minimum of four days without her computer would devastate her schedule. Heaven only knew how long it would take her to get back on track. Still, there seemed to be nothing she could say except, "Please try to have it ready as soon as possible."

Why, oh, why hadn't she backed up yesterday's work?

The technician carried the computer out to his van, then couldn't leave. Mick's pickup was blocking his way.

Margaret found Mick and Jackie still arguing in the den, Jackie dry-eyed and furious now, Mick looking utterly exasperated. "Mick, you have to move your truck," she said.

"Please, Margaret," he said a bit impatiently, "I'd like to stay and finish this."

She exhaled loudly and planted her fists on her hips. "I am not asking you to leave, though I probably should be. You've blocked my driveway, and the computer technician can't get out. Please move your truck."

"Oh." He had the grace to look sheepish for a moment. Then he glanced at Jackie. "I'll be right back," he said warningly. "We're not finished with this."

She humphed and turned an icy shoulder to him.

Margaret didn't even want to know what they were fighting about. She just wanted them to do it elsewhere. "Couldn't you take him to your place?" she asked Jackie when Mick had left the room.

"I never want him in my house again," Jackie declared dramatically. "If you had heard the things he said to me—"

There was a crash from somewhere in the house.

"Oh, Lord," Margaret said with a wince. "Kitten!" She ran.

The cookie jar was in pieces on the floor, bits of ceramic mixed among the chocolate-chip cookies. Kitten was in noisy tears. "I didn't mean to," she wailed. "I thought I could reach it. I'm so so-o-o-rry."

Margaret thought momentarily about bursting into tears herself, but she figured there were already two too many sobbing females in her house. "It's all right, Kitten. I'll take care of it."

She parked a still-sniffling Kitten at the table with a glass of milk and two of the cookies from the top of the pile and then set to work with broom and dustpan. The telephone rang just as she dumped the mess into the trash container. She picked up the kitchen extension.

"Is Kitten still there?" Tucker asked without identifying himself. "I told her to run over and look for her book and then get right back home."

"She's still here. Your brother's here, too. And so is Jackie. The computer technician just left," Margaret recited.

He must have caught her frazzled undertone. "Problems?" he asked after a moment.

"A few," she admitted.

"I'll be right there," he said.

"No, that's—"

But he'd already disconnected. She hung up her own phone, then just stood for a moment with her forehead pressed against a cabinet door.

"Margaret? Are you okay?" Kitten asked, her tears-and-cookie-streaked face creased with concern. "You look kind of funny."

Margaret sighed and straightened. "I have to go answer the front door."

Puzzled, Kitten tilted her head. "But the doorbell didn't ring."

"It's about to," Margaret answered. "Finish your cookies, Kitten. I'll be right back. And please don't touch anything else, okay?"

"Okay, Margaret," Kitten agreed meekly.

Margaret opened the door just as Tucker arrived.

He took one look at her face and pulled her into his arms. "What's wrong?"

She tried to remember the last time she'd been able to bury her face into someone's shoulder and unload her problems. She couldn't come up with one instance. From the time she'd been very young, she was the one who'd always had to be in charge. The one who kept everything under control.

So what had happened?

Even as she asked herself the question, she knew the answer. Tucker Hollis had happened. Her life hadn't been the same since he'd entered it.

She pulled herself out of his arms. "Mick and Jackie are fighting in my den. My clients seem to be conspiring to drive me insane. My computer self-destructed with a day and a half's work lost in it. The repairman said it might be four or five days before I get it back. And I've got a vicious headache. Other than that, everything's just great."

He looked at her with narrowed eyes. "Is your throat sore?"

She swallowed, only then aware of the discomfort. "Well, yes, a little, but—"

He placed his palm on her forehead. "I think you have a fever."

She sagged. "No. Please don't say that. I really don't have time to be sick."

"It's probably the bug Sam had. Margaret, I'm sorry. If I'd thought there was any chance you'd catch it, I would have— Well, I really didn't have any other option," he admitted ruefully.

Her head pounded. "I'll be fine," she said defiantly, speaking to herself as much as to him. "I'll take some aspirin or something in a minute. I have to start getting ready for my meeting soon—if I can get Jackie and Mick out of my den," she added as a duet of raised voices came again from that direction.

Tucker grimaced. "They are going at it, aren't they?"

Kitten walked through the doorway. Upon sight of her father, she promptly burst into tears again.

"I didn't mean to break Margaret's cookie jar," she insisted loudly, looking as pathetic as possible. "It was an accident, Daddy. I'm so so-o-o-rry."

Tucker blinked, then looked back at Margaret. "You really *have* had a lousy day, haven't you?"

She didn't feel the need to answer.

Tucker seemed to come to a sudden decision. He moved in long, determined strides toward the den.

Curious, Margaret followed, Kitten right at her heels.

Mick and Jackie were standing toe-to-toe in the center of the room, both talking too fast for either to possibly understand the other. Tucker put two fingers in his mouth and gave a loud, shrill whistle. Kitten put her hands over her ears.

Startled, Jackie and Mick fell quiet and turned to stare at him.

"What the hell is going on here?" Tucker demanded.

Jackie and Mick both started to tell him at once.

Tucker immediately held up a hand for silence. "Never mind. I don't care about the details. The point is, this is Margaret's house and you are in her way. Either break up now and be done with it, or take the battle somewhere else."

Mick slanted an apprehensive look at Jackie. "We aren't breaking up," he insisted. "I'm in love with her."

"If you were in love with me, you would trust me," Jackie retorted, her swollen eyes filling with tears again.

"Trust you? I thought we'd agreed not to date other people, and then I saw you at lunch today draped cozily all over some other guy in a restaurant. What the hell was I supposed to think?"

"He was my *cousin!*" Jackie yelled. "I'd have already told you that if you'd stopped yelling long enough to listen."

Margaret rolled her eyes and groaned. "Please tell me this wasn't started by Mick finding you with Phillip," she murmured in exasperation.

"See?" Jackie demanded of Mick. "I *told* you Phillip is my cousin. We've been like brother and sister since we were in diapers."

"Well, how was I to know that?" Mick demanded.

"You could have asked, instead of coming across like some macho jerk and yelling at me. I will not be treated that way, Mick Hollis. If you can't trust me to be faithful to you, then that's the end of it. It's over between us."

"Is that what you want?" Mick asked quietly, seemingly unaware that Tucker was watching them in disgust, Margaret in chagrin and Kitten in wide-eyed fascination.

"No," Jackie sobbed. "That's not what I want. I love you, too, damn it."

Mick wrapped his arms around her. "I'm sorry," he said. "I should have trusted you. I've been acting like a jealous idiot, but it's only because I've never been in love before. I got scared, I guess."

Jackie buried her face in his shoulder and mumbled something Margaret couldn't understand and didn't try to.

"Great," Tucker said, clapping his hands together. "Now, the two of you need to sit down and have a long, *quiet* discussion about your relationship. You may begin at my house. You're baby-sitting this evening."

Mick looked quickly around. Jackie lifted her head to peer inquiringly at Tucker. "What do you mean?" Mick asked warily.

Tucker put a hand on Kitten's shoulder. "Sam's home by himself, and Margaret isn't feeling well. You two are going to take Kitten home and stay with the kids until I get there after I make sure Margaret is all right."

"But—"

Tucker leveled his brother a look that made Mick fall silent. "You owe Margaret this after barging in on her like this today," he said. "Don't you agree, Michael?"

Mick swallowed. "Uh, yeah, I guess you're right." He looked apologetically at Margaret. "Sorry about this," he muttered. "I, er…"

"It's all right," Margaret assured him wearily. "I've just had a bad day."

"You're sick, Margaret?" Jackie asked in embarrassed concern. "Why didn't you say something?"

"I haven't had a chance," Margaret answered wryly. "And I'm not really sick. Just a headache. I just need a few minutes of quiet to get ready for a meeting tonight."

"You aren't going to a meeting tonight," Tucker informed her, his quiet tone underscored with determination.

She looked at him with narrowed eyes. "I beg your pardon?"

"We'll take Kitten home now," Mick said quickly, taking Jackie's hand and tugging her toward the door.

"Don't fight in front of my kids," Tucker said, glancing at his brother over his shoulder.

Jackie flushed.

Mick cleared his throat. "No, we won't. Come on, Kitten. Uncle Mick'll give you a piggyback ride home."

Kitten happily agreed. "See you later, Daddy and Margaret," she said, leaping onto her uncle's back.

Tucker turned to Margaret as soon as they were alone. "Now," he said, advancing toward her, "let's get you out of those clothes."

Margaret wasn't sure she'd heard him correctly. Surely Tucker hadn't just suggested… "I beg your pardon?"

He motioned toward the prim blouse and vest she wore with belted, pleated slacks. "You can't possibly get comfortable in your working clothes. Run upstairs and throw on some sweats or something. I'll make you some hot tea with honey and lemon."

"I don't even own sweats," Margaret said, though the thought of settling down with a cup of hot tea was almost irresistibly appealing after the day she'd had.

Tucker grimaced impatiently. "Then put on pajamas or something—anything loose and comfortable. You need to relax."

"I really should go to my meeting," she fretted.

"Margaret." Tucker's smile was just a bit dangerous. "Shall I help you undress?"

Something in his expression told her he was seriously considering it. And, oh, how she was tempted to let him. But the timing was definitely wrong.

She was frazzled, upset and probably sick. She needed to try to clear her head—and having Tucker undress her was certainly no way to accomplish that!

She cleared her prickly throat. "I'll, um, I'll be right down," she promised.

He nodded in satisfaction and turned toward the kitchen. "Your tea will be ready for you."

She let out a slow, unsteady breath as she headed up the stairs. After seeing him in action with Mick and Jackie—and herself, for that matter—she knew how Tucker's children and students must feel on those rare occasions when he really laid down the law to them!

She told herself she wouldn't make a habit of meekly cooperating with his orders. But just this once, after the day from hell, it was rather nice to have someone else take charge. Just for a little while.

Chapter Fifteen

The tea was strong, hot and wonderful. Margaret drew a deep breath of pleasure as she sipped it, letting the warmth soak into her scratchy throat and through the rest of her. She was dressed now in her velour lounging pajamas, soft slippers on her feet, her hair loose around her shoulders. Already, she could feel some of the tension leaving her neck and shoulders.

"This is very good, Tucker," she murmured. "Thank you."

Sitting on the couch beside her, he nodded. "You're welcome." He touched her forehead. "Did you take any aspirin? You still feel a bit warm to me."

"Yes, I took some."

He slid his hand down her cheek, the gesture a caress. "I'm sorry you had such a lousy day."

She almost shivered in response to his touch. "It wasn't your fault," she said, the huskiness of her voice having little to do with her sore throat.

"Drink your tea," he urged, touching her hand. "Can I get you anything else? Are you hungry?"

She sipped the tea, then shook her head. "I'm fine, thanks. I just needed a few moments to unwind."

Tucker waited until she'd finished the tea, then took the empty cup from her and set it on the coffee table. And then he pulled her against his chest, settling her cozily into his arms. She stiffened for a moment, but almost immediately relaxed. It just felt so very good to be there, she thought with a silent sigh.

He kissed the top of her head. "Ready to tell me about it?"

She started from the beginning. Oversleeping, dropping her foundation, no coffee waiting for her, the mess Greg had brought her, the computer's death, Jackie and Mick's arrival.

"And then Kitten broke your cookie jar," Tucker said when she fell silent before reaching that part.

"She didn't mean to," Margaret insisted, instantly on the defense on Kitten's behalf. "I told her she could have some cookies."

"Mmm." Tucker rubbed her neck with his free hand, his fingers pressing into the knots he found there. Margaret almost purred in reaction. "Anything else bothering you?" he asked.

She made a face against his shoulder. "Do I need anything else on top of all that?"

"No. But that's not all, is it? You're worried about us."

She started to deny it. And then she found herself answering honestly instead. "Yes. I suppose I am."

"You think I'm going to cause havoc in your life. That I already have, for that matter. You're wondering if you'll ever have peace and quiet again."

Startled by his insight, she lifted her head to look at him uncertainly. "Well...maybe," she admitted.

His smile was crooked, revealing only one dimple. It was still enough to make her heart jump. "I wish I could assure you that your fears are unfounded. Unfortunately, they're probably justified."

She frowned. "What do you mean?"

"Being involved with me isn't going to be easy, Margaret. I have a little trouble getting organized. I usually manage to get all the important things done, but it's in a way practical types like you would never understand. And I have two young kids, which means a variety of mishaps are always just waiting to happen."

"Tucker, you aren't making me feel much better," she felt compelled to tell him.

"I know," he said regretfully. "But I have to be honest with you. I could promise to try to become a model of efficiency and organization, but I'm not at all sure it's a promise I could keep."

"I'm not asking you to make me any promises," she whispered.

"No. But I'm making a few anyway. I promise to try to understand your need for order, and to do my best to help you with it, even if I sometimes fail. I promise to give you as much space as you need to keep you from going crazy in the confusion. I promise to remind you that it's just as important at times to laugh and play and goof off as it is to meet your next deadline or follow your established routines.

"But most of all," he continued steadily, holding her gaze with his own, "I promise to love you unconditionally, to be on your side whenever you need me and to devote the rest of my life to making up for whatever happened in your childhood to leave you so withdrawn and unhappy at times now."

It seemed as though all the stiffening went out of her. Even her jaw dropped. She closed it quickly, trying to push away from him in alarm. He held her tightly.

"I— I..."

Love? The very word petrified her.

Promises? She'd heard all too many of those over the years. She knew how much it hurt when they were broken.

Her eyes filled with tears. "I'm not ready for this, Tucker," she whispered, abandoning her efforts to free herself. "Not today."

"I know my timing could have been better," he admitted wryly. "But I couldn't wait. You looked so panicky and desperate when I arrived this afternoon that I had to let you know you aren't alone anymore. I love you, Margaret. I want to be here for you when you need someone. I think you need me."

It was emotion rather than illness that made her throat ache now. Fear.

"I don't need anyone," she whispered. "I've been taking care of myself for a long time."

"Are you ready now to help me understand that?" His tone was so gentle, so caring, that her tears welled again.

It wasn't easy for her to talk about her past. But she agreed that it was time Tucker heard about it so that he could understand her reluctance to risk the control she'd gained over her life in the past few years.

She couldn't look at him as she talked. Her eyes focused blindly on her hands, she drew a deep breath and told him about the two hopeless alcoholics who'd been her parents. Drawn together by their own weaknesses and cravings, they'd had little energy left for their only child.

They'd tried at times—how often had she heard them tearfully promise to give her a better life, a better future? But always they'd failed—another job lost, another home taken from them, another school left behind as they'd moved from town to town, always searching for something just beyond their grasp.

Margaret had moved out at seventeen, the day she graduated from the last of a long series of schools. Driven by a need for some sort of order in her life, and fueled by the encouragement of teachers who'd recognized her intelligence and abilities, she'd put herself through college. It hadn't been easy. Too often, her hardearned wages had been given to her parents, who'd still been able to manipulate her even after she'd told herself that she wouldn't let them ruin the rest of her life.

But they'd been the only family she'd ever known, and she had loved them in her own sad way. Just as they had loved her in theirs.

And then they'd died. It had been a freak accident just after Margaret's twenty-third birthday. Two days after she'd finally graduated from college. Her parents had been on their way to visit her—she'd always hoped the purpose of the visit would have been to congratulate her on her achievement rather than to hit her up for more money for their debts.

Somewhere on the road from Beaumont to Dallas, a tractor-trailer rig, driven by a trucker with a history of driving drunk, had swerved out of control, hitting her parents' car and another, killing five people, her parents among them. For once, Margaret's father had been completely sober. The accident had been caused solely by the trucker's impairment.

Though Margaret had been too deeply in shock to care about lawsuits and settlements, a suit against the trucking company had been filed on her behalf by the personal-injuries attorney who'd represented the survivors of the other victims. She'd received a settlement two years after her parents died, enough to pay for her house and get her started in her business. There hadn't been anything left over, but a permanent home and a secure future were all Margaret had craved. All she'd wanted for as long as she could remember.

She'd always considered it painfully ironic that her parents' deaths had given her what they had never been able to offer her while they'd lived.

"You see, Tucker?" she concluded quietly, despondently. "I don't know anything about a real family. I don't know about providing a stable home for children. I've never been able to observe firsthand a solid, healthy marriage. How can I risk hurting you or your children by trying to take on responsibilities for which I have no training or experience?"

"You're wrong, you know," he said conversationally, though his expression told her how deeply her unhappy story had distressed him. "You've proven without doubt that you can accomplish anything if you want it badly enough. With the childhood you endured, it wouldn't be any wonder if you'd given up, but you never did. You made a life for yourself—a good one. I admire you more than anyone I've ever known. I can't think of anyone who'd set a better example for my children."

"Tucker, I'm afraid," she said, her voice choked with emotion. "Can't you understand that?"

"Yes. I know how daunting it must be for you to consider taking on a ready-made family, especially after you've worked so hard for the peace you're afraid we'll shatter. There would definitely be trade-offs. I'm hoping you'll decide that the rewards would be worth the sacrifices. Doesn't your quiet sanctuary ever get lonely, Margaret?"

A single tear escaped her. "It gets very lonely," she whispered.

His arm was warm around her shoulders. "And wouldn't it be nice to know that you're loved?"

She swiped unsteadily at her cheek. "I've always

wanted to be loved," she admitted, remembering all the tears she'd shed as a child.

"You are, Margaret. I love you. I think I have from the moment I saw you. And Kitten loves you. Surely you know that."

Her breath caught with a hitch. "And Sam?"

Again, he gave her that endearingly crooked smile. "He's coming around. One step at a time, honey."

She leaned her head wearily against his arm. "I don't know what to say right now."

He brushed his lips across her overwarm forehead. "You don't have to say anything. I just wanted you to know."

"I—" She drew a deep breath. "I love you, too, Tucker. I have for weeks."

"I know," he murmured, a gleam of pleasure lighting his bright green eyes.

"You sound like Kitten," she murmured, closing her wet, burning eyes for a moment. "Just a bit vain."

"I'm hoping you'll help us work on that," he said, sounding amused.

She didn't smile in return. "I still need some time," she said without opening her eyes. "I'm not ready to make any promises yet. There's so much for me to think about, and I can't seem to do that tonight."

"You have as much time as you want," he vowed. "I'll probably turn into a frozen prune from all the cold showers I've been taking lately, but I won't rush you into a commitment you aren't ready to make."

"Maybe I can do something about those cold showers soon," she murmured, finally able to smile a little.

He groaned. "Don't even talk about that right now while you're in my arms and too sick to do anything about it," he begged humorously.

She snuggled more comfortably against him, her eyes still closed. "Just give me a few minutes to rest."

''Yeah, sure.'' He settled her against his chest and leaned back, obviously prepared to stay for a while.

Rather to her own surprise, she was smiling faintly when she drifted into sleep.

Margaret was sick all weekend. Fever, chills, sore throat, headache. Tucker was there for her, dividing his time between her house and his own. True to his word, he didn't press her about their future, but he made no secret of his love for her.

As much as she worried about what would eventually happen between them, she couldn't help thinking about how nice it was to have someone who truly cared that she was sick. She'd had a bad case of flu the winter before; she'd suffered through it alone. It would be all too easy to become addicted to having someone always there for her.

Had Tucker been right about the rewards being greater than the risks? She suspected that he was—but still she worried.

At her request, Tucker kept the children away while Margaret considered herself contagious. She didn't want to risk passing the illness to little Kitten, or possibly reinfecting Sam. By Monday evening, however, she felt well enough for them to visit.

Kitten threw herself at Margaret as soon as she opened the door to the family. ''Are you feeling better, Margaret?'' she asked anxiously. ''Did you get the pictures I drew for you?''

''Your father gave them all to me,'' Margaret replied. ''And I loved every one of them. Thank you, Kitten.''

Sam glanced a bit shyly up at her. ''I'm sorry I gave you my germs, Margaret,'' he murmured.

It was the very first time he'd called her by name, she realized.

"It wasn't your fault," she assured him. "Are you feeling better?"

He nodded. "I went back to school today. I'm only a little behind, since Dad helped me catch up. Mrs. Dixon said I'll probably still have *A*s on my next report card."

He was actually talking to her. Answering her with more than monosyllables. Margaret glanced at Tucker, finding him watching them with rather smug approval. She could almost see his thoughts in his eyes. *See? I told you he'd come around.*

One step at a time, she reminded herself. All forward. Maybe it wouldn't be necessary to take any more steps back.

She resisted the urge to cross her fingers as the wistful thought passed through her mind.

As it turned out, she made her decision on Thanksgiving Day. And it was a surprisingly painless process; somehow everything just seemed to resolve itself in her mind.

Pandemonium reigned in Tucker's parents' home as the family gathered for the holiday meal. The children, excited by the holiday, were more boisterous than usual. The adults talked and laughed and joked as dishes clattered in the kitchen. Parades and football games blared from a television set in the den.

It was one of the noisiest, least organized events Margaret had ever attended. But the deep love and genuine warmth in the household more than made up for the lack of order, as far as she was concerned.

Jackie was there with Mick. They had apparently made up their differences—at least for now—and were almost cloyingly affectionate. Mick's family had apparently accepted Jackie's presence in their midst; they treated her now like another member of the family. Just as they did Margaret.

One of the children spilled a glass of iced tea during the meal. Tucker and Mick got into a playful debate that seemed destined to lead to a food fight before Lillie firmly put an end to it, to Margaret's amusement.

Just before everyone finished eating, Debbie screamed and rushed to the kitchen, startling everyone. It turned out she'd forgotten to uncover a special casserole she'd prepared as a side dish, which she brought out then in chagrin and ordered everyone to eat, whether they were full or not. Her brothers teased her mercilessly.

"Tucker's brought you into a madhouse, I'm afraid," Lillie murmured wryly to Margaret as they carried dishes to the kitchen after the meal. "I hope you weren't expecting a quiet, formal Thanksgiving dinner."

Margaret's smile felt a bit tremulous as she contrasted this cheerfully chaotic afternoon with the too-quiet holidays she'd spent alone during the past few years.

"I wouldn't change a thing about today," she assured Lillie with total sincerity.

Lillie smiled and glanced over her shoulder at her boisterous family. "Neither would I," she murmured contentedly.

After loading his own dishes into the dishwasher, Tucker took Margaret's hand. "I'm taking Margaret out to see your rose garden, Mom," he announced.

"There are no roses in November, Tuck," his sister interjected sweetly.

He slanted her a look. "Butt out."

"Go ahead, dear. We'll finish in here," Lillie said mildly, lifting a silencing hand when Debbie would have responded to her brother's blunt command.

Tucker led Margaret out the kitchen door and across the spacious, beautifully landscaped backyard. A small, metal-sided storage shed stood in one corner of the yard; he pulled her behind it, out of view of the house, and then tugged her unceremoniously into his arms for a kiss that nearly singed her hair.

It took her a moment to catch her breath when he finally lifted his head. When she could speak again, she said weakly, "I thought you were going to show me the rose garden."

"There are no roses in November, Margaret," he murmured with a smile, rubbing his nose teasingly against hers.

She wrapped her arms around his neck. "Does this mean I've been shamelessly deceived?"

"Shamelessly," he repeated. "I've tricked you out here for nefarious purposes." He nibbled at her ear between words.

Her neck arched. "What—what nefarious purposes?"

He pulled her so close against him that she couldn't possibly doubt what he'd really like to be doing with her. "I have something to tell you."

She couldn't resist pressing herself a bit more closely against him. "What is it?" she asked huskily.

"There's no school tomorrow. The kids are spending the night with Mom."

She lifted an eyebrow. "And where were *you* planning to spend the night?"

His grin was downright sinful. "I was rather hoping to spend it with you. It gets awfully lonely at my place when the kids are gone, you know."

"There's always Boomer to keep you company," she murmured.

He chuckled, then gently bit her ear. She gasped. "Okay," she said. "You can spend the night with me. But only if you promise to do that again," she added with a slow smile.

He groaned. "You can count on it." And he kissed her again.

He drew away reluctantly. "I suppose we'd better go

back in soon. I just need a minute to, er, recover first.''
He set her firmly a few inches away from him.

She resisted a mischievous impulse to glance down.
''I've had a lovely day, Tucker,'' she told him, growing
serious for a moment.

He smiled and brushed a strand of breeze-blown hair
from her cheek. ''Have you? I'm glad.''

''You have a wonderful family. They love you very
much, you know.''

''They can be your family, as well,'' he said, his casual tone not quite matching the serious look in his eyes.
''All you have to do is marry me.''

She widened her eyes at him. ''Surely you aren't pro-
posing to me behind a shed in your mother's backyard?''

He grimaced, dimples showing sheepishly. ''Maybe I
should have put a little more planning into it?''

''Gee, ya think?''

He frowned, apparently uncertain how to take her
light response. ''Would you rather I bring this up at another time?''

She cocked her head, pretending to think about it. It
was hard to keep up her casual attitude when her heart
was beating so hard and fast she could hardly breathe.

''Maybe you should make an appointment,'' she murmured. ''You really should write a proper speech and
practice until it's perfect. And, of course, you have to
plan for all possible responses and counterproposals. Not
to mention—''

''You're teasing me,'' he said blankly, staring at her
in exaggerated amazement. ''I bare my heart to you, and
all you can do is mock me?''

''I can't help it,'' she confessed. ''You know how
impulsive and unpredictable I am.''

He snorted. The smile had returned to his eyes, along
with a gleam of what might have been excitement. ''I
suppose there's a point to this?'' he asked cordially.

"I'm practicing," she explained. "If I'm going to fit in to this family, I have to learn to tease and surprise people occasionally. Carefree spontaneity isn't easy, you know. It takes—"

The rest of her nonsense was smothered beneath his mouth. "I'm taking that as a yes," he warned her when he finally lifted his head for a gasp of air.

She clung to him for support, her knees having gone out sometime during the life-changing embrace. "Yes," she whispered. "I love you, Tucker. I don't ever want to go back to the lonely life I had before you and the children came into it. I don't know about being a good wife or mother, but I'll learn. I never give up when it's something this important to me."

"I can't promise that everything will always go smoothly," he cautioned. "It's going to be chaotic at times, Margaret."

"I know. I've had serenity and tranquility. It's been very nice—exactly what I needed for a while—but I'm stronger now. Braver. I'm ready to be surprised occasionally."

He smiled. "That I can guarantee."

She returned the smile. "I love you, Tucker."

"I love you." He lowered his head again.

"There you are!" Kitten announced a few minutes later. "Me and Sam have been looking everywhere for you two. What are you doing?"

Margaret and Tucker released each other hastily and turned to find his children watching them from the corner of the shed. Kitten looked curious. Margaret noticed that Sam looked somewhat resigned.

"We were, er, talking," Tucker answered his daughter, a tinge of color on his cheeks.

"Didn't look like talking to me," Kitten replied. "Looked like kissing."

"Okay, we were kissing," Tucker admitted with a strained chuckle. "You caught us."

Margaret was still watching Sam. He met her eyes, his expression thoughtful.

Their gazes locked.

She held her breath.

"Are you and Margaret going to get married, Daddy?" Kitten demanded. "People get married when they kiss."

Tucker, too, was watching Sam now. "That's one of the things we were talking about," he said carefully. "How do you two feel about it?"

Kitten grinned broadly. "I *like* it."

Tucker smiled briefly. "I figured you would. Er, Sam? What do you think?"

Margaret bit her lip, trying to read Sam's expression. It would mean so much to her if he could accept her— just a little, she thought hopefully. She didn't expect open arms, but a wary truce would be infinitely preferable to open rebellion.

"I've been sort of expecting this," Sam said after a moment.

Again, it was Tucker who responded. "Have you? So—what's the verdict?"

Sam gave a rather regal nod. "It's okay with me."

Margaret released her held breath in a gusty exhale. "You don't mind?" she asked, anxious for reassurance.

Sam shrugged. "You remember when you said the phantom should have wanted what was best for Christine, not himself? And at the end, he did?"

Aware that Tucker and Kitten looked confused, Margaret nodded. "I remember."

"I want what's best for my dad," Sam explained simply. "He's happy when he's with you."

Margaret blinked back tears. It was probably the sweetest thing anyone had ever said to her. "I'll do my best to make *all* of you happy,'' she promised. ''Thank you for giving me a chance, Sam.''

''Think we can go see *The Phantom of the Opera* sometime?'' Sam asked, not above taking advantage of her gratitude.

She smiled at him, recklessly vowing to herself to buy four plane tickets to New York at the very first opportunity. Maybe she'd give them to Sam as a Christmas present. ''You bet we can.''

Sam smiled at her, silently sealing the bargain.

Kitten threw her arms around Margaret's waist and hugged her tightly. ''This is great!'' she squealed. ''You're going to live with us now. We'll be a real family.''

There were still so many details to work out. When the nuptials would take place, whose house they'd live in, whether she'd continue to do business from home or from an office—but none of that mattered now.

For once, Margaret was content to leave the planning for later.

She returned Kitten's hug. ''Yes,'' she said, her throat tight. ''We'll be a family now.''

Kitten broke away to hug her father. Tucker swung his daughter high into his arms, making her laugh happily.

Sam stepped forward. ''Welcome to the family, Margaret.''

She hesitated only a moment before opening her arms. She was thrilled when he stepped into them. For the first time, she was able to hug him, and be hugged in return.

Still holding Kitten in one arm, Tucker slung his free arm around Margaret's shoulders, linking the four of them together. ''Let's go tell the rest of the family,'' he said, eager to share the news.

Taking Sam's hand in hers, Margaret nodded, smiling down at the boy.

They were halfway to the house when Kitten suddenly laughed. "Now I have a nickname for you, Margaret!" she announced gleefully.

Warily, Margaret eyed her. "What is it, Kitten?"

The child's smile was smug. "Mom," she said.

Sam's fingers tightened for a moment in Margaret's, and then he relaxed and nodded. "It's okay with me," he said with a shrug.

"It's okay with me, too," Tucker murmured huskily, looking at Margaret with so much love that she could almost feel it enveloping her.

Margaret drew a tremulous breath. "That's a nickname I can live with, Kitten," she murmured, still looking at Tucker. "For the rest of my life."

Epilogue

"Triplets!" Tucker paced distractedly around the bed-room, holding his head in both hands. "Triplets," he repeated. "Just as I've gotten accustomed to the possibility that we'd be having twins, the doctor tells us we're having triplets. That's three babies, Margaret! All at once."

Margaret knew how he felt. She was still dazed herself from the visit with the doctor that afternoon. Sitting on the edge of the bed, she rested a hand on her stomach, which had gotten rather large considering she was only four months pregnant. That had been the first clue that there would be more than the one baby she and Tucker had carefully planned.

After just over a year as a part of the Hollis family, she'd learned to expect surprises like this. But it had still shaken her.

"Oh, man," Tucker groaned. "This is unbelievable. We'll have to get a bigger house, of course. And we'll have to make plans. Schedules. We'll never survive if we don't carefully work these things out. Feedings, diaper changes, colic—"

Margaret lifted an eyebrow. "You can schedule colic?"

He shot her a harried look. "This isn't a joke. Do you have any idea of the logistics involved in taking care of three babies?"

"No," she admitted. "But if there's one thing I've learned during the past year, it's that parents must be flexible and adaptable. Schedules are important, and it's nice when everything falls into place, but there are times when it just doesn't happen."

He put his hands on his hips and turned to stare at her. "Am I hearing you correctly?" he demanded. "Are you advising *me* to stop trying to plan ahead?"

Margaret smiled. "Not exactly. I'm just reminding you about that old saying about the best-laid plans."

He moved to sit beside her on the bed. His expression was a bit rueful when he laid a tender hand on her stomach. "Bet you never imagined your own plans would change this much when I moved in next door to you."

She shook her head in wonder. "I couldn't even have imagined the changes in store for me."

His mouth curved into the smile that still took her breath away every time she saw those sexy dimples. "Ever wish you could go back to those quiet, orderly days before you met me?"

She covered his hand with hers, feeling the faint stirring beneath their palms. In her peripheral vision was a large framed photograph of Tucker, Sam, Kitten and Margaret, looking very much the close, happy family that they'd become. Outside the bedroom window, Boomer barked gruffly at a cat or a squirrel, still faithfully guarding his territory.

It hadn't all been perfect. There'd been problems, of

course. Minor conflicts. Adjustments. Chaotic days. She knew there were many more ahead.

Tucker's hand was warm beneath hers, and his smile was tender and intimate. She leaned forward to brush a kiss across his mouth. "I wouldn't change a thing," she assured him with all her heart.

He wrapped his arms around her and lowered her to the bed, his green eyes gleaming with familiar intent. "Since the kids are at my parents' house..."

She held him back when he would have covered her mouth with his. "Aren't we supposed to join them for dinner in less than half an hour?"

He was already busy with the top button of her blouse. "Looks like we're going to be a little late. Again."

With a mental apology to her mother-in-law, Margaret opened her arms to him. There were times, she decided happily, when spontaneity was decidedly preferable to following a strict agenda. It had taken Tucker Hollis to teach her that—and she planned to spend the rest of her life demonstrating her appreciation for the joyful surprises he'd given her.

And every once in a while, she thought with a soft laugh, remembering his expression in the doctor's office earlier, she just might manage to surprise *him*.

* * * * *

Silhouette's newest series

YOURS TRULY

Love when you least expect it.

Where the written word plays a vital role in uniting couples—you're guaranteed a fun and exciting read every time!

Look for Marie Ferrarella's upcoming Yours Truly, *Traci on the Spot*, in March 1997.

Here's a special sneak preview....

1

Morgan Brigham slowly set down his coffee cup on the kitchen table and stared at the comic strip in the center of his paper. It was nestled in among approximately twenty others that were spread out across two pages. But this was the only one he made a point of reading faithfully each morning at breakfast.

This was the only one that mirrored *her* life.

He read each panel twice, as if he couldn't trust his own eyes. But he could. It was there, in black and white.

Morgan folded the paper slowly, thoughtfully, his mind not on his task. So Traci was getting engaged.

The realization gnawed at the lining of his stomach. He hadn't a clue as to why.

He had even less of a clue why he did what he did next.

Abandoning his coffee, now cool, and the newspaper, and ignoring the fact that this was going to make him late for the office, Morgan went to get a sheet of stationery from the den.

He didn't have much time.

Traci Richardson stared at the last frame she had just drawn. Debating, she glanced at the creature sprawled out on the kitchen floor.

"What do you think, Jeremiah? Too blunt?"

The dog, part bloodhound, part mutt, idly looked up from his rawhide bone at the sound of his name. Jeremiah gave her a look she felt free to interpret as ambivalent.

"Fine help you are. What if Daniel actually reads this and puts two and two together?"

Not that there was all that much chance that the man who had proposed to her, the very prosperous and busy Dr. Daniel Thane, would actually see the comic strip she drew for a living. Not unless the strip was taped to a bicuspid he was examining. Lately Daniel had gotten so busy he'd stopped reading anything but the morning headlines of the *Times*.

Still, you never knew. "I don't want to hurt his feelings," Traci continued, using Jeremiah as a sounding board. "It's just that Traci is overwhelmed by Donald's proposal and, see, she thinks the ring is going to swallow her up." To prove her point, Traci held up the drawing for the dog to view.

This time, he didn't even bother to lift his head.

Traci stared moodily at the small velvet box on the kitchen counter. It had sat there since Daniel had asked her to marry him last Sunday. Even if Daniel never read her comic strip, he was going to suspect something eventually. The very fact that she hadn't grabbed the ring from his hand and slid it onto her finger should have told him that she had doubts about their union.

Traci sighed. Daniel was a catch by any definition. So what was her problem? She kept waiting to be struck by that sunny ray of happiness. Daniel said he wanted to take care of her, to fulfill her every wish. And he was even willing to let her think about it before she gave him her answer.

Guilt nibbled at her. She should be dancing up and down, not wavering like a weather vane in a gale.

Pronouncing the strip completed, she scribbled her

signature in the corner of the last frame and then sighed. Another week's work put to bed. She glanced at the pile of mail on the counter. She'd been bringing it in steadily from the mailbox since Monday, but the stack had gotten no farther than her kitchen. Sorting letters seemed the least heinous of all the annoying chores that faced her.

Traci paused as she noted a long envelope. Morgan Brigham. Why would Morgan be writing to her?

Curious, she tore open the envelope and quickly scanned the short note inside.

Dear Traci,

I'm putting the summerhouse up for sale. Thought you might want to come up and see it one more time before it goes up on the block. Or make a bid for it yourself. If memory serves, you once said you wanted to buy it. Either way, let me know. My number's on the card.

Take care,
Morgan

P.S. Got a kick out of *Traci on the Spot* this week.

Traci folded the letter. He read her strip. She hadn't known that. A feeling of pride silently coaxed a smile to her lips. After a beat, though, the rest of his note seeped into her consciousness. He was selling the house.

The summerhouse. A faded white building with brick trim. Suddenly, memories flooded her mind. Long, lazy afternoons that felt as if they would never end.

Morgan.

She looked at the far wall in the family room. There was a large framed photograph of her and Morgan standing before the summerhouse. Traci and Morgan. Morgan and Traci. Back then, it seemed their lives had been permanently intertwined. A bittersweet feeling of loss passed over her.

Traci quickly pulled the telephone over to her on the counter and tapped out the number on the keypad.

* * * * *

Look for TRACI ON THE SPOT
by Marie Ferrarella, coming to
Silhouette YOURS TRULY
in March 1997.

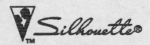

Harlequin and Silhouette celebrate
Black History Month with seven terrific titles,
featuring the all-new *Fever Rising*
by Maggie Ferguson
(Harlequin Intrigue #408) and
A Family Wedding by Angela Benson
(Silhouette Special Edition #1085)!

Also available are:
Looks Are Deceiving by Maggie Ferguson
Crime of Passion by Maggie Ferguson
Adam and Eva by Sandra Kitt
Unforgivable by Joyce McGill
Blood Sympathy by Reginald Hill

On sale in January at your favorite
Harlequin and Silhouette retail outlet.

COMING NEXT MONTH

#1087 ASHLEY'S REBEL—Sherryl Woods
The Bridal Path
That Special Woman!
Forbidden passions sparked to life when ex-model Ashley Wilde
reluctantly shared very close quarters with handsome rebel Dillon Ford.
Can their turbulent past together allow them a passionate tomorrow?

#1088 WAITING FOR NICK—Nora Roberts
Those Wild Ukrainians
Here is the story readers have been begging for! To Frederica Kimball, it
seemed she'd spent her entire childhood waiting for Nick. Now she's
all grown up—and the waiting is over!

#1089 THE WRONG MAN...THE RIGHT TIME—Carole Halston
It was love at first sight when virginal Pat Tyler encountered ruggedly
handsome Clint Adams. But the ex-marine gallantly pushed the
beguiling young woman away. He thought he was the wrong man for
her. Could she convince him he was Mr. Right?

#1090 A HERO'S CHILD—Diana Whitney
Parenthood
Hank Flynn died a hero—or so everyone thought. Now he was back to
claim his fiancée—and the daughter he never knew he had....

#1091 MARRY ME IN AMARILLO—Celeste Hamilton
Gray Nolan would do anything to stop his baby sister's wedding—
even seduce bridal consultant Kathryn Seeger to his side. But this
commitment-shy cowboy quickly learned that Kathryn had no intention
of changing his sister's mind about marriage, and every intention of
changing his....

#1092 SEPARATED SISTERS—Kaitlyn Gorton
Single mom Ariadne Palmer just discovered she has a missing twin
sister! Placing her trust in the mysterious man who brought her this
compelling news, she must learn what family *really* means....

If you're looking for irresistible heroes, the search is over....

Joan Elliott Pickart's

Tux, Bram and Blue Bishop and their pal,
Gibson McKinley, are four unforgettable men...on a
wife hunt. Discover the women who steal their
Texas-size hearts in this enchanting four-book series,
which alternates between Silhouette Desire
and Special Edition:

In February 1997, fall in love with Tux, Desire's
Man of the Month, in TEXAS MOON, #1051.

In May 1997, Blue meets his match in TEXAS DAWN,
Special Edition #1100.

In August 1997, don't miss Bram's romance in
TEXAS GLORY—coming to you from Desire.

And in December 1997, Gib takes more than marriage
vows in TEXAS BABY, Special Edition's
That's My Baby! title.
You won't be able to resist
Joan Elliott Pickart's TEXAS BABY.